A SMALL CASE FOR
INSPECTOR GHOTE?

A SMALL CASE
FOR INSPECTOR
GHOTE?

H R F Keating

WINDSOR
PARAGON

First published 2009
by Allison & Busby Limited
This Large Print edition published 2011
by AudioGO Ltd
by arrangement with
Allison & Busby Limited

Hardcover ISBN: 978 1 408 46162 4
Softcover   ISBN: 978 1 408 46163 1

British Library Cataloguing in Publication Data available

Printed and bound in Great Britain by
MPG Books Group Limited

CHAPTER ONE

Inspector Ghote, ensconced in his newly won cabin at Bombay Police Crime Branch, head down at work, was just aware every now and again of a smell. An odour by no means obtrusive, but there. There and, yes, somehow wrong.

Each time it impinged on him he gave brief thought to it. What can it be? Is there a dead pi-dog somewhere underneath the floor? Or a . . .

But, no. Get on with the work. *Bandobast*, the interminable juggling to fit all the cases under investigation to the available inspectors. Damn it, I am keeping waiting the Head of Crime Branch himself, Assistant Commissioner of Police Mr Ramprasad Divekar. And there is a lot more still to be done.

Down again went his head.

Yet, not very much later, he found his thoughts had wandered and he was reckoning that he had been working at his *bandobast* task now for—it must be—five weeks. I joined duty on the first day of the Hindu month of Chaitra and now we are well into the month of Baisakh, the annual promise of fresh blooming flowers and summer warmth. So it must be more than five weeks. Yes, almost six. And still I have not been given my first proper Crime Branch case. An investigation, not into any of the everyday murders that happen all over Bombay, but of a case involving one of the city's important and influential people. A crime that counts, some case of—

No, no, no. Get on with the work. My duty now.

What next? Ah, yes.

Once more he glued his eyes to the schedule in front of him. And, almost immediately, found that they had closed and he was giving a long exploratory sniff. Yes, definitely, smell still there. Drains? Everywhere in Bombay there is almost always a smell from defective drains, somewhere or another. But this doesn't seem . . .

No, get on with the work. Mr Divekar may at any time actually pick up one of the three telephones on his desk and ask me why I have not finished. And then I may find myself for even longer on *bandobast* duty, perhaps for weeks and weeks more.

For the fifth or sixth time he brought himself to concentrate on the particular memo from Mr Divekar that was lying in front of him.

Or can there be a crow that has somehow got into the cabin, and died here? But surely a smell of that sort must long ago have been dispersed by the fan in the ceiling.

He glanced upwards.

Damn it. Wretched thing not even switched on. Once again Bikram has failed to do what he very well knows is every peon's duty at the start of each day. Really, the fellow is altogether too incompetent. I cannot think how killed-on-duty Inspector Patil, whose place I have inherited, never simply got rid of him. Should I myself even be getting him hundred per cent chucked out now? Would that be the full demanding way to behave for a full Crime Branch officer?

On the other hand . . . Well, Bikram has a right to gain a livelihood, even if almost every *paisa* he gets seems to be spent on rum. Every day that goes by that disgusting stale odour is breathed out all over me.

But the fan.

Making his way across the narrow width of the cabin, he flicked down its switch. The three groaning blades above began reluctantly to stir the already-too-warm air.

Back beside his desk, Ghote squeezed himself through the narrow gap between it and the wall behind, slid down on his chair and took from his in tray the next bundle of orders sent down from Mr Divekar's huge airy cabin on the balcony directly above. Determinedly he worked on, thinking how to fit each new demand—more than a few superseding oncs already dealt with—into the complex pattern of possibilities.

Soon, the smell that had niggled and niggled at the back of his mind was altogether forgotten, absorbed as he was in officers' names, in requirements for periods of leave (casual or earned), in police dogs' availability, in transport demands, in cancellations and cancellings of those cancellations. With, ever present, the fear that finally one of his instructions might prove to be totally and impossibly at odds with another.

And then, all in an instant, it came to him what the persistent slight irritation, now once more blossoming in his nostrils, was.

It was the smell of blood.

Yes, it must be blood. I think I can recognise it clearly now, even though it is so faint. But where can it be coming from, if it is really the sweetish odour of blood? The three dirt-grimed blades of the fan slowly pushing the air round seem still not to be dispelling it, slight though it is.

3

But after all, he abruptly thought then, perhaps it is not truly the smell of blood? Words from his personal holy book, bought long ago from a pavement vendor, Dr Hans Gross's *Criminal Investigation*—just there on the cupboard top—had come back to him. *When it is a question of determining the correctness of a smell-perception great care is necessary, and all the more because the sensibility of the organ varies so much.*

So it may be blood, or . . .

But never mind that. I have by no means finished my work. Back to it once more. Do not think about the damn smell until I have altogether finished.

*   *   *

So now it was only when there were intrusive interruptions that Ghote even for a moment looked up. There was Mr Divekar's own Goan peon, smartly dressed Thomas, giving him from time to time a polite drawing-attention cough before putting another batch of orders into the tray. Why should it be Thomas coming now and not Bikram? he half-thought as he took the new papers, absorbed their instructions and began working out how they might be fitted in.

Then there was the tea boy. Suddenly and silently there, pouring with intent care the milky liquid from his heavy canister into the waiting cup, its inner surface still rimed with stains Bikram had failed to remove. Did I pay the boy before he went? Did I, or didn't I, even give him a word of thanks? I forget, already. But there's always his second round. Ask then if I paid before.

Next came a hesitant tap-tap on the top of the

4

batwing doors of the cabin and Sergeant Moos, Bombay Police fingerprints expert, came sidling in from the noisy compound outside. Ghote, in his very first week in the job, had learnt that Moos was notorious for always wanting any officer he could persuade to listen to give him 'two-three minutes just to mention something'. The 'something' always being a long, long explanation of some new intricacy arising from his *kaam*, the work he was wedded to as devoutly as God Krishna had loved his Radha.

'Sit, sit,' he muttered to him, scarcely looking up. Then, as Moos eagerly drew back one of the two chairs ranged in front of the desk, he let the droning of his voice become no more than the buzzing of the flies that constantly came in from the compound beyond the doors. But, when at last he realised that he was now ready to type out the result of all his crossword puzzle work, he found that at some point Moos must have simply drifted away. Did I murmur something to him by way of saying I had found it all most interesting? Heaven knows. I am just hoping that I did.

Pushing his chair the two or three inches clear of the desk before it knocked against the wall, he twisted round and reached down into the dark corner beside him for the much worn, keys-jamming typewriter he had inherited with Patil's cabin. But as his fingers sought for the worn leather strap of its cover something about the waste bin tucked beside it caught his eye.

Damn it all, it is full. The bin is full to very brim. And that idiot, Bikram, knows as well as he knows anything it is his duty to empty the bin each evening before he goes home. Or, more likely, goes to whatever beer bar it is where he gets his rum. And why, in any case, is the bin so crammed with rubbish? I certainly did not throw very much into it yesterday. Yet here it is, full to top.

And, yes. Yes, it is from there surely that the smell is coming. I am certain of it. And it is the smell of blood. My smell-perception of it is hundred per cent correct. I know this odour well enough from the murders and assaults I dealt with in my assistant inspector years up in Dadar. But what on earth is the crumpled newspaper doing in the bin, looking like the froth on a tall brightly layered glass of *falooda* from a juice bar? I never brought a newspaper into the cabin yesterday, nor on any other day. This is no place for idle reading. So why is there a newspaper in my bin?

Nose wrinkling at the smell, he grasped between finger and thumb one corner of the newsprint sheets and gave a gentle tug.

Ah, I see now. It is the *Matunga News*, the rag I used sometimes to see when I was posted in Dadar, next to Matunga itself. But how on earth did a paper from there, halfway across the city, get into my waste bin? And that photo on the page I am holding, surely it is of that politician about to contest the by-election for the South Bombay seat in the Legislative Assembly, the fellow who has earned the full wifely contempt of my Protima? Does he then come from Matunga?

Reaching down deeper into the bin with his other hand, he caught hold of what seemed to be the twine handle on one side of an old shopping bag. He pulled at it. Then, finding it unexpectedly weighty, he gave it a series of rather harder tugs. The bag's other handle, folded back, emerged. He

6

got hold of it and half-inch by half-inch pulled the whole bag up. He realised now that what he could feel at his fingertips at the edge of the newspaper sheets, was . . . was nothing else but cropped wiry human hair.

Wait. Wait a moment.

He dipped down deeper.

Yes, I can see clearly now that I am looking at the top of a man's head. Short greying hair in one tangled mass, and altogether dirty also, scurf-encrusted under an almost dry layer of blood. The cause of the smell. Definitely, definitely.

A stray puff of breeze from the compound beyond gave an extra impetus to the sullen air stirred by the slow-grinding fan. The *Matunga News* pages were flipped a little further apart. And suddenly Ghote's whole mouth went as dry as if he had been sleeping for hours with lips wide apart.

Scarcely knowing what he was doing, he let go one handle of the bag and reached blindly back for his long-neglected cup of milky tea, draining its whole clammy contents at a gulp. He had in one glimpse recognised whose head it was that he had hauled to the light of day. It was Bikram's.

CHAPTER TWO

The first thing that came fully into Ghote's mind then was, incongruously, *So this is why it has been the ACP's Thomas who has brought down my orders all morning.* Then other thoughts, more to the purpose, one by one made themselves manifest. Bikram is dead. His head has been hacked away from his body. Yes, when I got a glimpse deeper into the bag I made out that death did not come in one clean cut. Bikram had not, going home in his usual state of drunkenness, walking beside some railway line, fallen down and stayed there, out to the world. No, he did not come to die as a train rumbled by. He has been murdered. Brutally murdered.

And that should not have happened to him. It should not happen to anyone, any human being whatsoever. Bikram's life was sacred. Sacred despite the way he always contrived to get his peon's khaki shirt and shorts altogether more stained and shabby-looking than those of any of the others fetching and carrying from one Crime Branch cabin to another.

Yes, despite the drunkenness he was hardly able ever to disguise, Bikram was a man, a human being. He should not have been killed in that appalling manner.

He looked down again at the bloody mess of the head in the shopping bag on the floor now at his feet. Then he heaved it back again, out of sight beside Inspector Patil's still-closed typewriter.

Yes, he reasoned, twisting himself upright again, someone must have brought Bikram's head, in that bag, from wherever it was that he was killed. They must have carried it here, themselves looking little different from the thousands of other bag-carrying shoppers going each day to markets all over Bombay. But where had this particular one been carried from? Where precisely? Where was it that Bikram's killer hacked away his life? And then carried that shopping bag from wherever it was he had done it to . . . to here. Into my cabin. My

8

Crime Branch cabin itself.

But Bikram's killer, who can he be? *He?* Yes, it must be a *he*, a man, and one ruthless and brutally strong enough to have done what was done. But who can it have been? Who? And where was it that he put drunken Bikram's head into this particular bag and then carried it right into my cabin? Or . . . ? Yes, this is possible: did he get someone else to carry it here? But who could that be?

All right, the bag could easily enough have been brought into the Headquarters compound by almost anyone. Inside the compound there are, after all, living quarters for police lower-ranks. The occasional person could wander about there unchallenged at any hour of the night. And my batwing doors are, of course, open to the whole of the compound, which is why at night I have to make sure everything is under lock and key. Yes, if someone wanted—but why should they?—to put Bikram's head in the very place where the wretched fellow went about his duties, so far as he ever did, then my cabin is where, in the whole of Crime Branch, it could most easily be left.

But what reason would anyone have to bring Bikram's head here? In all probability it must surely have been for some specific reason, however it had been managed.

If whoever killed Bikram in this terrible way had simply wanted to get rid of the evidence they could have simply dropped the body and the head, too, into the sea surrounding almost the whole of the city. Very probably the body itself must already have been consigned to the waters, to be within a short time rendered unidentifiable. Provided it was

9

without a head. So that head would have had to be dealt with in some other way.

Whoever had hacked it from Bikram's body could hardly have taken it to the new Electric Crematorium that, in growing and growing Bombay, takes some of the burden off the Burning Ghat. But neither did the head have to be brought into Crime Branch. Yes, murder, or rather, patent evidence of murder, had been brought right into Crime Branch itself.

So . . . A new thought. Surely that murder must be investigated by Crime Branch, however far removed the case might appear to be from the important and influential affairs the Branch is actually here to handle. However much Bikram was at the very opposite end of that scale.

So what to do? One answer only. Report this discovery at once to the Head of Crime Branch. To ACP Divekar himself.

But then yet another thought. One almost as disturbing as the finding of Bikram's head, if in quite a different way. It is this: might it be that Mr Divekar would give the investigation to the officer who actually discovered the severed head? To me? After all, with the victim being no more than a peon, and a wretched enough one too, the case can really be only a small one. One, isn't it, quite suitable for a newly arrived officer to try his teeth on?

*   *   *

Ghote stood looking at the winding stone stair that led, from almost beside the batwing doors of his own cabin, up to the ACP's airily spacious one on

10

the balcony above. This will be, he thought, only the second time I have entered same. The first was after Superintendent Ghorpade, Crime Branch second-in-command, had shown me, with full explanations and much friendliness, all over our building. Then he took me to Mr Divekar for my official welcome. But that first meeting with the ACP turned out to be more of a warning than a welcome. A warning about the conduct expected of any officer working under him and the strict obedience he required, plus then a little of welcome also.

But now, up at the top of the winding stairs, on my own, unescorted, I must peer through the little square of glass in the ACP's door, as I saw Mr Ghorpade do, and make certain Mr Divekar is disengaged. And then . . .

Then I must give the door one good hard tap. A much harder tap than the one I gave when waiting outside before. My quiet knock then earned me, as soon as I stood before Mr Divekar, a sharply fierce shelling. Did I not realise it was necessary to knock loudly enough to be heard above the sound of the fans overhead? And those, I saw, were full seven-bladed ones, the whole row of them.

Inside, I must remember now, since I am wearing uniform, to give a full-hearted, snapped-up salute. Superintendent Ghorpade kindly informed me that, out of uniform, simply clicking heels sharply together suffices. But in uniform, as I was on that first day, a salute is always required.

Now, in answer to the ACP's *Well, Inspector?* I will have to tell him, altogether briefly and unhesitatingly, what it is I have, just only this minute, found in my waste bin.

11

Into Ghote's mind then came the image of the altogether imposing cabin he would have to enter, vividly as a film in a cinema hall. But not any of the black-and-white films I mostly have seen. No, this is in sharpest colour, tinged with menacing underlights.

First, the huge curving desk, with six chairs—if I counted right—lined up in front of it. Its densely black covering protected against sweaty hands by a wide sheet of gleamingly polished glass. The three telephones waiting on it, each differently coloured. Beside them, a set of four presentation pens juts up from a rose-pink marble holder, clearly never intended to be other than a sign of prestige. Then, directly in front of the ACP himself, there is that very, very large leather-cornered blotter, its absorbent white paper unsmirched by a single ink-spot.

Beside that, the film in my memory shows, there are two neat piles of round silvery paperweights, half a dozen of them, altogether necessary to keep in place under the beating air from those whirring seven-bladed fans above, the documents the ACP may need to consult. And, yes, each of the topmost little weights, I saw, was incised with the letters *RVD*, the ACP's own initials.

But what of ACP Ramprasad Divekar himself? I can hardly put a face to him, so overwhelmed I was then under that fierce shelling, and altogether worried as I am now by the prospect before me. Yes, he has grey, grey eyes. Or does he? And does he have, even, a moustache? Or is it that I am just only imagining the sort of moustache he ought to have? Bristling, well-trimmed to the last whisker, and angry? He was, I cannot forget, blastingly angry when I stood in front of him before because of my too-polite tap on his door.

But in two minutes only, less even, at the top of these winding stairs, I will be facing, once again, the man himself. There to tell him about the appalling discovery I have made. So now . . . now it is a matter only of going up these steps to the balcony and along to that door. Then to look through its single thick glass pane before giving the door a tap, altogether hard enough to be heard. Yet not too hard.

But no . . . no. No, there is something vital I must do before I am at all reporting. I must at once go back into my cabin and replace every item of the evidence just where it was before. Everything must be exactly at the same spot it was when I leant down to get hold of the typewriter and saw the frothy *falooda* mess of the *Matunga News*. There will be photographs to be taken. There must be also the possibility of fingerprints on the bin itself. And, oh God, there may, too, somewhere on those blood-marked newspaper sheets, be my own prints. They will almost certainly be also on the shopping bag's handles that I was holding so tightly.

A bad mistake for me. I should have known better than to touch those handles, even if I was at that moment not at all knowing I was about to discover Bikram's severed head. But perhaps even Sergeant Moos, Number *Ek* expert though he is, will be unable to lift even one decent print from among all that mess.

He turned and hurried back into the desecrated cabin, sweating suddenly with relief that out of sheer necessity the moment of confrontation above had been postponed. Then, checking that the batwing doors had swung firmly closed behind him, he snatched from his desk the wooden ruler he always used to underline any important phrases in the schedule, something Patil's typewriter never managed, and sliding it through the two twine handles of the bloodied shopping bag he raised it, and , with the most delicate care, replaced it in the waste bin, still waiting in its dark corner, not moved by so much as an inch from its original position.

One last fierce inspection. Yes, surely the newspaper sheets concealing poor Bikram's tangled, scurf-encrusted hair are now just as they were when I first lifted out the bag.

And left my fingerprints all over its handles, if nowhere else.

That will be something I will have to confess to. Confess—it would be best—in just a few minutes' time to bristling moustached Mr Divekar. Or not bristling moustached.

CHAPTER THREE

A tap on the door with the square glass panel in it. A good loud tap. Oh, my God. Too noisy? Have I gone too far in other direction?

But there came a barked 'Come!'

Straightening his bony shoulders, Ghote turned the handle and pushed the door open.

Yes, I did at least get that right. Exactly right. So, four smart steps onwards to bring myself up to the edge of the desk, just between two of the chairs

14

arrayed in front of it. Now, a truly smart salute. Right hand swiftly-swiftly to peak of cap. Did I tip it sideways? Yes. No. No, no, it did not move. Count: *ek, do, teen*.

Now, lower my hand. Lower it, for heaven's sake. Oh, but I have. I have. And Mr Divekar has said nothing, thank God. And now, I am face to face with him. No, no sign of a moustache. Just a steel rigidity of taut flesh beneath the sharp jutting nose. A truly British-style stiff upper lip, a grey-tinged barrier.

The whole of his body, for all that he is simply sitting in his well-polished, high-backed, red-leather chair, is, Ghote could not help feeling, just as stiffly upright as if he were standing to attention in front of the Governor of Maharashtra State himself. And those grey eyes that . . . yes, that glare out from under the fiercely tangled eyebrows, seem as incapable of showing understanding as any two glass marbles from some street urchins' game.

'Inspector Ghote?' The eyebrows sharply descended. 'Why is it that you have presented yourself, unsummoned, to my cabin? When I consider you fit to be relieved of *bandobast* duties and ready to take on one of the cases I might have assigned to young Patil—great loss to the Branch, first-class material—I will have you informed.'

'But, sir—'

Ghote forced his lips tightly shut. There could be no *but*s in the face of the Assistant Commissioner.

'Well, man? I asked why you have presented yourself in front of me.'

Now. So now, after all, it must be told.

'Sir, sitting in my cabin down below, I discovered

15

just only a few minutes ago . . . in my waste bin, sir
. . . sir, the cut-off head of my peon, Bikram.'

Is there some expression of surprise, even of
shock, in those two grey eyes? Ghote could not
bring himself to look at them directly enough to be
sure. In the blank silence that appeared to have
greeted his announcement all he could do was to
transfer his gaze, without noticeably moving his
own eyes or head, from the ACP's stony glance off
to the further reaches of the big room behind.

There, high on the wall, is the big blackboard, up
to which every morning the ACP's peon must
climb in order to alter the dispositions made the
previous day and show, to the last man, the
dispositions for the day ahead. The dispositions I
was working out myself. Yes, I can clearly see the
names of the dogs I was entering on my big sheet
not so long ago this very morning. There they are,
still, as they should be, the same as they were back
in British days, if not attached to the same animals.
Caesar, Captain, Rover. All as it ought to be. And,
oh, yes, I can see, too, the fat white-headed pin
that means *Bandobast Duties,* placed firmly against
my own starkly new name at the very foot of the
list of officers.

'The head? The severed head—did you say,
Inspector?—of your peon? So that's why all
morning the fellow has been absent when
summoned.'

Mr Divekar had spoken at last, if not in words
Ghote had expected to hear.

'Yes, sir,' he managed to bring out by way of a
reply. 'And I . . . '

His voice failed him. From a side door he had
seen the ACP's own Thomas enter the huge room.

16

But not carrying the stool he must use to get up high enough on the blackboard to make his daily changes. Instead, held rock steady in his right hand, there was the prettily flowered china teacup and saucer of the ACP's mid-morning refreshment. For one moment Ghote's mind switched down below to his own saucerless cup with the sharp-edged chip in it that always came just where his lip met the crudely coloured earthenware.

The cup that Bikram had been accustomed to plonk down on the desk, generally on top of a vital document. Dead, head-severed, rum-reeking Bikram.

But Mr Divekar, apparently heedless of Thomas entering, had more to say.

'Very well, Inspector, your peon's head—if I can believe you—appears to have got into your waste bin. But why in God's name have you come bothering me with that? What do you think it has got to do with me? Just dispose of the damn thing, man. Dispose of the damn thing and get on with your work. Why haven't I seen your final list of changes? Good God, it's halfway through the morning and Thomas hasn't been able to make a single alteration to the board there.'

'Yes, sir. No, sir. Sir, just as I was about to begin typing out the final version I was interrupted. By, sir, that discovery. In my bin, sir.'

Standing there, frozen to attention, Ghote, all thought of the confession about the prints he might have left on the shopping bag wiped from his mind, could do nothing else but watch Thomas as he approached the ACP's desk in a way so stealthy that he might have been an assassin about

17

to strike.

Now he seemed to be fixedly regarding a little round shiny leather mat, as black as the black covering of the huge desk, as if, by putting down on it the fragile weight of the cup, a bomb planted directly under the ACP's tall red-leather chair would be instantly triggered.

The forefinger of Thomas's left hand was sliding towards the mat. It touched it. Then it began quarter-inch by quarter-inch to push it sideways as if it had been placed by the smallest amount in the wrong position.

'Inspector,' Mr Divekar snapped out, apparently not even having seen Thomas, 'however glowing was the recommendation I had of you as being a proper officer to join Crime Branch, if you cannot attend to the first simple duty I have given to you, then you are not likely to be of much use to me in future. Yes?'

'Yes, sir. I mean no, sir,' Ghote jabbered out, his mind obscurely wrestling with the notion that he should warn the ACP of his peril, perhaps lean across the wide desk and give him, chair and all, a mighty life-saving shove. Or should I wheel round, fling myself on Thomas and knock him to the floor?

But Thomas had put down the cup exactly on the black mat's centre where plainly each day at this time it should rest, and no explosion had followed. It had been placed, Ghote now realised, where in no circumstances could any vigorous gesture the ACP might make send its tea spilling over the desk's immaculate glass surface. And now Thomas was withdrawing, silently as if on his feet were not *chappals* but the wheels of roller skates, muffled.

Ghote brought himself back to reality.

'But, sir,' he said, quietly argumentative, 'that severed head has been put into the very heart of Crime . . . sir, into one of the cabins in Crime Branch itself. Sir, isn't it a case for Crime Branch to investigate?'

'The head of a damn peon, Inspector? To be dealt with by Crime Branch? A branch set up specifically to investigate murders and other serious crimes involving persons of importance and influence? Crime Branch, that I, myself, am going to drive to a new pitch of efficiency. An example to forces all over India, to forces all over the whole damn world. Crime Branch, to be used to deal with thc death of an appalling scheduled caste peon? What are you saying?'

'But, sir, that head is evidence of murder. And, sir, even if it is not that of a person of influence, sir, should at least our nearest police station be asked to investigate? Sir, Tilak Marg PS?'

'And have this whole place trampled over by a lot of heavy-bootcd idiots from there? Inspector Ghote, you still have a lot to learn, a hell of a lot. Dismiss.'

*　　*　　*

Just dispose of the damn thing. Those had been Mr Divekar's own words, Ghote thought back in his little cabin, when I said I had found Bikram's head hacked from his body. The thought boomed and bounced in his own head, wanting an answer.

Yes, he felt, I can smell the blood still. Except, of course, I cannot. I cannot really. Yes, I smelt it when I put my nose down close to the waste bin

19

when I first saw that stained copy of the *Matunga News* covering up the far worse sight below. But by now the fan up there, almost useless though it is, has dissipated the last traces of it. Yet that smell of blood is in my mind still. In my mind, and crying out, not for vengeance, but for justice. Yes, Bikram has been murdered, and whoever chances to meet such a fate, however high or low in the ranks of society, deserves to have their death investigated, their murderer found and duly punished.

What did the ACP expect me to do when he said what he did? To take hold, once again, of the handles of that shopping bag, to haul it out and call for my peon to— But I have no peon now to call. My peon is deceased. His head, his head itself, is where, not so many minutes ago, I was carefully replacing it as evidence, as vital evidence to be preserved at all costs, in that very bin in its corner, positioned where sitting at my desk I could throw anything into it without even looking.

So what am I expected to do now? To take hold, myself, once again of those two handles at the sides of the bag, lift out Bikram's head and . . . And do what?

Dispose of it. To dispose of Bikram's head because he was no more than a 'damn peon'. Very well, calling him that is what many, many more high-caste people than Mr Divekar might do. And, in fact, I am not, as it happens, knowing precisely what caste Mr Divekar is. Names ending in *kar* are typical up and down the whole length of Maharashtra. But, however wide was the gap between Mr Divekar and rum-reeking Bikram, between Bikram and myself also, Bikram was after all a man. One fellow man to myself. And to Mr

20

Divekar.

More, he was a man, one human being, who was horribly done to death. You could hardly be more brutally killed than by having your head hacked off from your neck. And Bikram was, however much a disgracefully idle peon, a citizen of the Republic of India, the new and still young Republic of India. He was entitled to have his murder as thoroughly investigated as that of anyone among those 'persons of influence', Mr Divekar's own description. Bikram is entitled to have his death properly investigated by, at least, some competent officer from Tilak Marg PS, an officer of at least assistant inspector rank, as I was myself until the beginning of this month of Chaitra.

But I have been instructed, ordered, not to contact Tilak Marg PS.

So what to do? What to do? Because I am going to do something. Something more than just getting rid of that awkward piece of evidence.

Yes, this is it. I have, without at all thinking about it, decided.

I have decided that I, Inspector Ghote, an officer of Crime Branch, Bombay Police, am going to investigate, however much I am lacking authority to do it, the death of one Bikram, a peon.

CHAPTER FOUR

Ghote had hardly come to his decision to investigate, altogether on his own, the case of the murdered peon—a matter he saw at once as being just the sort of small affair that might, had it been

21

somehow connected to some more serious affair, have been given to him as his first assignment in Crime Branch—than he remembered ACP Divekar in the big cabin above barking out, *Why haven't I seen your final list of changes? It's halfway through the morning.*

Hastily he went over to his desk and stood in front of it searching for the rough copy of the schedule he had been about to type out when he had noticed the crammed state of his waste bin, soon followed by his discovery of Bikram's severed head. Then there had come the thought that this was something that had to be reported at once to none other than the Head of Crime Branch.

Damn it all, he said to himself as he looked in dismay at the memo slips and rough papers of his earlier changed and changed-about workings-out, why does everything on the desk have to be in so much of disorder? Impossible to find anything. But next moment he caught a saving glimpse of the large scrawled sheet he had been about to commit to neat typing as it had come to him that, however much apparently he had been mistaken, Bikram's murder was something he should report to Mr Divekar.

He went round and pulled his chair away from under the desk's kneehole to where its back all but touched the wall behind. He managed then, as always, just to squeeze down on it. Now, with the vital sheet ready at his elbow, he twisted round and reached down, teeth clamped in determination, to where Inspector Patil's keys-jamming typewriter still stood mutely next to the waste bin. The bin with, back inside it, the shopping bag and murdered Bikram's head.

One last fierce effort to eject with a single explosive puff from his nostrils any last possible traces of the odour of blood, and he hauled the typewriter from its place, twisted himself back round and dropped the heavy machine, with an all-too-familiar thump, into place.

Now, fast as I can, type out that list. With no mistakes.

*   *   *

Whether it was the violence with which he struck the keys, or actually his very lack of violence as he typed, in only a few minutes his task was accomplished. Rapidly he read over the sheet. No, not a single error, not even in the spelling of his own name, a mistake he frequently made. To his repeated surprise.

Now to call Bik— No, not to call Bikram. Never again to summon Bikram with repeated bang after bang on the shiny brass button of my bell.

Instead, he picked up his phone and succeeded, immediately, in getting hold of Thomas.

'I have one urgent document for Mr Divekar.'

'I will be down directly, Inspector. I know ACP *Sahib* is waiting.'

How different from . . . But do not think such thoughts.

As Thomas appeared, a new awful idea came to Ghote. Will he, so smart and so clean-looking as he is, be struck at once by a still just lingering smell of blood? The smell I myself can no longer detect? He looked, hard as he possibly could, at the fellow's face as he came towards the desk. Surely what is hidden in the waste bin, Bikram's head,

23

Bikram's head, Bikram's head, must, even if only to the smallest degree, still be smelling of blood, however long ago blood ceased to flow from those severed veins, however little I myself am still aware of it?

But what will Thomas do now, knowing, as he must from having entered the cabin above with the ACP's morning tea, that Bikram's head must still be here? Will he offer to take my bin and empty it? That would answer, in one almost miraculous moment, the problem Mr Divekar set me with that snapped-out *Dispose of the damn thing*.

He waited transfixed into immobility.

No change, surely, in that face gravely intent on this small extra duty the ACP had given him.

Or is there a change? Is there on it the minutest flicker of interest?

But, no. No, there is not.

'*Sahib*, the schedule for ACP *Sahib*?'

He Ram, what have I been doing? He has come to collect the schedule. It is here, here right in front of me, but it had altogether vanished from my mind.

Hastily he scrabbled at the typed sheet, got hold of it at last, despite the sweat that had appeared on his fingertips, and passed it to the tall, stately form of the peon in front of him.

'*Achchha, sahib.*'

And he had simply taken away the precious sheet. No solution there to the problem of what to do with the head in the waste bin.

Ghote leant back in his chair, as far as he could, and began seriously to think about what he had decided was now his duty.

All right, I must now dispose of Bikram's head,

24

in accordance with orders. But I will not do so straight away. Eventually, yes, I will dispose of it, somehow or another. But first I will keep same. That bloody object may be—must be—the beginning of the long train of evidence I shall have to find. The evidences that, one by one, will lead at last to a man standing in the dock charged with Bikram's murder.

But where to preserve this first piece of evidence? Where to go myself, with this appalling burden, and safely hide it so that any evidence to be drawn from it is available? And evidences there may well be. Evidences from the head itself, or from the shopping basket in which someone— who? who?—carried it, from whatever quarter of Bombay it was where it was hacked from Bikram's body, here to this very cabin in the middle of Police Headquarters.

Into his mind the answer to his dilemma appeared, as if in the cinema a film had abruptly been interrupted for an announcement *Is there a doctor in the hall?* There could be, he had realised, only one safe place to keep hidden the appalling grisly object.

In our flat.

In the flat we acquired, not much more than a month ago, after that long search, rejecting the too costly on the one hand and the altogether too small, and too disgusting, on the other. Our new flat. Our new home, the first proper one we have had, if you do not count our years in the Government-furnished place at the top of the accommodation block at Dadar police station. The first real home we have had.

What will Protima say when I have to tell her

25

what it is I want to hide there? Or, if I have managed to get the bag, and the bloodied head in it, into the flat without her seeing, and she then finds it? What will she say? What will she scream out about defiling our home before it is even fully furnished and where, in the wonderful old wooden, swinging cradle that we managed to find, baby Ved now sleeps so contentedly. Or does for the most part.

All right. Going to the flat is a terrible decision to have made. But I must go. I must transfer the impossible object from this cabin to the unsullied precincts of the flat hitherto solely dedicated to our family.

He pushed his chair back till it hit the wall behind, got to his feet and, shuffling his way round, went and peered over the batwing doors at the wide area of the compound beyond, with all the busy life it held.

A blue police vehicle, stationary almost directly in front of him, was abruptly started up and after a few moments moved noisily forward for some twenty yards, belching out black exhaust fumes. A khaki-coloured officer's car went shooting past it, the driver already looking tigerishly at the compound gates beyond. A pair of burly *jawans* were marching a group of handcuffed prisoners along, not without a good deal of forceful pushing and punching. At the far side, a pair of pi-dogs with no business even to be in the compound were furiously chasing each other round and round, their barking clearly to be heard above all the other noises. Little groups of wives from the living quarters were making their way out, carrying—oh, God—shopping bags barely different from the one

26

in which, before much longer, Bikram's hacked-off head will have to be conveyed past the gateway that khaki car has just swished through.

But it looks as though no one out there, going about their business, will take particular notice of a uniformed inspector making his way to the outer world, even if he is carrying an object as unlikely as a shopping bag. And this is almost certainly the time the flat will be empty, with Protima going to the market carrying, yes, her own shopping bag, and baby Ved in a fold of her sari.

Often and often she has told me how she is spending her day while I am at work here on my interminable *bandobast*. For her, shopping, especially when she is having to carry Ved everywhere, must be an altogether wearisome task. Yet it has to be undertaken. Much occupied as we are with the flat itself, we have not yet managed to find any servant at all.

So, time to go. No one out there, I think, who is knowing me well enough to ask me what on earth it is I am carrying in an old shopping bag.

If they do, can I say my wife is not well and I am going home having taken on one of her daily tasks? Yes, I could get away with that, if I make it plain I am in one devil of a hurry. And then it will really be hurry-hurry away on that half-mile walk to Bank Street Cross Lane and the old, dangerously tilting, three-storey building there. God, how many monsoons must have battered at its walls to wear it away so much. Pieces drop off almost every day.

But, once there, I should be safe, even as soon as I begin toiling up those bare wooden stairs to our top floor.

Right, then, nip back this instant to the dark corner behind the desk. Lift up the shopping bag and its heavy burden—wonder who owned it before—adjust its top carefully as I can to conceal the blood-spotted *Matunga News*. Then, my left hand loaded down, go over again to the doors here for one last check outside.

A minute later he thought, *Oh, my God, thank heavens I took this one last look*. Superintendent Ghorpade is there, unmistakable even across the whole compound from the way he has just walked all round a cluster of hens pecking at the gravel. Who else would give way to hens? Not scatter them, squawking, as he marched through? But, kindly man as he is, if he was spotting me he would have almost certainly come over to ask how I am getting on. And then—he might, he might—inquire what is in the heavy-looking bag I am carrying. He is the sort of officer who would notice anything out of the ordinary and want to know about it. The top-class detective. And I would be hard put to it, in face of that steady gaze of his, to make at all convincing my lie about Protima not being well.

But, no. No. Good. He has just turned in the direction—yes, it must be—of that out-of-the-way little building which Sergeant Moos has as his fingerprints den. Perhaps he has got some evidence for Moos's ultra-powerful microscope and his comprehensive card indexes.

Carefully, so as to attract the least possible amount of attention, he pushed apart the two doors in front of him.

All right, if I am leaving the cabin unattended and with no peon there, I should have locked every

28

drawer in the place, as we do at night. But, if I have to set down this terrible bag to go through all that complicated routine, I will risk someone stopping to look at me over the doors. So, for once, leave it. This is one first-class emergency.

Right, off now.

He froze. A shadow, long in the bright light from the sun now well above the compound's tall surrounding buildings, had thrown a dark patch across the doors' tops. Someone coming from round the corner. But who . . . ?

Oh, yes. Yes, it's all right. It's the damn tea boy. I had altogether forgotten he is always coming again at about this time.

But what if he had arrived just a few moments earlier? Found me carefully pushing down deeper into the bag the blood-marked *Matunga News*?

He wheeled round, ran across to the desk, squeezed into his chair, hefting the weight of the bag up to his lap—will it stain my trousers? Oh, God—then swung it round and, at last, was able to slide it once again into the waste bin.

He had barely straightened up when there came the boy's customary tap-tap on the top of one of the doors, the sound that, hard at work on the ACP's chart, I almost never notice.

Now the boy came in, tall tea canister swinging at his side, white or whitish shirt open across his bare chest, legs, below a pair of khaki shorts, equally bare right down to his grimed-over feet.

Must be careful. What if the bin is a little more prominent than usual and he just only catches sight of one corner of those blood-marked newspaper sheets?

Quick, speak to him. Distract his attention.

29

But what to say? What? My mind is one hundred per cent a blank.

'So . . . so it is you.'

'*Jee, sahib*. It is time.'

'Yes, yes. Time. So it is. And . . . '

Yes. At last this is it.

'And is this the end of your work for today?'

'*Nai, nai, sahib*. Morning-end only. You would not be happy if you were getting no tea all afternoon.'

Ghote managed a pale grin.

'Quite right, quite right. I am altogether depending on your visits. Nothing like a good cup of tea when you have been working hard.'

'But if I was not coming, *sahib*, you could be sending your peon, that Bikram, to fetch.'

So he does not know. Not many people must have learnt Bikram is no more. Really only from Thomas. What tremendous office *gup* the news will be when it begins to get out. It is not every day a peon is . . . Not every day a peon's head is found in a cabin waste bin.

He gulped.

To tell the boy, or not to tell?

He thought rapidly.

Yes, best after all to tell. Best to come out with it *ek dum*. Think how many miscreants I sniffed out, in my days up in Dadar, because they hesitated long before they explained themselves.

'I see you have not heard about poor Bikram.'

He paused, gathered himself together. Yes, I must tell it. Now. Die is cast.

'The truth is—be ready to take in same—earlier this morning only I myself was finding Bikram's . . . in my waste bin here . . . Bikram's cut-off head.'

30

He felt, for the first time, a surge of vomit beginning to rise up, barely able to be checked.

God, should I have drawn the boy's attention to the bin? Will he want to look at it? But, no. No, he has been shocked by what I have said. He almost dropped his canister on the floor. It tilted so much that tea spilt. And he has gone pale also.

'Listen, listen. You must not be taking this news too much to heart. Did you know Bikram so well?'

'*Sahib*, I was knowing a little only. But always he is . . . always he was . . . he was wanting to stop for chat. Even when he was having nothing at all to chat.'

The hovering vomit settled back. Yes, the boy has been able to take in the appalling news. Slowly the paleness is going from his cheeks.

'So, do not let it be worrying you too much, yes?'

'*Jee, sahib.*'

'And never mind about that spill of tea. And I shall not be wanting more tea today. I must go out. So, on with your round, isn't it?'

'*Jee, sahib.*'

And the boy was gone.

Ghote stood there for two minutes more, three, getting back his state of calm alertness. But Protima, he thought then, may soon be back from the market with her shopping bag, as heavy in her hand as mine is going to be. And with Ved in the fold of her sari also. My dreadful task is still to be done, and must not be delayed.

He hauled up the bag yet again, strode across to the peg where he had hung his uniform cap.

Be properly dressed. Nothing must draw attention to myself.

He settled the cap straight, went over to the

31

doors and took one more look to make sure it was as safe to go out as it reasonably could be. Then he pushed the doors wide and stepped through.

CHAPTER FIVE

Reaching the corner of Bank Street Cross Lane without any real incident, Ghote thanked his stars that not a single one in the flood of passers-by he had encountered seemed to have taken any notice of a police inspector in full uniform lugging along a bulging old shopping bag. Yes, he said to himself, as he turned out of Bank Street into the narrow lane where, barely twenty yards along, stood the ominously forward-tilting old house at the top of which was their flat.

Tomorrow, he said to himself, I will go to Headquarters dressed in mufti, just only shirt and pant, as I am fully entitled to do, like any other Crime Branch inspector. Or, no, I must take also my jacket to hold my notebook, my wallet, my pen and whatever other necessaries are there.

Not that there had not been one or two heart-thudding moments as he had made his way through the crowds. Once someone—he never saw who—had actually bumped against the cumbersome bag in his left hand. Did they cause some small bloody fragment to come out of it, he had asked himself? They could have done. The bag is old and worn, something could easily pass through the weave. A few minutes later it had suddenly occurred to him that some *paar-maar*—pickpockets everywhere in Bombay—might have

32

slipped a cunning hand into the bag. Is that thief at this moment looking with wonder at a long blood stain running right up to his wrist? And what will he do if there is? Go to the first blue-uniformed police *jawan* he can see?

Oh, for God's sake, how likely is that?

But, setting out at last on the climb up the bare wooden stairs of the crumbling old building to the third floor, he reflected—it was a comfort—that there had been no sign of Protima ahead of himself as he had entered the lane.

Then, in sight of the door of the flat, he suddenly thought, *What if after all she never left home?* It could be. Some small complication in little Ved's life—his need to be changed, a bout of hiccups— and she could have been delayed going for shopping. It might be anything. Anything.

What will I be able to say to her if she is coming to the door when she is hearing my key in the lock? What possible reason can I give for leaving duty in the middle of the day? And if . . . if, when her questions come pouring out, I am at last forced to tell her, straight out, point-blank, what is in this dirty old shopping bag I have in my hand and, worse, that I am intending to undertake a purely private investigation into the death of the peon whose severed head is here, what will she think? What will she have to say?

He stood there where he was.

The bare board of the stair beneath him gave a sudden prophetic creak.

No, I must go on up, he said to himself. I cannot possibly take Bikram's head away from here. Where could I go with it? How could I *dispose* of it? But, however Protima may answer whatever I manage to say, her words will come tumbling out in one long tossing, unstoppable stream. Whether of approval or of blank opposition there is no way of knowing. Will it be . . . *You are a police officer. You have been given an order. You must not disobey. You cannot disobey* . . . ? Or will it be . . . *Yes, yes, my husband, you have seen that this victim, however low down in life, is a man and must have the right to have his murder investigated down to the last drop* . . . ? Or, again, will it be . . . *In our home? Keeping the head of a dead man in our home? No, never. Never will I allow that* . . . ? No telling. No telling at all.

With features set in stony determination, he resumed his upward progress, each leg leadenly heavy as it rose step by step. At the top landing, however, just in case Protima was actually inside, he left his keys in his pocket and, instead, pressed the button of the buzzer. From inside there came the curious hiccupping low drone the thing invariably made.

He felt a burst of fury. A finger on a door button should produce a cheerful brisk buzzing. Not this damn half-noise that somehow tells of the flat beyond, by no means the place we imagined when we set out to find somewhere to live, all three of us, not too far from Crime Branch. The place is almost bare, hardly at all decorated. No getting over that. And it is also, deep down, not at all clean. The walls show patches of damp. The ceilings in the living room, the bedroom, the tiny kitchen and in the even smaller bathroom—scarcely space for shower pan and cracked grimy Western-style toilet—are all equally grey with ingrained dust that nothing can shift. And, of

34

course, there is nowhere big enough to put the refrigerator we both thought we would at last be able to buy. No, it has turned out to be as it was in the Dadar days, putting into the cupboard, with pierced metal sides we have fixed to the outside wall, a piece of turmeric so as to keep things fresh.

All right, I do now have the telephone I had hoped to possess. A telephone to answer when an emergency call comes, wanting me, a full Crime Branch officer, to go out on an investigation. But it seems the ACP is never giving me such.

The droning sound from inside was producing no response.

Achchha, at least I was right about Protima being out shopping.

So, pull out my key-bunch, find the one for the door, put it in the lock, turn it and then push hard at the door knowing it almost always jams, either from the heat or from the rain.

Right. Safe inside. So now where to hide the thing?

I do not know. I have no idea at all.

In the few weeks we have been here, with myself out all day wrestling with the *bandobast*, I am hardly fully knowing the flat's every nook and corner.

Then a ridiculous flash of recall, coming from nowhere.

Nook and cranny. Cranny. Not *corner.* That is how you have to say it in proper English. The white *sahib* who was brought in at Police Training School when there had been too many complaints about wrong usage in exam answers gave us a joke memory aid for that. Yes, this is it. *Remember, it's not 'crook and nanny' but 'nook and cranny'.* One

35

fine joke, if not actually funny. Plus also you have to know that a nanny is English for an *ayah*.

But forget all that. It must have come into my mind because I feel altogether at a loss about what to do. And that is: find somewhere to hide this horrible bag and the more horrible thing inside it.

Put it in the kitchen somewhere? Hardly. Protima spends hours there, must know every inch of it, the two cupboards, the big and the very small, and what is always in them. Also the space under the sink where the waste pail goes, the narrow corner where the gas cylinder is, the little gap under the cooking rings? God, no. Not anywhere there to put a severed head.

In the living room? Every bit as impossible. Protima is there at every hour when she is not cooking or busy with Ved in the bedroom. The bedroom? No, it would be a sin to put a murdered man's head where, beside our bed, Ved's cradle stands. The bathroom? Absurd. There is hardly enough room there for the jug to clean ourselves with.

Outside somewhere? If I can possibly hang this bag some two or three feet below one of the windows . . . ? No. No, in no time at all there will be a dozen crows fighting over its contents. And at once Protima will look out to see what all the noise and quarrelling is about. Impossible. Impossible.

But now I have eliminated each and every room in the whole wretchedly small flat.

He stood there just inside the door and tried to fight off the thought of what he knew now was the only hope he had left.

It was, it had to be, the bedroom after all. I was really seeing it in my mind's eye right from the

36

start. There, above the one tall fixed cupboard, full of Protima's saris (although also my Number *Ek* uniform has just one inch to hang), is a space between the top and the ceiling. It runs quite far back. All the empty baggages and boxes we used for bringing here our clothes, the sheets, towels and everything else we had in the Dadar flat are there now. Space altogether cram-full.

But, no. No, it is not. If I take down the cases there could well be room, I remember now, to hide the shopping bag right at the back. And then, surely, I could put at the front the cases and even the boxes, pushing them hard up against the hidden bag.

But . . . but isn't it that I was thinking, just only one-two minutes ago, that to hide the head of a murdered man in the bedroom where innocent Ved sleeps in his cradle would be one shaming sin?

He stood where he was just inside the flat's door, in silence.

But he knew that, sooner or later, there would be nothing for it but to pick up Bikram's bloody head in its bag and force it into that holy place. Yes, I must rest it, for just a few minutes, on the floor beside the cupboard, wherever I can see somewhere clear, and then get up on the bedroom chair—oh God, Protima sometimes sits on it to nurse Ved—and lift down one by one each and every suitcase and box. And finally I must hoist up that burden I brought here, push it as far back as I possibly can, and then replace every case and box, squeezing and squeezing them into place.

In a sudden explosion of action, just snatching up the bag, he ran into the bedroom, on his lips a muttered, half-forgotten, half-meant prayer of

37

intercession. From Ganesh Ghote to Ganesha, elephant-headed god, solver of all troubles.

Who provided at once a solution to a problem which Ghote had not yet even thought about. Yes, all right, it is quite likely the bag can be stowed away behind the baggages. But what if, in the time it may have to remain there, something inside it begins to fall through one of the cracks between the boards at the top of the cupboard? To leak not blood, but some appalling drops of . . . of something, slipping down through one of the narrow gaps. Some of those are dangerously wide. Then down will come bloody little pieces of . . . of something on Protima's close-packed saris below. On to the saris she wears every day, or on those she especially cherishes, like the ones she believes bring her luck at times when luck is needed, or the ones she wore first on some memorable occasion. Even on the one, most cherished of all, her red and gold wedding sari.

And God Ganesha's answer? Simple. As soon as the space above the cupboard has been cleared, find a sheet of something that will prevent any liquid or even solid leaking through.

Of course, where there might be such a sheet in the flat is another matter. But if Ganesha, the elephant-headed god who, thinking the serene Moon above was mocking him, was clever enough to snap off one of his own tusks and send it slicing high into the heavens to cut the mocking orb into the thin crescent it now shows at the start and ending of each month, then surely he can do something as simple as solving a small mystery like mine.

Ghote seized the chair then, took it over to the

38

cupboard, jumped up on it and began to rain down suitcase after suitcase.

In no time the space was there. Available. But still offering the danger of vile matter leaking down on Protima's saris. Even on my best uniform.

Jumping off the chair and going to search through the bare rooms of the flat, he at once rejected the rubber sheet Protima always used when bathing little Ved. How could I, even for a moment, have considered that? How could I?

A new despair settled on him. But in a moment, whether through the elephant god's aid or not, he spotted the piece of plastic which had wrapped, when they were on their way from Dadar, a precious statue of Ganesha himself, wedding gift from my mother. Though the sheet would not cover the full extent of the cupboard top, he managed to spread it widely enough to get, in two minutes, the whole monstrous bag safely confined on it.

Baggages and boxes in three or four minutes more pushed back up. Chair restored to its exact position. And it was done.

CHAPTER SIX

Walking back to Headquarters, no blood-heavy burden hanging from his hand, Ghote was able to step out at a pace that, he hoped, would see him into his cabin before anyone had noticed his absence. Some good, he thought before he could stop himself, in there being no Bikram to come blundering in with my half-washed teacup. But,

39

even when, safely past the batwing doors, he had seen on his desk no message in bright-red urgent ink, he felt by no means happy.

Have I, he asked himself, succeeded in hiding *it* well enough? (Not even in the depth of his mind could he bear to be more explicit about what that *it* was.) When I was lifting down those suitcases and those boxes plenty of dust was falling off. Surprising how much has collected in just a few weeks, yet with the whole house in such a poor state it is likely enough. But will Protima, when she is coming back from shopping and is putting Ved into his cradle, see on the floor that dust? She can hardly miss it, good housewife as she is.

And then will she . . . ? But, no, she never will. Even if she suspects the dust came from the top of the cupboard she would, to make sure, have to clamber up on the chair as I did, and I am very much doubting she would do that while Ved is there sleeping. So can I perhaps rest easy?

But did I leave other signs of something so much out of the ordinary happening while she was out? I must have disturbed plenty of things while I searched everywhere. Then there is that smell of death, too. Had I become so used to it I was no more noticing? It may still be there. And Protima has a keen nose. It is what is making her such a good cook. So, one sniff and she would not rest until she tracks down the evil odour.

Yet all I can do, here where I am now, is to wait. To wait and see if that has happened. But . . . but perhaps after all there may not be any smell for her to detect.

Say she does, though . . . What will she do? No doubt about it. She will go straight to the

40

telephone, the telephone I was so pleased to get installed, and she will ring me, although I have told her and told her not to call except in a first-class emergency. But, no, the phone on my desk here will suddenly shrill out.

Oh God, why did all this have to happen to me? Should I then give up the whole idea of tracking down whoever it was who killed Bikram? If you think about it, you could say his murder is no business of mine. All right, when someone out wherever it is Bikram stayed comes to realise he has vanished, they will probably report it to the nearest PS and lead to an investigation. No more my responsibility, if ever it was.

I could forget all about the poor fellow's terrible end. I could go back to the flat at the earliest safe moment, take down from the top of the cupboard that tell-tale shopping bag and somehow get rid of it. There is always the sea. Then I could let the whole business fade slowly away into my far past.

But I cannot do that.

I knew Bikram. I knew him well. I knew every waft of stale-smelling rum that came from his hanging-open mouth.

So I must just wait. Wait all the afternoon long. Wait and hope Protima does not for any reason, likely or unlikely, come to find Bikram's head there behind our baggages. But, more, I must begin to think how it came about that someone unknown killed Bikram, hacked his head from his body.

Carefully sliding down on his seat, he took a sheet of spare paper from the pile he kept in his desk, second drawer down. He looked at it, and put it back. Best never to leave anywhere any

41

written evidence of what it is I have chosen to do. That order from the ACP *Dispose of it* makes jolly good sense, for this at least.

But I am still going to do my level best to find the man who beheaded a humble *Dalit* like Bikram.

But how, after all, was that killer able to hack and hack at Bikram with no one witnessing it? And why did he need to do it?

Somehow everything that has been going on, my telling Mr Divekar that Crime Branch should investigate a murder in its very heart, the sharp order I was given to go and get on with my *bandobast* duties, and that threat even to get me altogether necked out of Crime Branch, plus my terrible trip with Bikram's head over to Bank Street Cross Lane and my search in the flat for somewhere to hide the bag—all that has put out of my head any consideration of what must actually have happened. Happened somewhere—but where?—in the huge sprawling city of Bombay, biggest in India.

So, now, let me think.

Achchha, first of all, the beginning of it, so far as I am able to imagine same. The moment of the murder.

How exactly was it done? Was Bikram attacked from behind, his murderer waving in the air some heavy sword? Or was it some other weapon he had? A butcher's cleaver? Not a few of those come out in places like Matunga and even Dadar when some street brawl begins. And did the killer cut Bikram's head from his body at a single blow? No. The head I hid, hid in my own flat, in the bedroom that is its centre, had been hacked at time and again. So was Bikram somehow put out of account

42

first? Perhaps just only knocked unconscious? And then, as he began to come back to knowing what was happening, was that deadly weapon held just above him as he looked upwards? And brought down on his naked throat? Once, twice, three times, four?

Did Bikram have time for a single terrified scream? A scream cut off like a klaxon switched into silence?

Yes, a fate such as that is one that no one, high or low, bad or good, should meet with. And it has fallen to me to find the man who inflicted it. But how to do it? How?

Head thrust despairingly into his hands, Ghote forced himself to confront his situation with something of calm orderliness. First of all, I am knowing, well knowing, how to conduct a murder investigation. There are rules for doing it. The rules I was learning at Police Training School. Rules I was following more times than I can remember in my years up in Dadar, where ordinary everyday murders happen often enough and where the simple application of those rules brought, almost always, a quick result. A husband kills his wife and leaves dozens of indications of what he has done. A wife, driven to desperation, kills her bullying husband and, numbed, awaits discovery.

But the rules I learnt at Nasik were based on there being a team behind the investigator in charge. Every resource that years and years of murder inquiries have found to be necessary was always there. But now I have no one to go to for specialist assistance. No one, even if I was in possession of Bikram's body as well as his head, to

43

carry out a post-mortem that would tell me from analysis of food eaten and part digested how much time passed since the *corpus delicti* was killed. Now I have no fingerprints officer at my disposal, let alone a world-class man like endlessly talking Sgt Moos. Now, should I perhaps need an expert tracker to follow a difficult trail of footprints, I would get no help at all.

A tiny clink of noise, distant it seemed as if it might have come from outer space, penetrated to his ears.

What . . . ? What it is? Why am I thinking I heard that sound? It is not part of my train of thought, the train I am trying to pursue.

I was in the middle of thinking, isn't it, how I can start a murder investigation altogether on my own. Isolated. How in any way to set about it? Where even to start?

He found then that his hands had dropped to the desk in front of him and his eyes were open.

And there, carefully pouring tea into his waiting cup, still marked with the stains Bikram never abolished, was the tea boy once again.

Chagoo? Yes. Yes, that is his name. Really I am knowing it perfectly well.

Oh, God, do I owe Chagoo any money? I forget. Forget altogether. This morning—I remember telling him I had found Bikram's severed head in my waste bin itself, and wondering if he had been too much shocked for a boy of his age. What age would that be? I have never asked. Ten, eleven? Twelve at most by the look of him. But he recovered from his shock then. Perhaps, after all, I did help him to do that.

And he told me that he knew Bikram, and that

Bikram was always ready to chat, even when he had nothing to say.

'Tell me, Chagoo,' he said in the Marathi he knew was the boy's first language, 'tell me, did I pay you this morning?'

A grin by way of answer.

'No, Inspector *Sahib*.'

'You should have reminded me to do it.'

'Oh, it was not mattering. I am well knowing you would pay soon. Not like those others.'

Those others, unnamed.

Ghote dug in his pocket, felt out a small round twenty-five *paisa* coin, as much he reckoned as he owed. Then, a sudden decision, he fished up a second one.

He handed both over. 'For you.'

'Oh, *sahib*, very good.'

Chagoo turned to go.

'*Wait*,' Ghote choked out on a flash of mental clarity.

'*Jee, sahib*?'

'There is something . . . You were saying this morning you often chatted with poor, murdered Bikram.'

Another grin, something of a sly one.

'Not so much of chat, *sahib*. More of listen while Bikram was saying this or that. Or nothing at all.'

'Yes. You said he was often and often half-drunk from rum.'

'*Jee, sahib*. You could even smell him coming round corner.'

Now for a first meaningful question.

'Tell me, do you know from where he was getting enough of money to be as drunk as he was almost all the time?'

45

'*Sahib*, he would not tell. Once I was asking, and he was becoming angry-angry.'

'So you have no idea of how? No idea at all?'

Chagoo bit in thought at his underlip.

A long silence.

And then, '*Sahib*, one little idea I am having.'

'Yes? Speak.'

'*Sahib*, I am thinking—it is thinking only—that however stupid Bikram is when truly drunk, when he is only a little bit drunk, or not at all, he can be too much clever.'

'Too clever? But too clever to do what?'

'Inspector, I am not knowing-knowing. But I am thinking this: Inspector, what if he was able to get money, much money, out of . . . out of someone? Someone rich-rich?'

Bright boy, bright boy. I do believe he may have guessed right.

'You know what they are calling a trick like that in English?' Ghote asked him. 'Blackmail, they are calling it. Black is *kala* and *mail* is meaning, more or less, a letter coming by post. Under Indian Penal Code, Section 383, blackmail is called *extortion*. But, whatever you are calling it, it is one very bad crime.'

'*Jee*, Inspector.'

Ghote considered rapidly what might follow from this discovery, if discovery it was. Wretched drunken Bikram, he thought, may have somehow come across something, perhaps even here in Crime Branch, some file carelessly left open or, say, a letter alleging some criminal activity left for a moment out on a desk. Anything that could have led him, even though no great reader, as I well know, to some knowledge which a wealthy

46

businessman perhaps would not want the world to learn about. So then Bikram might have come to see that this could bring him, over time, a steady income to spend on rum and more rum. But who on earth would such a well-off victim be?

'So,' he cautiously asked bright young Chagoo, 'do you at all know, can you guess even, who Bikram may have been *blackmailing*?'

Yes, the boy may have the answer. A wide-awake youngster, going here, there and everywhere with that long tea canister of his. He may even have wormed an answer out of rum-hazy Bikram himself.

But Chagoo's neat head made the circular motion that conveys *No*, or at best *Cannot say*.

And I am thinking that on this occasion it must mean definitely *No*.

CHAPTER SEVEN

It took Ghote more than an hour after Chagoo's plain negative, or fairly plain one, had seemed to block a possibly promising line of investigation to see what might, after all, be the way forward. At first, all he could do was to tell himself that, surely, he had learnt at least something. I have taken one step, the first, in my single-handed investigation. I think now I can accept it as a strong possibility that Bikram may have been blackmailing somebody. Feathering his own nest, as they say.

Feathering his own nest. The odd English expression had risen up into his mind from nowhere.

47

Why am I thinking of it, he asked himself? If anyone had inquired, I would have sworn I had never so much as heard the expression. But I must have done. Or perhaps I read it in some English book, and it lodged itself somewhere deep in me. Possibly, so ground-down as I was in thinking about Bikram's death, my mind has, of itself, found something altogether new to consider.

Then his same mind went skittering even more wildly off-track. He found himself thinking of a set of paintings in the Prince of Wales Museum that he had first seen when, as a young newcomer to mighty Bombay, he had cautiously explored the huge museum. There were twelve paintings in the set, each depicting a month in the Hindu calendar.

Young as I was, he thought, and certainly no art expert, I felt mysteriously sure then that the long-ago painter was no tremendous genius. He must have been—I was somehow certain—someone who had realised his skills could take him far, but only so far. And he had had the courage not to attempt to go any further. Perhaps that itself had been what so attracted me to those twelve paintings, making me go to look at them again and again in the years afterwards.

The one of the set that particularly comes into my mind just now, he admitted to himself, is of the month of Baisakh, the month we are now in. The painting showing, besides Krishna and his beloved Radha gazing into each other's eyes, trees everywhere springing into early summer leaf, full of fluttering koels pecking at will at the mango blossoms all around. Koels, the nightingales of India, as they call them.

Skitter, skitter, another memory arrived. One

48

day at Nasik I happened to mention to the Englishman teaching us correct usage that the koel, the Indian nightingale, besides singing so brilliantly, also has the habit of laying its eggs in the nests of harshly croaking crows. Did British nightingales do that also, I was asking? And got sharply corrected. *No, Ghote, the nightingale of England does nothing of the sort. You are confusing it with the cuckoo, which does in fact do that somewhat reprehensible thing.*

But why am I thinking about all this now?

Ah, yes. Yes, I know. It must be because I was seeing Bikram in a new light, as someone *feathering his nest.*

Achchha, but why was I not able to work out for myself that this is what Bikram must have been doing? Why did I have to be half-told it by a tea boy, probably barely able to read and having no more than a handful of English words at his disposal? Never mind, he gave me that first step, the one they say that counts.

But the second?

Let me think. Yes, it must be that *somebody* Bikram was managing somehow to blackmail decided he must be got rid of. Eliminated. That person must, of course, be someone a great deal richer than ignorant Bikram. So, how in the first place did Bikram even get to learn who it was he could blackmail?

Think . . . Yes, can there possibly be some other person altogether, who Bikram eventually got to know, able to work out that the secret he had discovered was such that the rich man it concerned would pay good money to keep it hushed up? Say, the victim is some well-off businessman, or

49

perhaps a politician, like for instance that chancy fellow, Pradeep Popatkar, so deeply in Protima's bad books.

But who could Bikram have come across with enough knowledge of the ways of the world to be able to tell him he had hit on a source of ever-flowing income? Wait. Think of this. Is it not unlikely that in one of the beer bars Bikram went to night after night he met, or even just heard talking, a man who boasted about the underhand things his rich, rich boss did, the dirty tricks of the business world. Say he is a clerk in the very office of the man whose secret Bikram chanced to come upon when some file or letter had been left where he could see it.

Think now. Surely Bikram's acquaintance might easily become his accomplice? With a job somewhere in the rich man's office he would be able to deliver, in safe anonymity, the necessary blackmail note. Between the two of them then they would have thought they had a wide-open path to supply themselves with incomes for life, one with his piece of valuable knowledge, the other with the means to deliver a blackmail demand.

But they must, the pair of them, have failed to reckon with their target's ruthlessness. As soon as he had absorbed the blackmail note that had, say, appeared on his finely glossy desk he would have thought he must get the whole business brought to a quick end. And the tried-and-trusted way to do that would be to hire a *supari*, a man who for a sum often thought of as no more than the price of a street vendor's handful of chewy supari seeds would, simply, commit murder. Leaving the person who paid him with his own hands kept clean.

And, yes, as part of the bargain this *supari*—there were plenty of them if you knew where to look—would have been instructed to cut off the victim's head. And then, yes, to take it to a place where it would attract maximum attention. So that anyone else who might have ideas about blackmail would be warned, if only through the newspapers, about what would happen to them.

But there is more. If Bikram's severed head has been put somewhere inside Crime Branch, is it not possible that the person being blackmailed has guessed that his secret, whatever it is, has been passed perhaps by some business rival, who till now has got no more than a sniff of it, to some friend or acquaintance in Police Headquarters? He would hope this insider might dig up enough additional facts to lead eventually to the prosecution of the victim, the fall of a hated rival.

Ghote jerked himself back in his chair, all but striking his head against the wall behind.

Have I got it?

Yes. Or at least I may have done.

Bringing himself to sit more upright, he looked at his watch.

Good God, already almost ten minutes later than my time for calling it a day and leaving for home. I must have altogether forgotten also to go for my tiffin at noon. And what will Protima be thinking, if in her busy day she happens now to have noticed the time?

Quickly he pushed all the papers on his desk into its drawers and shut them away. But, as he did so, it came to his mind that, now without Bikram to make sure as his last duty that every drawer and cupboard in the cabin was properly locked, he

51

would have to do more than just shut up the desk.

Swiftly he attended to the filing cabinet and the cupboard on the inner wall.

So everything done now? Yes, must be. Every key turned and put safely away in the desk. Yes. Or, no. No, by God. He turned back to the cupboard. My Gross's *Criminal Investigation* in its place of honour on top of the cupboard. How could I have left it out there? Anyone might have made away with it. I must have omitted it because I think of it as a fixture where it sits, radiating its wisdom every minute of my day.

He opened the cupboard again, carefully put the precious battered dark-blue volume safely inside.

One final look round. And off.

*   *   *

When, in something of a sweat from the speed he had walked over to Bank Street Cross Lane, he had thudded his way up the creaky wooden stairs, he found he did not need to take out his key-bunch or give a push to the buzzer button. Protima, with baby Ved firmly attached at her side, had jerked the door wide.

'Where have you been?' she shot out. 'You are late by more than one half-hour. What it is you have been doing? Talking *gup* with some other inspector, and forgetting even that you have a wife? And, yes, a poor little hungry son also?'

Which of this stream of charges to counter first? Point out it is not anything like by half an hour I am late, barely as much as twenty minutes? Say I am never chatting with any other inspector? Or say even, a small lie, that ever-friendly Superintendent

Ghorpade was catching sight of me and wanting a word?

But the thought that came immediately into his head, in a sunburst of relief, was that, because Protima had made her complaint, she could not have found the terrible hacked-off head in its shopping bag above the bedroom cupboard. And that was followed by an altogether more overwhelming thought. *I have decided beyond alteration that I am going to track down Bikram's killer and to do that I must sooner or later examine his hacked-about head. It may provide me with a clue. May? It almost certainly could tell me at least something. And, if I am thoroughly to carry out that examination, Protima will have to be told after all what is there in the bedroom.*

He saw then that, if it was at all to be told, the whole appalling story must be brought to light at once.

'Yes, yes,' he blurted out. 'I am late. But that is because something terrible has happened.'

In a moment Protima changed from vengeful goddess to anxious wife.

'What . . . ? What of terrible, husbandjee?'

So, with the flat's door barely closed behind him, he told her. He recounted it all, from the moment when, reaching for his typewriter, he had seen that *falooda* froth of newspaper at the top of his waste bin, to his discovery in the shopping bag of Bikram's mutilated head. Then on again to his rebuff from Mr Divekar, determined to have his Crime Branch tackle only the most important cases as he drove it to a higher and higher pitch of efficiency. And on, once more, to how his own suggestion that the murder ought to be a Crime

Branch case had brought that immediate instruction, *Just dispose of the damn thing.*

And here Protima stopped him flat.

'But he should never have ordered you to do that,' she exclaimed. 'Never. To go and dispose—was that what he truly said?—to dispose of that poor peon's head, as if it was a piece of rubbish only. It was wrong. Quite, quite wrong. No one, not even an Assistant Commissioner, should say a thing like that. All just so as to drive—you were telling—the Branch he is heading to more and more of efficiency. That man is nothing else than one of those rajahs from past days, seized by ambition to conquer each and every state they are seeing, and doing it with the blood of the people they are wishing to claim as their own subjects.'

Ghote felt he could not absolutely endorse Protima's charge. And in any case something more urgent had entered his mind.

I have not yet told her what I eventually did with Bikram's head. I have not said I brought it here. To our flat. I have not said why I had to put it on top of the bedroom cupboard. Worse, I have yet to tell her what I have become determined to do. To investigate, with help from no one since I cannot ask for any, Bikram's death.

He took a long and deep breath and told the rest of his story. In as few words as he could.

'His cut-off head?' Protima all but shouted. 'Up on top of the cupboard? On top of the bedroom cupboard itself?'

But, though the words might have been fiery with outrage, they were somehow not so. Despite their volume, bewilderment was the one thing they conveyed. And—could it be?—a little of

54

compassion for himself also.

Foolishly, Ghote responded to that hint by drawing attention to his baby son.

'You are not horrified? And, look, yes, little Ved is smiling even. It is the first time ever he has smiled. The first. He must be somehow knowing nothing too terrible is there on the cupboard.'

Protima gave Ved one swift glance.

'His first smile?' she said. 'That is the way with fathers. They are hoping and hoping always that the first smile will be for them. But, no, my husband, it is the first wind for you. And not at all the first. Wind and wind Ved has been having all day, even when we were going for shopping. I am not at all knowing why.'

'Oh, you may not be knowing,' Ghote conceded at once. 'But I am sure you are right. It must be wind, not smile. Yes, wind. But should you not be patting on back?'

'Patting and patting I have been doing ever since we were getting back from the market. But perhaps if I am putting him into his cradle now, he will go to sleep.'

Then a gasp, almost a shriek.

'But . . . but he cannot be put to sleep in that room, with that . . . He cannot be put in there when, just only feet away, there is the head of a murdered man.'

Ghote stiffened his shoulders.

'Very well, then. I will take down that shopping bag *ek dum*, and put it somewhere else. In the kitchen? Would that be a place for it?'

'No. Oh, yes, yes. There, if anywhere. That would be the least bad place.'

'But, first,' Ghote said, 'I have more to tell.

55

Something I am not sure you will like to hear.'

'Not like to hear? But what it is? Tell, tell.'

'In one moment. First, please go and sit there on the *takht* and put little Ved down beside you.'

Protima went across to the improvised *takht* which, on the day they had taken possession of the flat, they had constructed by piling together all the cushions they could lay hands on. She sat and put little Ved, already showing clear signs of sleepiness, down beside her.

'Yes, Ved's father?'

Ghote felt a little jab of self-satisfaction. The master of the house had given instructions, and had been obeyed.

Then, interrupted by frequent hesitations, he explained in full the decision he had felt himself unable to not take.

'Yes,' he concluded, 'I have definitely decided, howsoever difficult it may be, that I, on my own altogether, will track down the man who savagely killed my peon, Bikram.'

'Of course,' Protima said at the end of it. 'Of course that is what you must do. Any help I can be giving I will give. Even help, if you are needing, to take one good look at . . . at that head.'

CHAPTER EIGHT

Ghote felt his world, the stable world he had thought he existed in, had been turned upside down, *ulta pulta*. My wife, to me essence of womanhood, mother of my Ved, ever tears-ready, and, yes, ever rage-ready also, has declared she is willing to help examine Bikram's blood-soaked, horribly hacked-about head . . . It is seeming to be an impossibility.

But then he realised it was no impossibility.

To the roll-call of feminine feelings I just now found running through my head like a film shown at double speed—womanliness, tears, rages—I should have added something else. Woman's willingness, shared by nearly all of them, to examine, to touch if necessary, whatever wounds a body may have fallen victim to, whatever foul sores may have erupted and are requiring attention.

'You are here, here to help me when I am needing help as never before.' The altogether grateful words came.

So, after a hasty meal, before baby Ved was put into his carved swinging cradle to sleep the sleep of the innocent, Ghote set to work in the bedroom lifting down the squeezed-in baggages, thinking that, not so many hours before, he had in desperate haste pushed these same suitcases and empty boxes back into their places, with dust falling all around, apparently unnoticed.

'Let me look,' Protima said as he stepped down off the bedroom chair he had once more pressed into service.

Wondering at her yet again, Ghote pulled wide the twine handles of the shopping bag and let her pluck apart the topmost sheets of the *Matunga News*.

'But that is a photo of Pradeep Popatkar, the filthy cheat,' she said holding up the first page.

'Yes, yes. Your pet hate. The one your magazine *Daylight* was saying, just only this week, that he was doing very bad things, yes, up in Matunga. And also, *Daylight* was claiming, taking the financial help of the boss of big, big Moolchand Investments plc. But, listen, I am very much wanting to get this horrible bag out of this room where soon Ved will be sleeping-sleeping.'

'Yes, you are right. I will wait to look and look at it when we are in the kitchen.'

*   *   *

On the kitchen's small white bakelite-topped table, carefully scrubbed, the two of them began at last to conduct their examination. Ghote set down the battered old shopping basket on its side and carefully extracted the terrible object inside it, tugging as gently as he could at Bikram's roughly cropped, wiry hair, blood still a little sticky in the warmth of his tugging fingers.

'Yes,' he said, 'if I can remember enough now of what I was learning years ago at Police Training School, we may discover something worth knowing from the wounds inflicted by whatever weapon was used.'

'Then begin, begin. What first is it the investigator would do?'

Working as much as possible in the way a

58

forensic scientist had demonstrated years before in the lecture room at Nasik, Ghote, lacking all the scalpels and other instruments the scientist had employed, conducted as scrupulous an examination as he could of the neck of the severed head, even from time to time making use of Protima's little fine-sewing magnifying glass.

But, after something like two hours' painstaking work going over and over the now hardened surface, he gave one look at the blank open page of the notebook he had hopefully placed on a corner of the table, and had to admit in tumbling disappointment that he must have forgotten almost all he had once listened to so carefully at Nasik.

'We have discovered nothing,' he said. 'Nothing that I did not see before, even in the brief glance I was able to take at the head in my cabin. All I could have entered in this notebook, had it been at all worth my while, was that whoever hacked Bikram's head from his body needed four blows to do it. Yes, exactly four blows. Evidence, of a sort, I suppose.'

'But, no, there is something more to help,' Protima contradicted him.

She opened wide the laid-aside sheets of the *Matunga News*.

'Look, it is here. Here.'

'But this newspaper is only what the killer happened to use to wrap up the head before putting it in the shopping bag,' he said. 'All right, it is the *Matunga News*, and that may tell us where the killing took place. Or it may not. But—'

'No, no. It is nothing at all to do with which paper he was using. It is the photo. The photo I was telling you about before, the one of the man you were calling as my *pet hate*. Of Pradeep Popatkar. Yes, he used to be a person of much influence out at Matunga, among all the criminals and riff-raff that are there. But now, standing in the by-election for Bombay South, with all the rich pickings it promises, he is announcing he always had the greatest interest in this area where we now are itself.'

This was too much for Ghote. Tired out as he was with his loathsome task seeming all the more horrible each time, it had come home to him that he was working on the head of the man who had served him, however badly, ever since his first day at Crime Branch, and he rounded now on his wife, however helpful she had been to him.

'What you are saying?' he shouted. 'All that is nonsense only. Just because Popatkar has his picture in this newspaper it does not mean he had anything whatsoever to do with Bikram's murder, the murder I am determined to get to the bottom of.'

But, it seemed Protima had, in an instant, changed from loyal forensic assistant to wife determined her husband would do as she wanted.

'No, no. Popatkar is someone you should be taking very much of interest in. He is a one hundred percent no-good. Why do you think he has come down to here, here where you and I now are having votes, to try by every unfair means he can to win the seat, altogether in laps of gods with so many other contestants? It is because he will be able to sell his Legislative Assembly votes to whoever will pay most. His interest is in Pradeep Popatkar only. He is not at all knowing what, in

60

this world, is his proper place.'

Ghote was on the point of finding more sharp, and logical, words when Protima's denunciation took on a suddenly different note.

'No, Popatkar is not knowing his right place in the way you know yours, my husband.'

And Ghote experienced a rush of astonishment.

Yes, the thought streamed through his mind, it is true I have, almost from a child, wanted to find my own proper place in the world. To find it and to stay in it, not falling away and not also filling my head with thoughts that I must go higher and higher. But I had no idea at all that Protima has found this is so.

The least I can do, it struck him then, is not to tell her she is being ridiculous about who is standing in her by-election, fly-election.

'Very well,' he said, 'I promise I will pay some attention to Pradeep Popatkar. Yes, I promise.'

'Promises are not enough. You have made promises before. But now, when Voting Day is getting near, you must do your duty. Your duty to Bombay itself, to the whole of India even. You must see that Pradeep Popatkar is altogether thrown out. He must be made into one fine example of public disgust at the way politics nowadays are made the plaything of men grasping for money and yet more money. So, yes, you must vote against him. But you must also tell each and every one of your colleagues in Crime Branch to do the same. The ACP even.'

Ghote thought, with appalled dismay, of himself daring even to address Mr Divekar on the subject of politics, much less conveying to him Protima's demand that his vote must be used in the way she

61

herself wanted. Good God, he thought, now that I have it in mind, ACP *Sahib* is much the same sort of man as this Pradeep Whatshisname. Both of them, it seems, totally determined to do what they are wanting.

But how to respond to the fearful suggestion Protima has made?

Yes, only one way.

'But, Ved's mother. There is something urgent-urgent we have to do now. Now at this moment.'

'Yes. We must get something more to eat. We are needing that. We were having such a quick meal before. We should have just another bite. But not here at this table itself. No, we should sit in the next room, together on the *takht*. If those slippy-slidy cushions will for once stay put.'

'All right, we will do that. But first—'

'First, what?'

'Look,' he said, with all the urgency he could summon up. 'Look at that head there on the table still. You know, I was able to find just only that one place to hide it when I brought it here. In the bedroom. I was searching everywhere, and there was nowhere else. Nowhere else at all. And . . . and there is still nowhere else to put it where it would be safe from some visitor who may come. You never can be sure someone will suddenly be there. You know that.'

A long moment passed before Protima spoke.

'You are saying you are going to put that head, all blood covered as it is, into the room where Ved is sleeping in his cradle? No, no. I tell you no.'

Ghote hardened himself to the sticking point.

'Then explain to me,' he said, almost grating the words out, 'where can it be put, at least for tonight and perhaps for a day or two longer? You and I will be eating our *chota hazri* here, at this table tomorrow morning. Ved also may be here. Everything must be taken away now.'

He let his words hang there in front of her. And then—he hardly knew he was speaking again—he added something. Just a quick remark.

'And a good squirting of Flit should be given also.'

Protima was still standing, in the way he had in the past seen her, adamantly upright in front of him. But now—*Flit*. Homely Flit had got to her— she melted. Snow in summer.

'You are right, Ved's father. Right.'

Ghote needed to hear not another word. In scarcely more than a minute he was back in the bedroom—swift eye cast on Ved fast asleep in his swinging cradle—and then once more he pulled the room's chair into position.

*   *   *

So, first thing next day, *chota hazri* quickly eaten, Ghote was back at Crime Branch before any of his fellow officers, even before Superintendent Ghorpade, glimpsed coming in at the compound gate a few moments after himself. His cabin's doors still flapping together behind him, he took a long, quiet look at the whole of the little room and then a yet closer survey.

Everything, he decided at last, was just as it had been the day before when he had left in a rush finding he was already a little behind time. The drawers where I was putting my papers are as firmly locked as they were. Cupboard is locked also, dark-blue, mildew-stained *Criminal Investigation* (edited by RM Howe) safely inside it. Right, put it back *ek dum* in its place of honour.

Yes, even my desecrated waste bin is tucked away in its accustomed dark corner. One piece of luck, perhaps more than I deserve.

But—the thought struck him like a bolt of lightning—what if pernickety Sgt Moos is coming in now and noticing with those eyes, famously keen to spot even one trace of fingerprints, something on the rim of the bin. But, no. No, if Moos is coming, and he almost certainly will come before long, then all he will be wanting is yet another of his famous chats. He will make straight for one of the chairs in front of the desk—yes, both now in their exact positions—and begin at once recounting his newest triumph. Or perhaps his oldest.

But the bin? Has it been cleaned at all? That was one of Bikram's tasks, generally remembered, if carried out very badly. No, no one will have seen to that.

So, yes, part of my *bandobast* duties, I must arrange now for a new peon for myself, and straight away also. I cannot once more have Mr Divekar's Thomas taken away from his tea-bearing duties to bring down instructions to me.

Time enough at this moment to get what I have to do done? Yes. Must be.

*   *   *

Before an hour more had passed, with the ACP still silent above, Ghote had in front of him one Paresh, a man looking a good deal tidier than rum-smelling, shirt-stained Bikram had ever been. His face wore the would-be helpful expression Gujaratis tended to show, ever willing to please.

Yes, I am truly learning the ways of Crime Branch, Ghote thought. If I had needed a new peon four-five weeks ago, what would I have done? Nothing. I would have flapped and floundered only. But just now it took me no more than some minutes to telephone Tilak Marg PS and search out this suitable fellow, to get him installed on the Crime Branch roll of peons, to state his rate of pay—one step up from Bikram's—and have him here in front of me to be given instructions for his each and every duty.

'Right,' Ghote said, 'First thing is: my waste bin. It is altogether needing cleaning. I do not believe the fellow I was having before you was ever doing same. Not once.'

A few minutes later, as quietly smiling Paresh came back, scrubbed-clean bin in his hands, another idea came into Ghote's head.

Just only fifteen-twenty minutes ago I was seeing to it that Paresh was entered in internal records. But it was not simply his name, *Paresh Maskawala*, that was written down there. It was his address as well. And, if I was seeing Paresh's full details, someone at some time must have entered Bikram's facts. So, back to Records. Then in hardly any time at all I will know where Bikram was staying. As soon as I am free after that I have only to go to wherever that is and I will very likely learn a whole lot more about Bikram than his bare name. Perhaps there will even be some clue to who is the person he met somewhere who gave him that access to the unknown businessman whose secret he happened to chance upon somewhere about Crime Branch.

A good step forward.

No, not one step only. Perhaps a good many steps in the investigation into Bikram's murder that I promised myself, Protima also, to undertake. To undertake on my own.

But Paresh had come in with more than a brightly clean waste bin. He had also quietly put on the desk the day's first bundle of memos from the ACP. Top priority.

*　　　*　　　*

Usually it took a full two hours, or even three, to compile the ACP's list. But now Ghote found he was reaching down for Inspector Patil's ancient, frequently jamming typewriter after a little more than ninety minutes.

Then—damn any waiting for the ACP's last-second corrections—I have in my grasp now a just-possible lead to Bikram's drinking friend, whoever he is, who must have given him his access to whatever money-dripping *crorepati* he was hoping to blackmail.

Yes, back now *ek dum* to Records. Do it for myself. Try telephoning them and God knows what complications will be there.

Among all the dust-thick cardboard files of Records, pieces falling off them left and right, the occasional overstuffed one spilling out half its contents, he located quickly enough the record book into which not long before he had watched Paresh's particulars being entered. More, flicking furiously back through its dozens of dusty pages he found within ten minutes the name Bikram Bhatt, with particulars that confirmed it as his own Bikram. If I'd ever heard the name Bhatt I had at once forgotten it, such a common one. Must be thousands of Bhatts in Bombay. But, yes, yes, yes, here is the address he gave when he got the job.

A disappointing one. It was Hut 191 in a slum out in Matunga. No more than that. And how maddeningly big any slum out there was likely to be. Bikram's one might well have many, many more huts in it than a hundred and ninety-one. All right, he had stated to the Records clerk who had entered his name that the slum was 'off Lady Hardinge Road', but that was hardly any help.

Well, I am actually knowing at least something about that British Lady Hardinge, honoured by the name of a road up in Matunga. My father, who loved all curious facts, told me once that there had been two Viscount Hardinges, each a Viceroy of India. So Lady Hardinge must have been the wife of one of them.

But that is hardly a help to me in finding Bikram's Hut 191.

Yet I must find it. I must go out to Matunga and find it. But, damn it, even Matunga itself is one hell of a long way from here.

Quickly he scrawled the scanty address in his notebook and made his way back to his cabin. There he banged hard on the rounded, shiny bell to summon Paresh.

Almost at once Paresh appeared. Good, Ghote thought. How often did Bikram come this quickly? Never. Never once.

'Paresh,' he said, 'I am going to be away from my desk for some time. If anyone is asking for me, say

67

you are not sure but you think I have had to eat my tiffin at home because my baby son—'

He stopped himself.

To invent some imaginary sudden illness for little Ved may somehow bring about just such a disaster. Very small children can, in one moment only, fall victim to a whole medical book of dangerous illnesses.

'No. Say this, that I have had to go back to my flat, not far away, because my wife is not feeling too well and—yes, this is it—we have no servant just now to look after our baby.'

'Yes, Inspector, I will give that message,' Paresh replied, simultaneously conveying by a fleeting look that he had guessed his new boss was going somewhere quite different from the destination he had specified. Perhaps to place a bet on whatever proves to be the winning number in the daily list of Cotton Exchange prices, the so-called *matka*, the big pot who anyone buying the single right ticket might win. Or, did Paresh think I might be going to buy this wife of mine a fine present to cover up some altogether different activity?

Ghote ignored it all. Quickly he locked up his desk, papers pushed away into it.

It will be hours, it must be, before I am back. Will Paresh be able to ward off inquiries? He must. He will have to.

*   *   *

The address he had got for Bikram was vague as could be. It was as if the rum-soaked fellow had been none too clear when he had given where it was that he did live. But that Hut 191 had to be found and visited, and as soon as possible. If Bikram, a short time before he was killed, had met in some bar near Headquarters a man who worked in an office headed by a *crorepati* with a secret that he did not want at any cost to come out, then finding that drinking companion quickly was worth almost any effort. Whoever the fellow was he could well lead directly to the *goonda* who had been paid, first to hack off Bikram's head, and then to put it somewhere inside Crime Branch, as a warning to any other would-be blackmailer anywhere.

Or, Ghote thought in a sudden jab of suspicion, perhaps—could it be?—to take it into Crime Branch because there is actually someone here to be given such an unmistakably direct warning.

But, no. I am soaring up into heights that are thick with doubts, misconceptions and wild surmises. No, Matunga first. I must be going to Matunga to hunt down Bikram's actual home, and then to get, if I can, a name and a description that will make it possible to find in the neighbourhood of Crime Branch this beer-bar friend Bikram confided in. If such a friend does exist.

Just managing to prevent himself running until he was out in the bustling streets, it came to Ghote that time was altogether limited. Good God, it is one long walk from here to Churchgate and Bombay Central where I must get a train to Matunga. That alone will take half an hour, and that will be a half-hour when I am absent from my desk, and it will be a much longer time that I will have to be out in Matunga. Even when I have reached there I will need perhaps the whole of the rest of the morning, most of the afternoon also, to

69

find, first whatever slum it is *off Lady Hardinge Road*, and then to locate its Hut 191.

How will Paresh, quick thinker as he seems to be, manage to account for such a long absence should Mr Divekar ring with a summons to me at last to take on a real Crime Branch case, unlikely though that is?

The next moment he spotted, in all the jostle of traffic in the wide road beside him, the yellow roof of a taxi. Wildly waving his arms, he managed to attract its driver's attention.

All right, fare will cost me altogether too much. But it will, at least, get me directly to Lady Hardinge Road.

CHAPTER NINE

At the ramshackle entrance to the slum to which the taxi had finally brought him, without too much of the taxiwallah leaning out and asking and asking of passers-by, Ghote stood for a moment appalled at what lay before him. How will I, once past this apology for a gate, in such a chaos of huts of every different shape and size, be able find Number 191? Some even look as if they cannot have attached to them any number at all, so much like are they to those single pieces of heaven-knows-what covering beggars sleep under in the monsoons. All right, there are huts I can see a little way further inside that have at least the appearance of dwellings, however much they are constructed from whatever their owners have managed to find in Bombay's numerous rubbish heaps, or to steal perhaps. But many more are scarcely huts at all.

So what use will it be to me to know the number in this slum that Bikram was giving as his address when he first secured his job as a Crime Branch peon? Hut 191, there must be huts here going up from number 191 to number 1901 and beyond. None of them, as far as I can see, made out of anything more than beaten-flat tins supplemented by flapping gunnysacks and ripped and torn tarpaulins.

Yet before the afternoon is over I must get to that number 191. Even then I will be altogether late—oh God, it will mean another taxi—and if Mr Divekar has rejected Paresh's excuses on my behalf, as he well may, it could very well mean he will carry out his threat to have me sent back to Dadar PS. To that flat at the top of the barracks block, much less agreeable even than the Bank Street Cross Lane with all its disadvantages.

Shall I give it all up? Here and now? Turn round, find a new taxi and get back to my cabin and whatever petty tasks await me? It would be the sensible thing to do. It is madness to hope, among all this riot of buildings—only not even proper buildings—to find the place where Bikram used to stay. And, yet more foolish, go on to find that drinking companion of his who might, or might not, turn out to be a clerk in some rich man's office able safely to demand from his boss some fat sum.

Impossible. Surely impossible.

So, turn round and look about in Lady Hardinge Road for the yellow roof of a taxi? Yes, there in just a few minutes at worst a bright yellow, easy-to-spot vehicle is bound to appear.

71

But, no. No, I am not going to do that. I am instead going to take the utterly ridiculous course that may, just may, lead me in the end to the man who hacked off Bikram's head.

Because I have sworn to find him. Because I have told Protima that is what I am going to do, and, as I knew she would, she has backed me to the hilt. Whatever a *hilt* may be.

He pushed his way through the ramshackle gate and advanced into the slum's depths.

And, as if the gods had backed his decision, within less than two minutes an urchin boy, naked all but for a pair of ragged once-red shorts, appeared from out of one of the apologies for homes. Seeing, not five yards away, a *sahib* properly dressed in clean shirt and trouser, he went at once into his begging routine.

But with a grin lighting up his whole dirty face.

'*Sahib*, *sahib*, one *paisa* only. Give, give, *sahib*, no father, no mother. There is no one but you, *sahib*, give five *paisa*, give ten. Ten for my sick-sick mother.'

Ghote looked at him, his skinny legs, his bare feet, the toes gripping the dirt and dust of the path.

'But you were just only saying you have *no father, no mother*. So how is it you are wanting ten *paisa* because your mother is sick?'

At once the boy gave him a broad smile.

'*Sahib*, Ma also is hungry. Twenty *paisa*, for her, yes?'

'No. But I tell you what I will do. If you will help me find Hut 191 . . . You are knowing your numbers, yes?'

'Oh, yes, *sahib*. *Paisas*, one. *Paisas*, five. *Paisas*,

72

ten. *Paisas*, twenty. Yes? *Paisas,* one hundred and ninety-one even. I will take you there. And then you must be giving *paisas* one hundred and ninety-one, isn't it?'

'Find me that hut and you will see. Perhaps.'

'Come, come.'

Eagerly the boy set out, hurrying by hut after hut, pushing his way past anyone they met, and turning at last into a cross-path far narrower and very much dirtier than the one leading from the slum gate. But he seemed quite confident he was going towards some point he had in his mind.

Ghote, panting a little at the speed he was being made to go, could still not help asking himself if he was being tricked by a tricky guide.

Am I in the end going to be left, lost and abandoned in the middle of this man-made jungle? Have the gods I thought had come to my aid when I found this boy now turned blind eyes on me?

A prayer? A prayer to Ganesha, solver of all puzzles?

Whether he had actually voiced that prayer, or whether it had been no more than something hovering at the edges of his mind, he was never to know. At just that moment the hurrying urchin came to a sudden stop and extended a wretchedly thin arm with one dirt-nailed finger pointing.

And, Ghote saw in an instant, that the dirty but direct finger was aimed at an almost unnoticeable length of wood propped against the side of a hut as precarious as any round about. On that, in faded white or yellow paint, there had at some time long ago been written the numbers *1 9 1*.

He fished into his trouser pocket for money.

Not, he decided for one rupee and ninety-one

73

paisa. After all, some credit may be given to the elephant-tusked god above. But for—yes, I have found what I was seeking—a whole rupee coin.

His guide took it, in an appallingly grubby hand, and thrust it deep into some recess in his stained and torn red-faded shorts. Then in a sort of dance he stepped back ten yards or more and waited to see what was going to happen.

*   *   *

Carefully Ghote approached Hut 191, his heart beating a little faster at the thought of what he might learn from whoever it was he thought he could just detect inside it, past the drooping remains of a green cotton sari that was all that served as a door. It is possible, he forced himself to admit, whoever I can hear in there, humming and moaning so drearily, will deny any knowledge of Bikram. After all, that bare address was entered in Crime Branch internal records something over two years ago, the whole time that poor dead Inspector Patil had to endure Bikram's rum-affected services, or lack of services.

But no point in delaying finding out whether the person inside—yes, it sounds like a woman—will know anything either way.

He issued a loud sort of cough and gently moved aside the green sari door-curtain. Peering into the shadowed darkness beyond, he found that the bright sun of the cheerful month of Baisakh overhead made it, by the sheer contrast, almost impossible to see anything. From one small hole in the hut's roof, one of dozens there, a sole chance-directed dazzlingly thin sunbeam lit up a small brass vessel on the floor. Which made it yet more difficult to see anything at all.

Taking half a pace backwards, he shaded his eyes with one hand and plunged in again.

Yes, I can see better now, a little. There is—I was right—a woman inside. Quite fat, elderly, in a pale-coloured sari of some sort and, yes, she is beginning now to rise up from the mattress where she has been sitting or sleeping. She has quickly pulled the *pallao* of her sari over her head. But she must be able to sec myself clearly enough.

'Please,' he said quickly, 'I am looking for the hut where a man named Bikram was—' He checked himself. 'No. Where Bikram *is* living.'

Still the time to produce the well-intentioned lie.

'Gone,' came the voice from the dark beyond. 'My son has gone.'

A voice heavy with resignation.

Ghote realised at once that her ambiguous *Gone* would now have to be replaced by the definite news it was his duty to bring.

'I regret,' he said, pushing his way by a single crouching step further into the darkness of the hut, 'I have to tell you . . .'

This is the moment.

'Bikram's mother, here is the sad truth: Bikram is dead. Yes, he has gone. Gone for ever.'

He had expected a wailing of tears. But there came only silence. A long weighty silence.

He waited, saying no more. It seemed best.

Then at last the sound of words came across to him. Low-voiced words, filled with resignation.

'It was his fate. It had to come. Bikram, my son, my only son, was, all his life, seeking to be killed.'

Killed? Had she said *killed*?

75

Ghote, not without reluctance, put then the first of the questions he knew he had to ask, contriving only to make it not too painfully direct.

'Yes,' he said, 'Bikram has been killed. He has been . . . Someone has murdered him, I have to tell.'

He expected now the delayed outburst of tears. But, instead, a dry, almost passionless voice emerged from the scarcely penetrable depths at the back of the hut.

'Yes, one day it was going to happen. I am knowing it. From as soon as he could go out on his own he was always getting into troubles. He was led away too easily. By the boys who were worse than himself, by the men who were far worse than himself. From the time he was eleven-twelve only he was drinking. And soon it was rum. Rum. He was loving rum. But he should not have been murdered for that.'

'No,' Ghote said. 'No one is deserving of the fate that came to him.'

Then the tears, the gulping sobs, did come.

For two or three minutes, perhaps more, perhaps less, Ghote remained crouching just inside the hut's entrance, listening helplessly as the stricken sobbing went on and on.

At last he ventured to speak.

'Bikram's mother, can I be fetching someone . . . ? Do you have a neighbour I can ask to come to you? Or . . . or anyone?'

Another heavy sob. And another. But then a single loud sniff.

'Faiza. Just only in next hut.'

A Muslim woman, Ghote registered. Unexpected. But in this huge, jammed-together

76

mix-up of people religious differences will be only the slightest of obstacles to friendship.

'One minute,' he said.

He retreated backwards out of the hut's narrow opening and rose stiffly to an upright position, back and knees slightly protesting. He looked round, noticing that the watching urchin boy had gone, events perhaps too much for him.

There were, he saw, huts to left and right, each within a foot or so of Hut 191. Which one is the *next hut*? There is nothing to distinguish any one of those close by from 191. Almost every hut I have seen, he thought, has been little different from this one where rum-loving Bikram was, most probably, born. Only the pieces of covering that keep out the weather—and God knows what happens under the monsoons—consist each one of different thrown-away objects. Faiza's hut could even be the one I can just see at the back there, in the parallel narrow lane. Or any other one here.

But his dilemma was, in a moment, solved.

A woman, a Muslim in long black *burkha*, one cheap toe ring glinting just a little on her left foot, had emerged from the hut on the right.

'It is Faiza?' he asked.

'*Jee, sahib.* And you are police? I was hearing it all through the walls.'

Yes, Ghote thought, it must be altogether obvious who I am. Who else would come with such a terrible message to a woman in this slum? But leave that aside.

He did, however, repeat, perhaps more clearly, the news Faiza had apparently heard through the two sets of insubstantial walls. It was impossible to tell from beneath the shrouding time-shiny folds of her *burkha* what exactly had been her reaction. But without a word now she strode past and ducked down into the hut that Bikram would never come home to. In a few moments he could hear the two women inside sharing, with new tears, their grief.

No privacy anywhere in a slum.

*　　　*　　　*

For more than a few minutes Ghote stood where he was, oppressively aware now of the heat of the sun, wondering what he should do.

Should I simply go? My duty done? But I had hoped to learn more than those few details of Bikram's life. I thought, when I impulsively hailed that taxi making its jostling way through the never-still traffic outside Police Headquarters, that I would at least be able to discover a great deal more about Bikram's life. Where perhaps he sometimes went in the evenings after he had left Crime Branch? Whether he also had friends out here? Drinking with them the rum that, his mother had said, he was loving? Perhaps drinking with one known to be a clerk in some *crorepati*'s huge office?

It all should have been so easy. I know well how to question a reluctant witness. I could have learnt so much. But now . . . now, if I call it a day, as it will be difficult not to do, I shall go away altogether empty-handed. But I cannot at this moment thrust my police officer's head past that sari-protected doorway and order those two weeping women to be silent while I ask my interfering questions. Nor would they pay me any attention. Grief has its priorities.

78

He stood where he was, now fully aware once more of the pervasive smell of things rotting, of excrement, animal and human, of foulnesses he could not even name. And, yes, the damn sun is altogether too hot. I should have been wearing something on my head. I would have had my cap if I had been in uniform. And I should not have to be standing outside here.

I should be, not even in my cabin, not even in our flat, hot though that gets in this weather. No, I should be, somehow, in a cool building like the one in my favourite painting of the month of Baisakh, that tall pale-purple house where Krishna and his Radha are able to sit in happy comfort. A *punkah*, I think, gently wafting air over them as they gaze and gaze into each other's faces.

But I am here, in this fetid slum, hotter than I should be at this beginning of the summer season, sweating from the crown of my head right down to my feet in my too heavy shoes. And with no idea how I am to proceed in my all but hopeless quest.

CHAPTER TEN

Abruptly Ghote became aware of a woman's voice, almost at his elbow, asking some repeated and repeated question.

'You are police, police in the slum? Police?'

He turned and looked at her.

She seemed little different from any of the dozens of women he had gone brushing past as that ingeniously begging boy had led him, at such a rushing pace, from near the slum gates to where he was now standing, sweat-covered and blankly depressed. He noted her sari, once patterned orange, was as sun-bleached and sad as any of the others he had seen in the slum, whether on young women or old. But that, he thought, tells me nothing. What age will she be, this gratingly questioning woman? He found it impossible to assess. She might be as young as thirty. She might be a good fifty. Only the nose on that sun-hardened face, thin and determined as a jabbing knife, makes me inclined to the higher figure.

'Yes,' he answered. 'Yes, I am police. But how are you knowing same?'

'Oh, *sahib*, that is easy, even when you are not wearing uniform-uniform. Who but a police would come alone right into the heart of this slum? No *jawans* all round with *lathis*—whack, whack, whack—to protect?'

Is that true, he asked himself? Have I been so daring as she was saying? And, he added, *so foolish?*

'*Achchha*, if you are police,' the old woman said with fierce determination, 'you can find the shopping bag Atul stole from me three days past. I was thinking I must in the end go to my MLA for some help. But that tub of ghee, Pradeep Popatkar, is off to try his luck in South Bombay and no more caring for us. So it is you must do it.'

Find her shopping bag for her? This woman is asking me to do that because she is thinking Pradeep Popatkar will not listen to her now he is contesting the South Bombay seat (no wonder he is in Protima's black book). This woman is asking a full Crime Branch inspector to find for her one stolen shopping bag. Am I under some mirage after being so long in the hot sun?

But, no. In this month of Baisakh it is not really so hot, nothing like what is to come. Yes, I was feeling somewhat overwhelmed, but that was not caused by sun.

And . . . and let me get it straight. Here, in this slum, where Bikram was living, there is a woman who is believing a man called, yes, Atul, has stolen her bag . . . Her shopping bag?

A shopping bag? A shopping bag? Could that possibly be the very one I was finding in my waste bin? But, no, that would be a coincidence hardly to be believed. There must be, even in this slum itself, hundreds and hundreds of shopping bags little different from that one in my bin. Every woman must have something of the sort. But, on the other hand, how many of them will have had theirs stolen?

Oh, if some slum woman's bag gets lost or somehow ruined, what is she likely to do but to get hold, if she can, of some other woman's decent bag? In a slum like this you cannot expect anything but dog eat dog. Yet this woman here has said a man, a man called Atul, suddenly stole her almost life-necessary bag.

I think I will ask a little more.

'You are wanting me to find a shopping bag you say someone called Atul stole from you? But why should a man, any man, steal a shopping bag? You must give answer. Tell me everything about this theft you say was happening.'

'Everything? But there is no more to say. It was Atul. Atul. He snatched my bag from my very hands.'

'Very well, Atul did that, if you are saying it. But

81

what other name is he having? Atul only is not enough. Give me full name, address also.'

'It is Atul only. He is always called just Atul. Why would he need some other name? Everybody is knowing him well enough. Too well even, the take-anything *badmash*.'

'Very well, if he is Atul only, he is Atul only. But where could I find him?'

'Address you are not at all needing. Atul is here. In the slum. I was just only seeing some minutes past.'

'Where? Where? Take me to him, and I will see if he has done what you were telling.'

But now, instead of producing any answer, she stood back and looked at Ghote, with a plain air of summing him up.

'But if you see him face-to-face,' she said, a glint of cunning in her eyes, 'he will be able to see you. And *ek dum* he will know you are police. I knew you were, yes? You could not be anything else.'

Ghote considered this observation rather too pointed for his liking.

But she is right, he thought. I do have the bearing of a police officer. Because that is what I am. Through and through. And I am happy to be such.

'If this Atul will know me as a police officer,' he said, 'then he will. But do not think that will make anything of difference. Just only take me to him, and we will see if he is the man who snatched this bag of yours.'

*   *   *

Straight away the old woman began to thread her

82

way along the lanes of the slum. Tramping beside her, through, when he had to, whatever squelchy mess presented itself, Ghote realised that, after no more than five minutes, he would no longer be able easily to find his way back to the gate. But he let himself be led further and further on. At least this determined creature, he thought, appears to know very well where we are going.

They were going, it seemed next, to a part of the slum even more vilely smelling than anywhere yet. Ghote frequently had to check an impulse to put his handkerchief to his nostrils, feeling that would hardly add to the impression of a police officer capable of dealing with this Atul.

The air, never wholly without stinks and smells of all kinds, had become, under the beating sun, twice, three times more sharply disgusting.

'We are near,' the old woman said triumphantly, apparently altogether unaffected by the stench.

Then Ghote saw a hut where, all over its walls, wettened lengths of cloth, crudely dyed in glaring colours, had been draped to dry.

Oh, yes, that is the reason for the nauseating smell. I know well that dyeing processes can create highly unpleasant odours. I should have guessed we were near somewhere where they are at work dyeing.

Led round to the back of the hut, Ghote knew at once who he would find there, provided Atul was still where the old woman had seen him earlier.

And, yes, the path widened into a small open patch behind the dyers' hut—the stink of dye in the air yet—and a tall man, half a head at least above the average, tangle of unwashed hair crowning him, arms thick, it seemed, as tree

83

branches, was leaning against a feebly struggling palm tree. But something more than his height made it plain that here must be indeed the brutal bag-snatcher. Prominent in his mouth, inclined as it was to loll open, were two spiky rows of long yellow teeth.

Crocodile teeth, Ghote thought.

Then he took in the look on the unshaven face just a few feet away, and knew that, just as he had said to himself *I will know this fellow again if ever I come to see him*, Atul was thinking much the same about himself. *Yes, policewallah. Has to be. And, OK, I will know him again.*

Then, with the rapidity of a tiger spotting a sun-dazzle from a hunter's *machan* high in the jungle, Atul was off, long legs pelting over the mud and rubbish of the dark lane beyond.

For a moment Ghote readied himself to go in pursuit. But then he realised a chase would be futile. He knew nothing of the ins and outs of the slum all round. But Atul must be bound to do so, to their last wriggle.

He turned to his guide, who had put herself carefully behind him.

'*Achchha, chalo,*' he said.

Let's go. It was all he needed. She set off once more. He followed for a while, but soon stopped her to put a question that might confirm the thought he found now quivering in his mind. Have I, by a series of fortunate chances, actually come face to face, not just with that shopping bag thief, but with the man who hacked off Bikram's head itself?

But, as he was about to put his question, second thoughts came.

84

'I have things I want to ask you,' he said to the woman. 'But it is not here itself where you should be telling me what I am wanting to hear. Anybody may be listening when the walls of each and every hut are so thin. So come with me right out of the slum. We will find some *dhaba* where we can sit with a cup of tea. Or a Pepsi, even, perhaps a *vada pav* for you to munch. Yes?'

'Yes.'

The woman turned at once and began to hobble off, slowly enough now after her hurry to make sure Atul was still where she had seen him before.

*   *   *

Outside the slum, it took Ghote some time to spot a *dhaba* he thought would suit his purpose. It was one given a certain respectability by a blackboard outside saying *No* to a long list of activities. *No smoking, no fighting, no spitting, no handing water to people outside, no sitting long.*

But will I, he thought, perhaps need to sit long? However, cannot spend more time looking for a better place.

Inside, he settled his witness at the most isolated table he saw and ordered Pepsis as he had promised her and one of the deep-fried, butter-filled buns called *vada pavs* that sustain fifty thousand Bombayites every midday. Then at the last moment, remembering he had had no tiffin himself, he asked for one more bun.

Sitting back, he realised suddenly that, in his excitement at the tantalising, if unlikely, possibility that the stolen shopping bag might lead him to Bikram's killer, he had altogether failed to get his

85

witness's name. A simple error in police work that brought the blood flooding up to his cheeks. Not a good omen for someone who has undertaken, on his own, an investigation that ought to have gone to the whole of Crime Branch.

He waited now till the Pepsi and *vada pavs* had been set in front of them. Then, as his witness sucked up her first long drink from the plastic straw in the bright-red can, he asked, 'Kindly give me your good name.'

Blank silence from above the condensation-rimed can.

What on earth has . . . ?

Then it came to him. No slum-dweller wants their name in police records.

'No, no,' he said. 'I will not at all be putting down your name anywhere, I am asking just so that I may be knowing who I am talking to. Just only tell me your name, and, look, you will see me writing nothing down.'

Useful to have one good memory, he murmured to himself then.

'It is Rekha Salaskar,' his witness answered guardedly, slowly putting the Pepsi can back on the table, though clutching it still with hard-fixed fingers.

'Rekha, good. So, Rekha, tell me all you can about this—what is his name?—Atul who took from you the shopping bag you must still be so much needing.'

'Atul? He is one bad-bad *badmash* with that twisted look he has with his teeth, so yellow, jutting out this way and that when he is smiling his wicked smile. As soon as, just only three days past, he got one look at my shopping bag he was tugging

86

it from my hands. Look, my fingers are marked still.'

Ghote regarded, with his best show of interest, the hand she held out to him, the other still firmly round the Pepsi can. It was true the fingers showed ugly marks from, no doubt, having had a bag's rope handles tugged viciously from their grasp. In fact, he thought, not much different from the marks left on the fingers of my left hand from all time I hurried from Headquarters to Bank Street Cross Lane, that heavy bag with Bikram's head in it. And, yes, three days past. That must have been the evening when Bikram's head was cut from his shoulders, yes.

'You are right,' he said, 'a man who snatched your precious bag with so much of force must be a brute itself.'

Tears came then.

'My beautiful bag,' Rekha sobbed. 'Old-old, yes. I was having it for years, even when my husband was living. The best I was ever buying. So big, all-all I was getting at the market was going inside. No one could take-take anything from it, so deep down all was lying. And strong also. Even when, once, a handle did break and I was having to tie ends together, even then it never broke again.'

Yes. Yes, Ghote thought then, it must be that the one chance in one thousand I was thinking of has come up. The bag I was lugging all the way to the flat and up all those stairs did have a knot in one of its handles, an old, tightly tied one. I can still feel the place where it rubbed against my little finger.

The identical bag. It must be. It may . . . it may very likely be.

87

'Yes,' he said to Rekha then, 'I have seen your bag. I have carried—' No, careful. 'I have carried something heavy in it. There was on one of the handles just such a knot as you have mentioned.'

'So, give. Give.'

Ghote shook his head.

'No, I am sorry you cannot have just now only. One day your very bag may be evidence in court. Evidence of murder. A murder, I am thinking, Atul himself may have committed.'

'Then he must be hanged in Thana Gaol itself. To steal a good-good shopping bag from an old helpless woman. He is a devil, that one.'

Not so very old a woman, Ghote thought. She would have made it hard indeed for this Atul to wrench her bag away.

'All right,' he said, 'tell me more about Atul. Anything you are knowing. He stays in your slum somewhere?'

'No, no. Often he is coming there, but he must be staying somewhere else.'

Ghote waited to see if she had more to add. But it seemed to be beyond her powers to bring anything more to mind.

'You have seen,' she said. 'He is big. Big and tough also. Arms like tree trunks only he is having, the *shaitan*. He is liking and liking, you know, to go out into the streets and join some fight.'

For a moment Ghote absorbed this. If in the end it is coming to an arrest, he thought, I may not find it so easy to subdue someone so much bigger than myself.

But, when I was looking at Bikram's head on our kitchen table and the way it had been hacked and hacked from his neck, I knew then that the man I

88

had to find would be no weakling. Nothing has changed.

But I must, if I can, find out yet more about him, if he is the man I must in the end arrest.

'So,' he said, 'when Atul pulled your bag from your very hands was he running off? Or walking only?'

If I can, he reasoned, put into Rekha's mind now a sharp picture of that moment, she will perhaps be able to tell me at least in what direction he set off with her bag. Did she attempt to go after him? Or would she have cried out at him *Bring it back, bring it back!* and have attracted attention? Other witnesses? And better ones?

But, no.

'I was weeping and weeping. Hot-hot tears I was weeping then. What else could I have done? My bag. The most precious thing I was having.'

'Yes. Perhaps, if I am not able to give it back, I may find another for you.'

Short of money though we are with so many things needed for the new flat, he thought, I must at least be able to find a rupee or so to get a bag like the one Atul snatched, with no doubt already in his mind the need to convey, unseen, the severed head to whatever public place it was part of his bargain to take it. So that rupee or so may be money well spent. The more Rekha is thinking about her loss the more she may remember about Atul.

'But, tell me,' he said. 'if Atul is not staying in your slum, why is he coming there so often?'

Rekha took a third or fourth hungry bite out of her *vada pav*.

'Oh, that is easy,' she answered, muffledly. 'The

89

big *shaitan* with those thick, thick arms he is so much liking to show, breaking and breaking anything he can find to break, is finding in our slum good friends, friends to take when he is wanting to go out for fighting.'

Not, Ghote acknowledged, exactly what I was hoping to hear.

He tried another line.

'And Bikram, whose mother you may have just now heard weeping and lamenting, was he one of the friends Atul was choosing to take fighting with him?'

He knew, knowing Bikram, what the answer would be: *Not at all*. But he felt in this way he might learn something more.

And he did.

Rekha put down the all-but-empty Pepsi she was about to drain to its last dregs and laughed a cackling laugh.

'Oh, yes,' she said. 'I am again seeing Atul in my head now. I am seeing him laughing and laughing with those big teeth he has, like a crocodile's only, when in joke he was asking Bikram to come with him and Bikram was answering *No, no. I cannot. I have one importan-important job. I am working at police headquarters, in Crime Branch itself*. Atul was laughing and laughing then.'

A link. Another link. One good link more.

Ghote hugged to himself what Rekha had said. Yes, now yet more is becoming clear. An unknown *crorepati* must have sent some trustworthy messenger to find a *goonda* to eliminate this peon who had learnt more than he should. The messenger must have thought Atul was a likely man for the job. For the elimination. And, after it, the task of letting someone—someone in Crime Branch itself?—know that the person Bikram had been trying to blackmail was very well able to deal with any such attempt. Yes, link after link in the chain I may one day be putting round Atul. And—

His thoughts came to a sudden halt. He asked himself: succeeding in putting round someone else's also? Round the big man who was able to send down orders to the useful street-fighter?

But, no, I will not let that thought too much enter my mind. Not yet. Enough for now to think about Atul.

So, have I learnt as much from Rekha as she is likely to be able to tell me? And at any moment—I can see the thought forming in her mind—she will demand another Pepsi, even a second *vada pav*. If I am to get her one good new shopping bag that will be quite enough to have to pay out. I am no longer able now, working for myself only, to claim expenses. Not by any means.

He rose quickly to his feet, noticing with a pang of regret the bun on his own plate was only half-eaten.

'You have been one hundred per cent helpful to me,' he said to Rekha. 'I may even need to see you again.'

'Yes, yes. When you have found out where Atul is staying.'

A promise. Of a sort. Will she be able to keep it?

He decided to beat a rapid retreat before any further demands could come.

CHAPTER ELEVEN

Ghote, hurrying along to his cabin after his taxi from Matunga had set him down, found for the second time in two days that it seemed not to matter whether he was or was not at his desk. The only sign that anybody knew of his existence was a full cup of tea, cold as a puddle, in its place at his right-hand side.

Yes, at least the tea boy has been here, and, thinking perhaps I had left the cabin for only a few minutes, he poured my cup and left, unpaid. Something to be put right.

He brought himself now to ping his bell for Paresh and, when almost instantly the man himself appeared, Ghote confirmed that no one at all had wanted to see him. Nor had any messages been left, beyond a few orders sent down from the ACP for the next day's *bandobast* schedule.

'Just only once,' Paresh concluded, 'Sergeant Moos was putting his head over your doors and then leaving.'

'Moos? Of course.'

When Paresh had gone Ghote sat on where he was, ignoring the small pile of orders which he should perhaps have been dealing with at once. No point, he thought, Mr Divekar is bound to alter them.

So no harm done by my long absence. None at all. But what if it had come into the ACP's mind as a new case came in that this might be just the thing for Inspector . . . Would he remember my name even? Yes. Oh, yes. Inspector Ghote, the officer I find no good in.

What if, then, no one had been able to find me? What would Mr Divekar have done? Necked me out of Crime Branch straight away? Very possibly. And if tomorrow, inside office hours, I am needing to take some urgent steps in this private investigation of mine, perhaps even just only honouring my promise to Rekha Salaskar by taking her a bright new shopping bag, and I am found then out of my seat? Will Mr Divekar *ek dum* turn me out of his cherished Crime Branch? The end of all the ambitions I have had from the time when, myself a small boy only, my father was teaching the many illegitimate sons of a maharajah whose murder was investigated by that British police officer, Mr Howard, he so much praised to me.

So should I again risk such a thing?

Should I risk the whole police career I have such hopes for? And what about Protima? She has those same hopes for me, and even—she was once saying—for baby Ved also. One day for him to be Inspector Ved Ghote, Crime Branch. No, her hopes flew higher. Perhaps even to ACP Ved Ghote.

It would be absurd to risk myself missing all that, just because I have taken it into my head to investigate the killing of my drunken incompetent peon. And, if what clever little Chagoo was suggesting about him is true, not just incompetent and habitually drunk but a blackmailer also.

No, no. Deciding on a private investigation was being altogether too ambitious. To think that I could succeed, all on my own, when Crime Branch itself is refusing to pursue matter.

So, yes, this is it. As soon as my time for finishing duty here has come I must go straight home and tell Protima that all the horrible work we were doing on the kitchen table last night was unnecessary. I must say I was being foolish—no, plain wrong—in thinking I could investigate on my own Bikram's death. I must tell her that Mr Divekar was right when he said Bikram's head should be *disposed of*. I will have to tell her then that I will take it, at once, to the Electric Crematorium and there let it be burnt to ashes only.

But, no. No, no, no, no. Bikram's head, the head of a stupid drunken idiot is, as I was first thinking, the head of a man, of a human being. However lowly he was, however not at all up to his work, however much a slave to God Rum, he was still deserving to have his murder investigated. To the utmost.

No, I will not go back to Protima in a little while and say it is all over, finished with, to be for ever forgotten. No, I will not go to the Electric Crematorium. Would it even be open at that time of the evening? But in any case I will not go there. Instead I will investigate Bikram's murder until I find, as the British were often saying, every avenue is exhausted. Or until I am able to arrest his murderer, to arrest, I am almost believing, one Atul, a *goonda*, with in my mind a solid chain of evidence, complete in every link.

And what if that is leading also to that hidden figure at the top, perhaps, of a multi-*crore* business? Yes, even then I will pursue the case to the end. No one has the right to order the murder of even such a low-caste individual as Bikram. Yes, that is what I must make clear to Protima.

*   *   *

So, less than half an hour later, with little Ved, thoroughly kissed and petted, put into his big swinging wooden cradle and rocked to swift sleep, Ghote led his wife back into the next room, sat her on the frequently slipping cushion pile of their temporary *takht* and told her of his discoveries in the distant slum off Lady Hardinge Road.

'So,' he ended, with a tinge of pride, 'what I must next do is to find this man Atul and—'

'No.'

'No? What are you meaning *No*? Is it that you are saying I should not, on my own, try to bring Bikram's murderer to justice?'

For a moment all his former doubts about the possibility of conducting an investigation on his own, about the rightness even of doing so, came flooding back to his mind. He began to experience a burden-lifted sense of relief.

But it was not to last. And he was happy, in fact, that it did not.

Protima's answer had been swift.

'No, husbandjee, you cannot have been thinking I was meaning you should not go on with your investigation. No, of course, you must do what you are knowing you must do. But finding that man is not the first thing to be done.'

'Not?'

'No, first and foremost, you must take out of this flat Bikram's head.'

'But—'

'No. Can you smell nothing even here with bedroom door shut? Did you smell nothing at all while we were rocking little Ved to sleep? I was all the time worrying and worrying that the smell coming from the cupboard top would stop him ever going off.'

It dawned on Ghote then.

Yes, now I am thinking about it, there was an odour in there. But somehow I was all the time discounting it. I suppose I was not willing even to think about Bikram's actual hacked-about head. I was not willing to think what should be done with it. Because, yes, it is certain it cannot stay where it is for very much more of time.

Yes, definitely, sooner or later I will have to think what to do about it.

'You must take it at once to Electric Crematorium.'

It was nothing short of an order. A command.

And it left him bewildered.

'But,' he managed at last. 'But is that place still open? All over the city shops are pulling down shutters. It is getting late.'

'Very well. Tomorrow at five ack emma, the way you are always saying the time.'

'But . . . but the head is evidence. Evidence of murder.'

'No, no. If somebody is wanting proof Bikram has been killed, there is you and me who have seen his head. Have seen and seen it. On my kitchen table. Our words will be enough of evidence. No, first thing tomorrow: the Electric Crematorium.'

Through his head then there marched all the troubles he had had in simply taking the head from his cabin to . . . to its twice-used resting place on top of the bedroom cupboard. Of how weighty that shopping bag had been, and that bag, too, was something that at least must be preserved as evidence, blood-smelling or not.

No, no. Think how the fingers of my hand were so deeply marked by that thick twine handle I was gripping, by the time-hardened knot Rekha had made. What if the *paar-maar* who tried to rob the bag . . . Or, no. No, that was just only a fear I was having, of a hand slipping in and coming up against Bikram's clotted hair, of the blood perhaps still oozing from the cleaver marks at the neck. No, it was altogether someone else who bumped against the soft side of the bag. Or perhaps even that never happened. And, no, there was no pickpocket either.

But, whatever did happen or not happen, it had been one nightmare journey.

And I am not going to make it again.

*   *   *

Standing outside the still-locked gates of the Electric Crematorium at that very early hour next morning, grasping once again the blood-spoilt shopping bag, Ghote found himself possessed of a violent desire not to be where he was.

How can I, he thought, hand over this appalling thing? All right, last night Protima neatly wrapped up the bloodstained *Matunga News* in the thick brown paper she had remembered putting away 'in case', and hid the package in the drawer under my second-best pair of mufti trousers. Damn her.

And, now, what if I see, in just only some minutes' time, a funeral party arriving? They may come before I am having a chance, with some explanation or other, to hand over the head. Can I snap out *Crime Branch order*? What if the body on its litter is arriving before even I can do that? With mourners chanting *Ram nama satya hai, Ram nama satya hai*, God Ram's name is truth, Ram's name is truth? But perhaps at this strictly modern place that custom is no longer observed, as it must be over at the Burning Ghats at Back Bay.

But, even if I am managing to hand in here one head in a shopping bag (and wanting bag back), will they make some sort of a damn fuss? Call the nearby PS? I am not at all able to think what they may do. And it is cold standing here. I must be shivering. Sun not up yet. Month of Baisakh, after all.

Suddenly he found he could no longer endure it. He gave anxious glances to left and right, ran forward and tipped the head in one violent jerk out of the bag close up against the Crematorium's black-painted gates.

He would have liked to have run off then. To have run, clutching the empty bag—evidence still—all the way back to Bank Street Cross Lane. But some last streak of responsibility trapped him. One more long look.

He chose a slightly more distant spot from which he would be able, when the city began to come to life as it would all too soon, to keep those black gates under observation without being noticed himself.

Barely ten minutes later he saw a peon swing the gates back. And, transfixed, watched the man react then with a start to the bloody object right under his nose, saw him eventually bend down and, with fingers accustomed to such tasks, lift up poor Bikram's head by the wirily stiff hair.

Lift it up, and carry it away.

*   *   *

'So,' Ghote said to Protima after he had carefully hidden Rekha's precious bag under the wrapped-up blood-spattered pages of the *Matunga News* beneath his second-best pair of trousers, 'now that Bikram's head is no more existing I must start to be finding this man Atul.'

'But how will you do that?' she asked. 'Find a man you are hardly knowing anything about, somewhere, anywhere, in this city of four millions of inhabitants?'

'I am a detective,' Ghote answered.

But the boastful words were not enough to satisfy his sharply probing wife.

'Very well, but how does a detective go about such a task? As go about it you must.'

'I . . . I would . . . It is not at all easy to explain. Not to someone who is not a full police officer.'

'But you can try. I may not have had lectures and demonstrations at Nasik Police Training College. But I have a brain in my head. I can understand things.'

A flicker of rage went through him. After all that I am just coming back from doing, to be asking and demanding like this.

'Oh, if you are so clever,' he said, voice rising, 'then you tell me what it is I should do.'

It took her barely two seconds of brow-wrinkled thought.

'Other peons at Crime Branch may certainly

99

know this—what was his name?—this Amul—'

'It is not at all *Amul*. It is Atul, Atul.'

'Atul, Amul, what it is mattering? If Bikram was a friend of that man, then one at least of his fellow peons must be knowing about him. You have only to ask and ask.'

*   *   *

Ghote, in his cabin later that morning, did as his wife had told him. He consulted first Paresh, little though it was likely that, as a newcomer to Crime Branch, he would know much about his fellow peons.

'Ah, Paresh. Just the man. Tell me, are you beginning to know the other peons here?'

'*Jee, sahib*. Many I am knowing. There are those I was friends with already from when I was at Tilak Marg PS, just only round the corner as you must be knowing. And there are already many here who have been altogether friendly.'

So far, so good. But what if, when I am asking and asking the sort of questions I must, it comes into Paresh's head that there must be some reason for them? What if, after just only some puzzling, he begins to suspect I am, on my own, investigating Bikram's murder? He will know that I have not at all been ordered to do so. So what then? Will he talk about it? With his new-found friends among the other peons? And then will it, as such things always are doing, gradually mount up higher? Higher and higher, until it reaches ACP Divekar himself and gets me necked out of Crime Branch once for all?

But that is a risk I must be taking. If only so that

100

I can tell Protima I am doing what I have said I would do.

'So,' he said, looking straight at the spick-and-span fellow standing attentively in front of him. 'So, you are hearing many things, is it, about Bikram?'

Paresh gave a discreet little giggle.

'Inspector, such things.'

Should I now giggle also? Perhaps not. But I can allow a small smile to appear.

'Oh,' Paresh went on, 'the amount of rum that man was drinking. It was a wonder, they all say, he was able to keep on his two feet.'

'Yes, yes. I was seeing same for myself. One bloody nuisance the fellow was.'

'Oh, *sahib*, yes. Yes, yes and yes.'

A strong note of disapproval from this good, sober Gujarati. Fine. But he is taking in everything also. He cannot fail to be taking in that I am wanting to know so much. And what will he think when I am asking where it was that Bikram was doing all that drinking?

But risk it. Must.

'So, tell me, where was Bikram doing so much of rum-drinking? Do you know? Do others of the peons know?'

This will be more than bright-eyed Chagoo has told me.

No change in the expression of mild gossipy interest on Paresh's face. Thank goodness.

'Oh, yes, *sahib*. Bikram was always boasting and boasting about his drinking ways. Inspector Patil, he was saying was knowing nothing about them, and as for—'

An abrupt halt.

Ghote had no difficulty in thinking what were the

words that Paresh had politely stopped himself saying. *As for this new Ghote fellow, he is even less knowing anything.* All right, you were in truth thinking such, Bikram. Dead, mangled Bikram, your head by now ashes at the Electric Crematorium. But, if you are dead, Inspector Ghote is alive. Alive, and about to find the man who was hacking off that head of yours.

'So where was Bikram doing this drinking of his? Was it in one place only? Or all over this part of Bombay?'

'*Sahib*, as I am understanding it, most of the time he used to go to a place quite near here called Beauty Bar. It is inside that big building in Waudby Road, where there are, looking on the street, the fine windows of a Number *Ek* sari shop.'

'Oh, yes,' Ghote said, putting into the words as much merely mild interest as he could manage, 'I think I have seen that shop.'

Casually taking up a pencil, he began to look at the first of the ACP's urgent memos that came to hand.

Paresh knew how to take a hint. When Ghote ventured on a quick look upwards he was not surprised to find him no longer there.

He plunged back into making out the ACP's schedule. But, in the depth of his mind he thought, *As soon as I will not be missed here I will visit that Waudby Road building, visit it and the Beauty Bar inside it.*

But then, before he was more than halfway through his laborious *bandobast*, the phone beside him shrilled out.

Dazedly, he picked it up. 'ACP here, Ghote. Come up.'

CHAPTER TWELVE

'Right, Ghote,' Mr Divekar snapped out, seated as ever upright as a statue in his tall red-leather chair, 'got an investigation for you. This Darab Dastor murder. You've read about it, of course.'

Ghote had not. No time for the newspaper after his trip to the Electric Crematorium at that chilly early hour, only a brief return to his warm bed. But the name Darab Dastor was familiar. He fought to find an answer that would not be altogether a lie but would imply, without more said, that he had in fact read the account of the murder in one of the day's papers.

The ACP looked up, shooting out his fearsome glare.

'You do read the newspapers, Ghote? Make yourself aware of what's happening in Bombay?'

'Oh, yes, sir, yes.'

'Victim edits some damn weekly or other,' Mr Divekar spluttered on. 'What's the wretched thing called? Yes, *Daylight*, that's it. Should be *Midnight*, all I hear about it. Getting hold of perfectly reasonable official decisions and making out they're scandalous.'

His outburst had given Ghote just the extra time he had needed in which to think.

Yes, of course I know about Darab Dastor. Protima is always reading *Daylight*. Yes, she was extolling Dastor just only a day or two ago when he was attacking her unfavourite politician, Something Popatkar. She is his great admirer.

But then the full meaning of what the ACP had

103

said broke in on him. I have been given—yes, I have—the investigation into Darab Dastor's murder. For myself. And it is sounding to be one important affair. The editor of *Daylight*, very much read in entire Bombay.

Then a descent. Falling, falling down into the chasm.

I cannot accept it. I must instead be tracking down the man Atul. I must be. It is my solemn task. I am dedicated to same. But . . . but how can I say this to Mr Divekar, Mr Divekar who was telling me to dispose of Bikram's head as not at all a case for his Crime Branch?

'Yes, sir,' he managed at last to bring out. 'I am well knowing about Darab Dastor.'

It is not, he thought, what I was intending to say. But was I, in fact, truly intending to say that other thing? Or should I now be trying to show to my utmost that the Darab Dastor case is exactly right for me? If it is? Or could I somehow reject it? Say I am not feeling competent when it is a matter of scandals left and right?

'My wife is always reading *Daylight*, sir,' he brought out, temporising.

Then, foolishly, he added something more. 'She was altogether admiring Darab Dastor, a Parsi of course.'

'Admires a damn Parsi, does she? One of those goody-goody, we-can-do-no-evil hypocrites.'

The ACP gave him a long, steady, assessing look.

'Right,' he said at last. 'The Dastor case plainly not for you. But . . . but, yes, there is something else. Yes, this will do.'

Yet a trace of indecision seemed to Ghote still to be lingering on the inflexible face looking up at him. If indecision was a possible thing for Mr Divekar to show.

But, if it was, it seemed to have existed for not more than a second or two.

'Right, there's this other affair just come up to me. Murder case, of course, but Cumballa Hill PS doesn't appear to be making much progress with it. Seems a simple enough business, though. As it happens, I know a bit more about it than you'll see in the newspapers.'

He paused for a moment. Then came to a sharp decision.

'The victim,' he said, plainly treading carefully, 'is actually . . . Yes, some sort of far cousin of mine. Fellow called Krishna Tabholkar. Cousin by marriage at least, and that's why I've been keeping a bit of an eye on things there. Right, then, here's the file that Inspector . . . Damn it, what's the fellow's name? Ah, yes. Rahe. Rahe. Here's Inspector Rahe's file. Make sure you master it, and then go up there, to Cumballa Hill, and . . . Let me see. Yes, take Sgt Chavan with you. Report any progress to me, of course.'

He thrust a slim file across the wide expanse of his desk.

*   *   *

Back in his cabin, Ghote sat struggling to swish away every thought he had ever had about murdered Bikram in favour of the as yet barely known man, subject of the boldly labelled *Tabholkar Murder* dossier right under his eyes. Yes, he thought, when I stretched out my hand to take this slim file everything was decided for me.

105

Hunting down Atul is no longer my task, not for however long this Tabholkar case may take. Instead, I have been given my first Crime Branch investigation, and it is something I will have to succeed in. Failure will be as bad as being discovered by Mr Divekar altogether absent from my desk. Yes, here is my test.

And, perhaps it is the best thing for me. First, to do my level best to solve the murder of this Krishna Tabholkar, distant-distant relation of the ACP. And only afterwards to allow into my head once more my vow to find the killer of my wretched peon.

Lips gripped together in a single straight line, he opened the file labelled *Tabholkar Murder*.

It did not take him long, burrowing into its surprisingly few and uninformative pages—yes, poor police work, no doubt about it—to have its contents planted solidly in his mind. Krishna Tabholkar, a young Bombay University lecturer and researcher—not that Rahe had stated in what field of research—had, it appeared, been stabbed to death, some weeks ago. He was, Rahe's report stated, by chance alone on the evening of his death in his newly built house up on airy Cumballa Hill, wedding gift for Juliette, sole daughter of Nathumal Moolchand, Head of Moolchand Investments plc. Ghote could almost smell the awe rising up as Inspector Rahe had typed out those momentous words, *Moolchand Investments plc*. The firm was perhaps the biggest enterprise yet that had been built in the new extension seized from the sea at the tip of the city's southern peninsula.

And, yes, I was hearing something about it

myself, not long ago.

Right, got it. Protima mentioned that her pet hate, Thingummy Popatkar, was getting some backing from Moolchand. She had. Well, well.

But he had also paused in surprise in his reading of the file when he had taken in the so English name, Juliette—surely, Mr Shakespeare's *Romeo and Juliet*—that had been given to the daughter of an obvious Marwari like Moolchand, one of Nature's hundred-per cent merchants and moneylenders.

Then something else struck him. Even if Nathumal Moolchand, a pillar of Bombay's Marwari community, had chosen such an altogether English name for his daughter—or had that perhaps been his wife's choice?—it was still very hard to see how it had come about that he had given her in marriage to a man with the everyday Marathi name of Tabholkar. Nothing more—this file is stating—than a lowly paid university researcher at the beginning of his career. But, more, Moolchand then had gifted Krishna Tabholkar with a house, a newly built house on breezes-kissed Cumballa Hill, haunt of the well-off of whatever origin. A house far more luxurious than any junior university lecturer might expect to own. But that is what he has done, and there it is.

He read on.

Then, it seemed, a little less than a full year after the young couple had moved into the house, there had come the evening of Krishna Tabholkar's death. It had been the custom, according to the evidence of their servants, a married couple, Gopal and Ritu, for the two lovebirds, as they

107

plainly were, to spend almost every evening at home, though by contrast both servants always had, every Tuesday, an evening off duty.

On the night of the murder Juliette Tabholkar had, Inspector Rahe stated, been telephoned by her mother and asked to go round to her invalid Aunt Smita's nearby flat, not much more than ten minutes away, as her aunt had not answered the regular 8.30 p.m. call made to inquire after her. Juliette had set out at once, despite it being already dark. Almost immediately afterwards the two servants had left on their regular off-duty visit to their daughter, who was, as it happened, a maid at the Moolchands' residence on Malabar Hill. That had left Krishna Tabholkar alone in the house.

Juliette, Rahe's report said, had found nothing amiss with her aunt and had returned in little more than half an hour. But when she entered the house she had discovered her Krishna lying dead in the entrance hall, a dozen deep stab wounds in his body.

Rahe had rapidly come to the conclusion that the murder must be the work of a chance intruder intent on, in the words of the Indian Penal Code, *house-breaking by night*. Nothing had been found, however, to identify the perpetrator, and eventually Rahe had been reduced to giving a hard time to every single man on the station's Bad Character Roll. To no effect.

There the investigation had come to a standstill until, perhaps in view of Mr Divekar's distant relationship to the victim, the file had been passed to Crime Branch.

Very well, Ghote thought when he had reached

108

the final page, on the face of it Inspector Rahe has got it right. A terrible chance tragedy. It cannot have often happened, if it had even happened once, that Krishna Tabholkar had been alone in that new fine house. Certainly, if the intruder had appeared on any of the six evenings a week when the two servants had been there, he would, had he even dared to try to break in, have been met with vigorous opposition. Gopal—the file had stated— was aged forty-one, so quite capable with Krishna Tabholkar, a good deal younger, of fighting off any *goonda*, however much armed with a knife. But, as it was, the thief had got clean away, it seemed, with a number of the couple's costly wedding gifts. The file had carefully listed them.

Ghote slapped its pages together.

Let me collect Sgt Chavan and go to scene itself.

*   *   *

Up in the airy coolness of Cumballa Hill, jumping out of the blue-painted police vehicle he had chosen to use, with at his side Sgt Chavan, morose and surly, Ghote was met with an astonishing surprise. Taking a first quick appraisal of his crime scene as he stood on the wide pavement outside, he realised that the house in front of him was, of all astonishing things, an almost complete replica of his favourite Month of Baisakh painting in the Prince of Wales Museum, made hundreds of years ago.

He stood, blinking.

Am I imagining it all? It cannot be, it cannot, that the house the painter once saw, surely only in his imagination, was somehow here all along on

Cumballa Hill in Bombay itself.

True, there is no golden chariot in the sky above carrying past the newly bright Baisakh sun to bring joy to the world below. Nor are the walls of this house here, now I come to think more clearly, wide open for inspection in the way that they are in the painting. Nor are there in front of this place, on an everyday Cumballa Hill side turning, any blossom-bedecked trees full of singing koels. Neither, come to that, is there any such little open *shamiana* shelter in front of the trees where Krishna and Radha are gazing into each other's eyes, simultaneously with themselves doing so in an upper room of the house.

But, set aside such devices of the long-ago painter's imagination, the two buildings are extraordinarily alike. Each of them three storeys high with attractive-looking flat roofs edged by low walls. Both painted in the same pleasant pale-purple colour.

He shook his head, closed his eyes and opened them again. No change.

Then at last a possible explanation presented itself in his bewildered mind. Yes, all right, this house, solidly here in front of me, does resemble, to a considerable extent, the dwelling imagined by that unknown artist all those years ago. But, in fact, it is a building of the twentieth century, erected no doubt by dozens of labouring men and women with on their heads piles of bricks or buckets of cement, mounting ladders or descending to the foundations. But, of course, it will have been designed by an architect commissioned, yes, by wealthy-wealthy Marwari businessman Nathumal Moolchand, Moolchand

Investments. It must have been an altogether splendid wedding present for his daughter and the poorly paid young university lecturer she had been determined to marry. A small enough man-made miracle, if one that had required the outlay of a large, large sum.

Sharply he dismissed from his mind a half-envious comparison between the jewel-like house he was standing in front of and the poky flat at the top of the Dadar PS accommodation block, the first home he had shared with Protima, never mind the scarcely better one they had now in Bank Street Cross Lane.

'All right, Sergeant,' he said to Chavan, coming fully back to the real world, 'in we go to find out what exactly happened here on the night of the murder.'

His ring at the pale-purple house's doorbell brought in a moment a neat, well-built man in smart white shirt and shorts, whom he recognised from Rahe's meticulous, if almost useless, report as forty-one-year-old Gopal. He gave the man his own name, and Chavan's, said that they were from Crime Branch taking charge of the investigation into 'the sad death of Mr Tabholkar' and asked if Mrs Tabholkar was at home.

'Inspector *Sahib*,' Gopal answered, with a certain caution, 'I would tell *memsahib* you are here.'

After a rather longer wait than Ghote had expected Gopal returned and said, 'Juliette Madam is ready to see you.'

Yes, Ghote noted, following him inside the place, almost as elegant indoors as the house in the Prince of Wales Museum painting—if without the aroma of God Krishna at play with his Radha.

111

Though, yes, some aroma is here. Cigarette smoke? Perhaps it is just only that.

A moment later he found himself face-to-face with, not the legendary Radha he had still somehow half-expected to meet, but with the oddly named Juliette, widow now of Krishna Tabholkar, simple university lecturer.

He saw an elegantly beautiful young woman, although dressed from head to foot in the white sari of a widow without the least adornment. She was nevertheless, he thought, clearly the carefully nurtured daughter of a Marwari *crorepati*, testament to the past exertions of a carefully chosen *ayah*, to the full care of an expensive nursery school, to the unsparing efforts of higher-educational establishments—Cathedral School, almost certainly, perhaps later even somewhere abroad—of dance teachers, beauty parlours and top coiffeurs.

Whenever it had been that young Krishna Tabholkar had chanced to meet her, he must have been immediately dazzled. But how had it been that Juliette, who would surely have expected any future husband to be in the same bracket as her rich-rich father, had plunged instead for a mere junior university lecturer?

Unanswerable question. The unfathomable mysteries of sexual attraction. After all, how was it that I myself came to feel so overwhelmingly attracted at college to a Bengali girl like Protima, in theory distanced from me by a dozen different language and social barriers?

'Madam, good morning,' he said. 'Allow me to introduce myself. Inspector Ghote, from Crime Branch, now in charge of the investigation into your husband's terrible death. Madam, allow me to offer my deep condolence.'

Juliette Tabholkar inclined her head.

Now, Ghote told himself, now I must begin to ask this mourning statue my questions from the world of violence and crime.

'Madam, I regret, but it is necessary that I should ask you, in perhaps more detail than Inspector Rahe was able to, about that terrible evening.'

'If you must . . .' A small trickle of icy water.

Ghote gave a *hem* of a cough.

'Very well. Then, madam, am I right in understanding that it was during a period of one half-hour or a little more, while you were out of this house yourself and both your servants also, that the killer . . . That the crime was taking place?'

'It was, Inspector.'

That, and no more.

This is going to be difficult. Perhaps naturally. Juliette Tabholkar must still be in shock, even after some weeks have passed. But in so much of shock as to be turned into as much of ice as this? She could be, but . . .

But ask a sharper question, see how much response it is getting.

'Madam, was it customary for you to leave this house on your own during hours of darkness?'

A quick look now from the shuttered eyes in the pale flawless face.

'Inspector, all this has been gone into by . . . by that man, Inspector . . . Your colleague.'

'Madam, it has. But, in a full-scale investigation such as people of influence and distinction are meriting, more precise questions have sometimes

113

to be asked than Inspector Rahe put. So, madam, can you be telling me . . . ' He paused. Spare her somewhat? No. I think not. 'Madam, was it your custom to leave this house during hours of darkness, altogether on your own?'

And it was plain she found the bluntly put question hard to answer.

At last she managed something.

'Inspector, it may not have been anything I would have done in the ordinary way. But . . . but, Inspector, these were no ordinary circumstances.'

Then, before Ghote could point out that, when she had left to go walking in the dark to her aunt's flat, the circumstances were in no way as extraordinary as they became when she found her husband stabbed to death, Juliette Tabholkar turned sharply away.

She went over to one of a pair of small, softly comfortable armchairs in the far corner of the spacious room and sat down.

Message plain: matter has been dealt with.

But why, Ghote asked himself? Why is she behaving with so much of rejection when my question, if put with firmness, was altogether polite?

All right, the only way to get answer is not to let her win.

He went over in his turn and stood looking down at her in the chair she had chosen (if only at the flat we had two such, instead of our tumbling-down *takht*).

'Madam,' he began, his mind still envious of the two well-upholstered little chairs, the seat of the second showing the deep impress of someone who had sat in it not long before, 'if this crime is to be

114

fully investigated, you must answer with altogether same fullness. Was it your custom to go out alone? How was it that, on that of all nights, you were going out in such a way?'

A look of fury, plain fury, on the face of the widow.

'Oh, if you must know, no, it was not any custom of mine. Is it likely in the ordinary way I would do such a thing? No, this was an occasion on its own. You have, no doubt, read in Inspector . . . in Inspector Whathisname's report that I was that evening telephoned by . . . by my mother, who had failed to get through when she was calling my elderly, not-at-all-well aunt, as she does every evening. Why should I not have gone to see her, and at once? Her flat is just only a few minutes from here. My mother was worried, very, very worried about her. Does that answer your question? Altogether as fully as you are wanting?'

Ghote felt he must persist.

'But your husband,' he said. 'He was here, yes? Why was he not going?'

'Why? Why? Why? Inspector, the husband you are so casually mentioning, my very own husband of one year only, has been knifed to death. Knifed to death not very many days ago. Do you really have to ask me these questions?'

'Madam, I regret. But, as I was telling, questions are necessary if the murderer of your husband is to be found. So, why was it you went through the dark of late evening to your aunt? Why was it you who went, and not your husband, a man able to take care of himself if some *goonda* was there?'

'Inspector, it must be in Inspector Rahe's report that when I reached Smita Auntie's flat I found all

115

that was wrong was that she had taken a sleeping pill and had not at all heard her telephone. Inspector, I cannot provide you with answers to all the questions it is entering your head to put to me.'

Just noting that no sleeping pill had been mentioned in Rahe's report, together, no doubt, with a good number of other pertinent facts, Ghote plunged on.

'But, madam, I was not putting any question about what you found when you reached your aunt's flat. I was asking only why it was you yourself who went and not your husband.'

'Let us just say, Inspector: it was myself who was going and not . . . not my beloved Krishna.'

A widow's tear glinted under her left eye. Glinted, but did not fall.

'Madam, you are distressed,' Ghote decided that he had to say. 'Madam, we will leave you now and talk with your servants.'

CHAPTER THIRTEEN

Led now by surly, hunched-shoulders Sgt Chavan towards the kitchen area at the back of the house, Ghote began to wonder why the fellow a pace in front of him was so unforthcoming, so evidently morose. Is it just only his nature? Or is there some reason why he is being like this with me? Is it perhaps he is resenting having to work with this newly come inspector to Crime Branch, and one who has been—it must be known to all—allocated week after week to simple *bandobast* duty? Or . . . a worse thought. Has the ACP instructed this man,

116

not simply to be useful to me, but to report any and every failing I may show?

He straightened his shoulders.

Very well then, I will not show any failings. Especially not with these servants I am about to question.

For a moment, as he followed noisily tramping Chavan, Ghote imagined that in this duplicate house to the one in the painting he so much liked he would also find Ritu, the woman servant, crouching down to scrub and scrub with a handful of ashes at the well-used cooking pot in front of her.

Then, as Chavan thrust aside a bright-coloured bead curtain and strode without so much as a cough of warning into the kitchen ahead, he saw Ritu wheel round from the smart new-looking sink at which she was standing, her hands dripping from the steaming water topped by a rich layer of bright bubbles.

Yes, he thought, in this twentieth-century version of Krishna and Radha's house there is no squatting to scrub with ashes a vessel that needs cleaning. Instead, yes, I recognise it, on the window shelf above the sink there is a packet of that Surf stuff they are always advertising nowadays.

But Gopal, who had been sitting at the table in the centre of the room with the remains of a recent meal on it—a table much bigger than ours at Bank Street Cross Lane, Ghote registered—had also, startled, jumped to his feet, actually knocking over his chair.

Well now, Ghote thought in a rapid aside as he stepped in, is that crude barging-in behaviour of Chavan's something to his detriment that I should be mentioning to the ACP?

A moment's consideration. No, perhaps better not. If Chavan truly may be the ACP's trusted informer.

'Good afternoon,' he said quickly to the two servants, realising how late in the day it now was. 'Sit, sit.'

'Gopal,' Ghote went on as the man swiftly righted his chair, 'you are already knowing who I am. But let me say to your wife—It is Ritu, no?—that I am Inspector Ghote of Crime Branch and I have come, with Sergeant Chavan here also, to conduct a more rigorous investigation into the sad death of your *sahib*, Mr Tabholkar.'

'Inspector,' Gopal replied, 'we will answer your each and every question.'

Ritu, big and well-fleshed, face radiant with smiles from double chin to dancing eyes, merely giggled.

'Good, good,' Ghote said.

There was a third chair at the table. He took it.

'So,' he said, 'I am interested in you being out of this house on the night Tabholkar *Sahib* was stabbed to death. Both of you went together? Was this the night in the week that you are always out?'

It was Ritu who answered now, all eagerness to tell the story.

'Inspector *Sahib*, it is always on Tuesday, every Tuesday, we are going, Inspector, back to where we used to work, at family house, Malabar Hill, before Juliette Miss was leaving to come here to this house that Nathumal *Sahib* built for her and her new husband. Oh, Inspector, such a love match it was. Such Krishna-Radha love. And he being called Krishna itself. Inspector, it was like a story-

118

story only. But, you see, our one and only daughter, Rupa, is one of the maids at Nahumal *Sahib*'s big-big house, so that is why, when Moolchand *Memsahib* said we should go to be servants for Juliette Miss when she was becoming Tabholkar *Memsahib*, she was telling we could return each and every Tuesday because she and *sahib* are always going to cinema on Tuesdays.'

Trusting he would be able to sort out later the account Ritu had tumbled out, Ghote asked her a question from the mental list he had told himself he must get answers to.

'So, tell me, Ritu. You had both gone out that night before your *memsahib*'s mother was telephoning to ask her to go to see if her auntie was in trouble?'

But his question received a reply—it came from Gopal—he had not expected.

'No, no, Inspector, it was Moolchand *Sahib* himself who was telephoning.'

'Moolchand *Sahib*?' he asked, puzzled. 'I was understanding it was Juliette *Memsahib*'s mother who spoke.'

A minor mix-up? But if so I must be careful about what either of these two are telling me. Servants are not always accurate in what they are saying.

But Gopal broke in again.

'Inspector *Sahib*, perhaps it was Inspector Rahe who was telling you this. But he was sometimes getting wrong the answers we were giving. He was in a very-very hurry always.'

'Yes,' Ghote said, telling a small lie for the sake of the reputation of the Cumballa Hill police, 'in early stages of a murder investigation speed is of essence. So perhaps Inspector Rahe is not at all to blame. But you are certain, is it, that it was Nathumal Moolchand *Sahib* himself who spoke to his daughter?'

'*Jee*, Inspector. I was very much surprised when, just as we were going out from kitchen on our way to visit our Rupa, it was his loud voice I heard when telephone rang. You can hear same all over the house when he is telephoning to here.'

But, Ghote thought, in Rahe's report it had stated that Juliette's mother made that call. Best not to pursue the matter now. I do not want to put into these servants' minds that there can be anything any police detective whatsoever fails to notice.

'So,' he said, 'you both went out on that usual day to go over to your old Malabar Hill house to spend the evening with your daughter? Yes?'

'Oh, yes, yes,' Ritu came in cheerfully. 'One nice-nice visit. But then when, late-late, we were coming back here, what were we finding? Tabholkar *Sahib* had been murdered. Inspector, it was terrible, terrible. Blood was still there all over floor, and that Inspector Rahe was telling I must not wash off same. Terrible, terrible.'

'Terrible for you it must have been,' Ghote acknowledged. 'But tell me, if you still can: when you reached the road outside here as you had left the house, did you see anybody waiting and hiding nearby?'

It was Gopal, the calm, who took it on to himself to provide the answer.

'Inspector, we did not.'

'But there could have been someone there? It was well dark already, yes?'

'Inspector, in the dark there could have been someone, but how could we—?'

Irrepressible Ritu broke in.

'Inspector, it was dark-dark dark. Inspector, one elephant could have been waiting there and we would not have seen.'

'Very well, I will accept that.'

He stood up to go.

What I am wanting now, he said to himself, is some time to think. In this place that so unsettlingly echoes that painting in the big museum I have not at all found everything as Inspector Rahe described it.

He looked at his watch. Good heavens, past four o'clock.

An idea came to him. This is long past my time for tiffin. Where better to make up for that than at home in Bank Street Cross Lane? But Chavan? Can I for just only one hour get rid of the ACP's hunched-shoulders spy? Damn it, yes, I can. I am a full inspector at Crime Branch. Whatsoever order I am giving must be obeyed.

*   *   *

At home at last he found Protima busy in the kitchen picking over rice for their evening meal. No servant to do such work. Must find one. Must. But this also: Protima has no idea still that I have been given my first Crime Branch investigation. A small case only, not at all as important as the murder of *Daylight* editor, Darab Dastor, but it is my case. And already I am finding out things that happened in the house on Cumballa Hill that Rahe was altogether missing. Then another thought, a blacker one . . . The Krishna Tabholkar murder is not the case of the Drunken Peon's Beheading. And that is what I was swearing to myself I would probe to the utmost bottom. And swearing to Protima also.

Perhaps a mistake after all to come here to the flat. But it is a mistake I have made, and I must explain it.

The moment Protima opened the door he spoke. Nothing else for it. The sweet-and-bitter news must be told.

'Listen, Ved's mother. Listen. Something good. Very, very good. This morning, almost first thing, ACP *Sahib* was summoning me to his cabin, and . . . and he was giving me investigation. The first I am getting in Crime Branch.'

'No, do not tell what it is,' Protima broke in, widely smiling. 'I am able to guess. Yes, it must be the murder yesterday of that wonderful man, Darab Dastor. The death of the editor of *Daylight* is crying out for one thorough investigation.'

And she is almost right, Ghote thought with dismay. I would have been investigating that affair except that, foolishly, I was mentioning to Mr Divekar that my wife was very much admiring Darab Dastor because he was a Parsi, and in one moment then I was given instead the Tabholkar case, the remains only of one already investigated. Or half-investigated.

'Yes, yes,' he said. 'The Darab Dastor murder would have been a fine job for me. But unfortunately it was given to someone else. I am investigating the murder up in Cumballa Hill—it was some weeks back—of a man called Tabholkar, a young Bombay University lecturer.'

122

'A lecturer only? And you were not given the murder of the editor of *Daylight*?'

'But this is a case involving people even more influential than Darab Dastor. Krishna Tabholkar was married, just only one year past, to the only daughter of that very well-known business boss, Nathumal Moolchand, Moolchand Investments. You must have read about him more than once in the paper. All the big deals he is negotiating.'

'Oh, yes. Heard and heard about I have. That man is supporting Pradeep Popatkar in the by-election here, supporting him with all his millions. It was in *Daylight* itself. Why are you—?'

She came to a stop, and began again, more urgently. 'Why are you bothering with that man's murdered son-in-law when you are meant to be using every minute you can find to investigate the wicked death of your Bikram?'

Ghote found in his head no immediate answer.

'But-but . . . well, when I have dealt with the Tabholkar murder . . . '

'The Tabholkar murder. What is that but a second-class case that is being blown up into one first-class matter because the victim happens to be married to the daughter of a *crorepati*? All the wealth he has makes him into a man of influence. Influence, influence.'

'But, no. No, that is not it at all. Krishna Tabholkar has been killed just as Bikram was. Both are victims deserving to have their deaths investigated and investigated until the perpetrators are found. Each is as urgent as the other. And when Mr Divekar himself was ordering me to go up to Cumballa Hill and take on an investigation where the local police have not done enough of

123

work, then I should go to that just as urgently as I am going later, in secret, to find Bikram's killer.'

And, somewhat to his surprise, Protima accepted his argument.

'Yes. Yes, I suppose,' she said. 'So, tell me, are you already finding out whatever the police at Cumballa Hill were getting wrong? A Crime Branch inspector should have no difficulties there.'

Then, settling down on the piled cushions of the home-made *takht*, Ghote recounted to his wife the whole of his morning's activities from the moment that, with Sgt Chavan at his elbow, he had rung at the bell of the house—he decided not to mention the extraordinary similarity to the Baisakh painting—to the moment he had hit on the curious circumstance that it had not been Mrs Moolchand who had told Juliette that her elderly sister had not answered her phone, but loud-voiced Nathumal Moolchand himself.

Protima looked wise over that, though she had no comment to make. What had piqued her curiosity, it turned out, was Ghote's casual mention a little earlier of the neat and comfortable-looking armchairs, to one of which Juliette had retreated in the face of his persistent questioning.

And now, feeling the cushions of the *takht* once again slipping aside underneath him, something struck him about those chairs. The one Juliette had not chosen had had two deep troughs in its seat as if somebody heavy had dropped down on it, whereas Juliette's one—I was getting one glimpse before she sat—had shown no such signs.

He almost asked Protima about how such chairs might react to people who sat in them.

124

But she had something else she wanted to bring to the fore.

'Yes, yes. Very fine chairs, you were saying, and very, very expensive also, of course. Didn't you say that the whole house was in tip-top condition? See what it is when a poor university lecturer gets to marry a *crorepati*'s only daughter. Suddenly the young man is becoming also rich-rich, and without one hand's turn to deserve same. And where, where, do you think all the money spent on his new house was coming from? From cheating the public. I tell you that.'

But Ghote, for once, paid his forceful wife not the least attention.

Yes, he was thinking, surely someone must have been firmly seated in that little, softly upholstered chair next to Juliette's at some time not long before I was ringing at the bell there. And, wait, now I am thinking, there is this also. When Gopal was admitting us there was a longer interval than I was expecting between the time he left the front door to ask his *memsahib* whether she would see me and the time when he had returned. An unaccountably long interval? And didn't I—now I am coming to think more—hear as we were waiting some sounds of hurry-scurry coming from inside? Of course, I may have been mistaken. Or the sounds may have been just only the noise made by some rapid tidyings-up. But I do not think so. The place looked fine as I walked through to see Mrs Tabholkar, that white-sari ice-pillar. Except, yes, there was a smell of cigarette smoke, and certainly that chilly pillar was not smoking. No sign of an ashtray near her either when she was first standing to meet me nor when she went to sit in

125

that chair in the far corner.

I had actually wondered about checking all that with Chavan when we were leaving. Asking if he heard anything, smelt anything. But then I decided not to. Anything I said was likely to be told to Mr Divekar, and, if he is to learn of the faint suspicion I am having that the grieving widow might have had with her a gentleman, then it must be from myself only. Or I may altogether lose any credit due to me.

But in any case is my suspicion correct that Juliette Tabholkar had with her a man whose existence she could not allow anyone to know of? After all, this Radha had been married for little more than a year to her Krishna. And it is surely doubtful that young Tabholkar had become too much interested in the sort of milkmaids the god of old all too often played with: his famed *gopis*. If Tabholkar had shown some lack of interest in his new wife surely it must have arisen, not because of other women, but from the ever more promising research he was undertaking.

He hardly heard what Protima was saying as she chattered away until, abruptly, he realised from the tone of her voice that she had asked, perhaps for the second time, a sharp question. Nor did he know even whether he had murmured some answer.

The fact was that his head had begun to buzz, more and more urgently, with a whole heap of new questions to be answered.

CHAPTER FOURTEEN

At Crime Branch next day the first thing Ghote did was to get at least one answer to the questions that had been buzzing in his head. He looked up in the telephone directory the number of Bombay University. If I am right in thinking, he told himself, it is at all possible that stabbed-to-death Krishna Tabholkar had ceased, even by a little, to be the ardent lover of his Juliette-Radha and that she had sought solace with someone else, then it is one matter of urgency to find out whether Tabholkar's research was growing so increasingly successful that it had begun to occupy his mind to the exclusion of everything else.

He got his answer with surprising speed.

'Yes,' Professor Venugopal, Krishna Tabholkar's supervisor, told him without hesitation, 'poor murdered Tabholkar was the most promising researcher into quantum mechanics, or wave mechanics if you prefer the term, that I have had for past ten-fifteen years. One day, even soon perhaps, he would have completed work on a discovery such as to make his name for ever. What a pity. What a pity.'

So quantum mechanics—whatever they are— with that promise of worldwide fame could very likely have been triumphing in the young researcher's mind over the love-fire he had formerly believed he felt for his Radha-Juliette. Had she then come to think she was owed from her Krishna more than he was giving her? Yes, it is easy to see a spoilt *crorepati*'s only daughter feeling she was entitled now to seek a new up-to-date Krishna, under whatever name.

One definite fact for the case I am beginning to see taking shape.

And what next? Yes, to find out, if I can get any clue, who is Juliette's, not new Krishna, but new Romeo.

But how to do it? How?

Wait, now back in my head there is fat and cheerful Ritu's romance-clouded description of the newly-wed Tabholkars' blissful life. *Oh, Inspector, such a love match it was. Such Krishna-Radha love.* Now, if that love has become less than what it was, is it not likely Ritu will be taking an equally close interest in any new development?

Yes, back to Cumballa Hill and contrive somehow to have a confidential talk with giggly Ritu. But with Chavan at my elbow? No, somehow, though no doubt I will find the ACP's spy will, asked or not asked, be coming with me anywhere I go. I must contrive to find him a task providing some good reason why he should be elsewhere.

*   *   *

It was, in fact, Chavan who solved the problem himself. Up in Cumballa Hill Ghote was standing for a swift moment looking up—he could not resist it—at the pale-purple house so closely resembling the one imagined by that painter of the far past. Can it be, he was thinking, that the architect that Nathumal Moolchand employed to design this house knows that Baisakh painting? Did he, simply for his own sly pleasure, do his best to bring it to life in today's Bombay? And did Moolchand,

128

thinking of little other than business, business, business, just accept the design for the house as being the best money could buy? Is he so uninterested in painting or in literature or anything of that sort that the only writings he takes any note of are—if what I once read in some scandal page is right—the *scripts* for games of cricket from which, it was hinted, he was able to make fat sums by knowing in advance a game will end in some altogether unexpected way (with the aid of a judicious bribe given to the right batsman).

'Inspector!'

Chavan had seized his arm and was hissing urgently into his ear.

'Inspector, behind the house. A man. Creeping. Could be our killer, yes?'

And, without another word he was off, running crouched along the road looking for somewhere to get in behind the row of smart houses.

Good God, is he right? Is there really a chance intruder here, the intruder Inspector Rahe spent so much time failing to find? Or am I, on the other hand, right about the significance of the deep twin depressions in that soft chair seat, plus also the length of time it took Gopal to return after he had first answered the doorbell?

Not a hard decision to make. Chavan must be off on wrong track. And it is up to me to get to see Ritu again just as soon as I can.

He opened the gate into the little garden in front of the house—no bushes full of singing koels—and went swiftly over to ring and ring at the bell.

Gopal came to the door, looking alarmed.

'You are wishing to see Juliette Madam once more?' he asked, calming down once he realised

129

who had rung so urgently.

'No, Gopal, I am wanting one more small word only with your wife.'

'*Sahib*, she is cleaning the vessels after . . . after *memsahib*'s late breakfast only. Can I be answering the questions you have?'

'No. No, thank you. It will not at all worry me to speak with Ritu while she is working.'

Then, a quick idea.

'But there is something you should perhaps do. Sgt Chavan is going round to the back of the house because he believes he has spotted someone hiding there who may be the intruder who was killing your master. Go round and see if you can help.'

Gopal went through the pretty strip of garden, turned sharply and hurried off.

Thank you, Ganesha, solver of difficulties. If you exist.

Prayer of gratitude offered up to *Swarga* above, or to nowhere, Ghote hurriedly made for the kitchen.

He found plump Ritu, her hands deep in the bubbles glinting on the water in the sink. Yes, packet of Surf still on the ledge above. But the vessels in that water and on the draining board, plates and the quarter-plates, cups and saucers. Surely there are too many of them? Twice as many as necessary for a late breakfast for Juliette on her own?

'Ah, Ritu. I was hoping I could find you. There is something, something quite small but quite important, you may be able to help me with.'

'Inspector, if I can do it, I will, very, very gladly.'

She wiped the Surf bubbles from her hands and a huge smile lit up her face.

'It is like this,' Ghote said, 'you were telling when we were talking before how very much in love your mistress and new master were in this new house of theirs. A story to warm the heart.'

'*Jee*, Inspector *Sahib*. Radha had found her Krishna, and such even was his real name. A wonderful thing. You see, I was not too happy to be leaving the big Moolchand house on Malabar Hill and to be coming here. But when I was seeing all that was happening I was . . . '

A coy blush swept up from her neck to her very hair.

'You are knowing it is one of my duties to make bed each day, Inspector? And . . . and always . . . ' giggle, giggle, 'it was needful to put new sheet.'

She reached forward and gave him a vigorous nudge with her podgy, dimpled elbow. An unnecessary nudge if ever there was.

'Yes, yes. I am following,' Ghote was quick to put in. 'But . . . '

Is this my opportunity? Arrived at in less than two minutes? It may be. It may be.

'But, tell me, was this happening every . . . every night, right up to recent days?'

Her eyes widened.

'Inspector, how did you know?'

*   *   *

Standing just outside the kitchen, Ghote let all that had just been confirmed for him, almost positively, run and run through his head.

Yes, Ritu's *How did you know?* can mean one thing only. That the night-after-night lovemaking of the first months of the marriage of Krishna and his Radha-Juliette had come to an end. So, what is more likely than that Nathumal Moolchand's spoilt daughter has taken a lover? A lover who, very likely, was here in the house with her when I was first ringing at the door yesterday morning? A lover whose precise name I do not at this moment need to know. Only that he almost certainly exists.

Very good. The clue of the crushed-down seat cushion is shown to have been hundred per cent good. And already it has been added to by the clue of the double load of vessels under washing.

So can it be that the cricket-fixer, learning of his daughter's new lover, most probably a man from the wealthy circles she has always moved in, would have seen him as the sort of husband Juliette should always have had, instead of the poorly paid lecturer she had unfortunately succumbed to? Would Nathumal Moolchand ever have believed her choice for husband was a scientist likely to discover something in the field of quantum mechanics that, in Professor Venugopal's words, would *make his name for ever*? No, a man like the cricket-fixer never would have done.

So . . . so, can I go one step further? When Juliette told her father she no longer loved her Krishna did he simply decide to have that incorrect husband removed?

Easy perhaps to see that he might have done. A man of his sort, into not only cricket-fixing but, no doubt, into other under-the-table business dealings—strike-breaking, even eliminating a rival—would know where, at a safe distance, he could lay his hands on a killer for hire, a *supari*.

Yes. Yes, come to think, he would need a man like the cleaver-wielding Atul I have sworn to find and arrest. Could, in fact, Nathumal Moolchand's *supari* be none other than Atul himself? But, no. No, no, no. Do not confuse two altogether separate matters. My hunt for ruthless Atul is not likely to be linked to the *supari* Nathumal Moolchand had to hand, a man who—if he truly exists—was the intruder who had dealt those dozen deadly knife blows to innocent Krishna Tabholkar, destined for great scientific fame.

Then he realised what it was he had to do. The enormous thing.

I have got to question Nathumal Moolchand, the *crorepati* whose name is always in the newspapers as if there as of right. And, more, I have got to ask him as many simple-sounding questions as I can about his daughter and the murder of her husband in the house he built for her on Cumballa Hill. I have got to ask him this and that concerning the events of that night without . . . without once referring to his telephoning Juliette, on the Tuesday when the two servants would be off to visit their own daughter. That call when Gopal heard him sending Juliette out of the house to see if something was amiss with her mother's invalid sister, and thus leaving Krishna Tabholkar alone there to be killed.

Will I be able to do it? And should I, before I attempt to put questions to such an influential figure, ask to see the ACP to consult him about an interview that may have tremendous repercussions?

If I do that, will I at once be taken off the case? I could be. Even if the ACP agrees that Moolchand has questions to answer, that he really must account for stating over the telephone, when

133

Gopal heard his booming voice, that Juliette's aunt was in trouble and she should go to her. Will I be allowed to ask those questions? Myself, the newest recruit to the Branch, untested, untried?

No, I will not be. I can hear him saying so.

Then must I go to the Head of Moolchand Investments on my own, and without any official backup? Yes, I . . .

But, no. No, I should not go straight away to the cricket-fixing *crorepati*. There is one other witness I should see first. Juliette's Smita Auntie.

*　　*　　*

It was, Ghote found testing the time it would take to go from the pale-purple house to the block of flats where Juliette's aunt lived, a much longer walk than he had expected. Once he had got directions from staid Gopal, back from his fruitless attempt to spot Sgt Chavan's intruder, it took him a good twenty minutes to get there, even at a brisk pace and by daylight.

That puzzled him once more. If walking to her aunt's block takes as long as this, there was even less reason for Juliette to go out, in the dark of the night, when her vigorous husband was there to go in her place. And no one has said to me that Krishna would not have known his wife's Smita Auntie well enough to look in on her and see if she was ill. So why had Juliette gone herself, leaving, as it happened, her Krishna alone in the house where Inspector Rahe's *intruder* had come and stabbed him to death?

Perhaps now, as soon as I have located the flats block—yes, *Sunnyside*, Gopal said it is called—I will be getting answer.

And at Sunnyside he found straight away that the invalid was not even lying down. She was up on her feet, happily pottering about the sunshine-filled flat. For once, Ghote thought, a name for a block of flats, Sunnyside, that is no sort of a lie. But will I find other sorts of lies here? Lies not told by this lady, her full shining face showing no more than a spider's web of fine wrinkles, her body under its cheerful red-and-blue striped sari betraying few signs, if any, of whatever disease she is suffering from. Altogether she seems to be a by no means inactive person.

So will I now uncover fully whatever deceptions there were in the telephone call that sent Juliette out of her house for as long as—it must have been—three-quarters of an hour at least? Three-quarters of an hour, during which the husband whom she had come to feel was no longer her loving Krishna had been murdered?

Introductions over, 'Miss Chunnilal,' Ghote said, registering from that name Nathumal Moolchand must have found a wife from as long-standing a Marwari family as his own, 'I regret, but it has become my duty to discover each and every last fact concerning the sad death of the man your niece was marrying.'

'Yes, yes, Inspector Ghote—I have got name right?—if there is anything I am knowing that you are wanting to find out, I will tell you it as best I can.'

'Thank you. So, first, let me ask about the visit your niece was paying to you that night when she was hearing you had not answered your usual 8.30 p.m. call. It was—'

'Inspector, I was getting no call that evening. I remember thinking it was surprising, but I just only supposed my sister had for once forgotten, and I was—yes, yes, I remember perfectly now—I was at once beginning my game of Patience. I had decided to play the hardest one of all that night, and I was making early start.'

Into Ghote's mind there came the memory of something Juliette Tabholkar had claimed. She had stated that when she reached Sunnyside that fateful night she had found her aunt had taken a sleeping pill. That, he knew now, was simply not so.

But this was no time to make fresh inquiries of Juliette about those circumstances. Now it must be more questions for this enthusiastic Patience-player.

'That is most interesting, madam,' he said. 'So you were surprised, is it, when your niece, Juliette, was coming at about nine o'clock?'

'Nine o'clock, Inspector? No, no, later than that. Nearer to half past.'

'Ah. Good. But I am understanding you were very much asleep when your niece was coming. So, if I may ask, how were you able to be so sure of the time?'

'Asleep, Inspector? I have told you: I certainly was not. Do you think I am so much an old woman that I spend all day and all night dozing only? Not at all, not at all. No, when Juliette was speaking on the entryphone that we are having—these are hundred per cent modern flats, you know—I was sitting here wide-wide awake. My Patience was working out so nicely I could not stop. But I did look at the clock then, and it said it was just after

136

half past nine.'

Ghote pulled out his notebook and wrote down the time, by no means just as a politeness to Smita Chunnilal.

'And you say you were still playing a game of Patience then? You are sure of that?'

'Inspector, that game I play is so difficult that it hardly ever comes out right. Do you think when, that night, it was almost-almost finished when the entryphone buzzed that I would be putting the cards away, as if the game did not at all matter?'

'No, madam, no,' he said. 'I am sure you would not do that. And, after your niece had gone— without actually seeing you, did you say?—you did finish it?'

He wanted, if nothing else, to hear the happy answer.

'Inspector, I did. I would not have abandoned that game if the very ceiling had fallen on me.'

Another discrepancy, Ghote noted. Had not Juliette at least implied she had seen her aunt, spoken to her face-to-face, been told she had taken a sleeping pill?

But all he said was, 'Quite right, madam. I am very glad to hear.'

And not only glad, he thought, because you are a bright and cheerful invalid lady, but also because your one hundred per cent clear answers are making another fine solid brick in the case I am building up in my head. Yes, Juliette had been out of her house far longer than she really would have needed to walk quickly here, see her aunt briefly, and then return. So had it been indicated to her by her father that she should be away from the pale-purple house for as long a time as she could manage? To be away from it while her no longer wanted husband was there all on his own?

CHAPTER FIFTEEN

As soon as he could after hearing about the triumphant end to the Patience game, Ghote left Smita Chunnilal. He had wanted even to run straight out of the flat just calling out a swift goodbye, but he managed in the end to keep the fierce excitement out of his eyes long enough to make his farewell polite and grateful.

His suppressed excitement lasted, however, only until he stepped out of Sunnyside's double doors. At once it came to him then that, knowing now how false was the account Rahe had been given of that night's events, nothing should be allowed to stand between himself and questioning Nathumal Moolchand, distant head of mighty Moolchand Investments.

Bracing his bony shoulders, he decided he must go, without any delay whatsoever, straight to Moolchand Chambers, described all too frequently in newspaper columns as the tallest and most modern building among all the high-rises coming up on the reclaimed land at the far tip of Bombay's southern peninsula. He decided, too, that he would take Sgt Chavan with him.

Very well, taking Chavan to Moolchand Chambers may give the ACP's spy a chance to report something not at all authorised which I am going to undertake. But it will also serve one very useful purpose. Hunched-shoulders, sullenly

138

determined Chavan will perhaps remind the powerful *crorepati* at his desk in Moolchand Chambers that the Bombay Police, and its Crime Branch in particular, has more forceful ways of finding out what it wants to know than just only by asking questions.

So, with Ghote choosing to take the wheel, they embarked on the long drive down from Cumballa Hill to the edge of the sea at Chowpatty Beach, its wide stretch of sand dotted now with the richer Bombayites taking early advantage of the first summer weather. Then, with Chavan sitting all the while staring morosely straight ahead, it was along the wide sweep of Marine Drive, wide but intolerably thick with traffic.

Abruptly it came into Ghote's mind, as he jockeyed the car along, that the situation with Chavan was nothing less than ridiculous.

Here I am, saddled with this morose hunched figure, neither of us having a word to say to each other. Chavan is tongue-tied because, almost certainly, he is under the ACP's orders to report on my every move. And I myself am condemned to equal silence because I believe this is what Chavan's duty is.

Right, time to break apart the absurd cocoon of silence.

'Tell me, Sergeant, am I right to think ACP Divekar has told you, in confidence, that he wants you to report to him all about myself?'

Chavan swung round in his seat.

'But-but, Inspector, no. No, no.'

'Really and truly *No*?' Ghote asked with a smile into which he put all the friendliness he could muster.

And, after perhaps five seconds, the answer came.

'Inspector, when ACP *Sahib* is giving me one order what must I do?'

'All right, that is a hard question to answer. And I tell you one thing: you must, of course, always give the ACP something.' He paused. 'Something, but perhaps not everything, yes?'

Suddenly Chavan smiled, the sun of Baisakh appearing through sullen clouds.

'*Jee*, Inspector.'

*   *   *

As they wriggled at last across to the eastern side of the now narrowing peninsula, with the wide spread of the harbour beyond, Chavan began, as they passed Colaba Causeway's long lines of shops and ever-crowded pavements, happily commenting on the activities of the various touts and card sharps, as well as peddlers of comfort-inducing *charas*. Better, much better.

Then, at last, they reached the city's busy newly claimed area of high-rising tall blocks, and the pathetic, barely roofed *jhopadpattis* that sheltered the workers building the towers.

They were able, when it came to it, to pull up exactly opposite Moolchand Chambers.

Good God, Ghote could not help saying to himself as he looked up and up at the white-gleaming building, how many chambers must be housed under this enormous Moolchand umbrella? Little though the bulk of them will have anything to do with Nathumal Moolchand himself, beyond paying him very heavy amounts of rent.

140

But somewhere on the best-position, one floor above ground level, there must be the offices of Moolchand Investments, with Nathumal Moolchand sitting spider-like in the middle.

So, it is out of the car, cross the road—watch out for all the sand-and-cement trucks pushing past—and then into the reception area and ask for '*Shri* Nathumal Moolchand, Inspector Ghote, Bombay Police Crime Branch, Sgt Chavan also'.

All easily done. In no time Ghote found himself watching one of the elegant receptionists behind her massive marble counter pick up a telephone. He stood then admiring the brilliant yellow of the full, nine-yard silk sari she wore. Oh, how sick with envy, he thought, it would make Protima.

Then things began to go wrong.

The receptionist put down her phone.

'*Shri* Moolchand's secretary says *Shri* Moolchand cannot see you.'

The answer seemed to Ghote almost as extraordinary as a sudden appearance in the road outside, not of any laden truck, but of a huge liner from the harbour hard by.

'Cannot? Cannot?' he stuttered in amazement. 'But he is there? It is *Shri* Moolchand himself who has told his secretary I cannot see?'

'Yes, Inspector. Or, in fact, it was one of his secretaries.'

'But why? What he is saying is preventing? If he is just only occupied for some minutes, I can easily wait.'

'She was saying only that he cannot see you, Inspector.'

Ghote gave a quick significant glance down to Chavan beside him, looking, yes, thoroughly menacing, shoulders more formidably hunched than ever.

'No,' he said. 'Call up again. Find out for how long it is that *Shri* Moolchand cannot see me. I can sit here one hour, two even.'

'Very well, Inspector, but . . . '

She picked up her telephone again, dialled the single number that was all apparently needed and spoke, very quietly, at greater length.

So, has she taken note of Chavan standing menacingly beside me?

Waiting, Ghote began to ask himself why Nathumal Moolchand, the great man, was behaving in the way he was. Could it be that, knowing, as he probably did now, that Crime Branch had reopened the Cumballa Hill investigation he was truly fearing the crime he had plotted—if that was what he truly had done— would come to light in its every detail?

In its every detail? A new thought came to Ghote.

When, at the pale-purple house, I was about to ring the doorbell, my eye was caught by the glint of its bright Yale lock, and I thought for a moment how this house, looking so like one from hundreds of years in the past, must in reality differ in all sorts of modern ways from that imaginary one. But now only it comes back to me that the door showed no sign whatever of Inspector Rahe's intruder having broken it open.

Did the fellow enter by smashing a window, then? But, if he did, surely Krishna Tabholkar would have heard the noise. He would most probably straight away have rung the police station. And, in fact, Rahe's report, with its long

142

list of possibly stolen objects, said nothing at all about any smashed window. So did the intruder hammer at the door and then, when Krishna opened to him . . . ? But an intelligent scientist was surely unlikely to have immediately opened his door wide in answer to some violent knocking in the hours of darkness. He would at least have called through the door asking who was there.

So did the intruder—is it possible?—have a key to that Yale lock? But how could he have one?

An answer came to Ghote as soon as the question had entered his mind. If a rich man builds a house for his daughter and his new son-in-law what is more likely than that he should keep a spare set of keys? He might need, if the happy pair were away somewhere, to get into the house for a hundred and one good reasons. And so . . .

'Inspector?'

It was Nine-yard Sari, telephone receiver back on its rest, giving him an impatient look.

'Yes? Yes? What it is?'

'Inspector, it is once more *No*. *Shri* Moolchand cannot see you.'

So much for the threat demonstrated by Chavan's aggressive presence.

'No,' Ghote said, losing nothing of his determination, 'let me speak with Mr Moolchand himself. I must hear from him, and no one else, that he will not see an officer from Crime Branch.'

A sigh from deep within the brilliant yellow sari.

'I will try, Inspector. But I cannot do more than say you are wishing to speak directly with *Shri* Moolchand.'

He listened then to his message being repeated.

Eventually Nine-yard Sari put down her receiver.

143

'Inspector, *Shri* Moolchand is sending down *Shri* Kanjilal, his personal assistant.'

Yes, I have done it, Ghote thought. You have only got to persist and persist and you can obtain whatsoever you are wanting. In my case, a face-to-face interview with Nathumal Moolchand. This personal whatever-he-is will in a few minutes only be taking me up to Moolchand.

He heard the whirring of a lift, the clunk as it reached its destination. Its doors began smoothly to open.

A rather short man, wide-mouthed, wearing round spectacles in a round face—a squat frog, Ghote could not help thinking—came across to the reception counter.

'Inspector Girish?' he asked, all too loudly.

For a moment Ghote thought there must be some sort of mix-up. Can there be a Gujarati Inspector Girish here also for some reason? But a Gujarati inspector in Crime Branch? There must be plenty away in Gujarat itself, of course, but a soft-spoken Gujarati in tough Bombay . . . ?

No, he realised. No, this squat frog with his big horn-rimmed specs and his wide flappy lips must have forgotten the name of the man he has been told to take up to his boss.

Unless . . . ? Unless this is a deliberate insult?

No, let me see.

'Is it Inspector Ghote you are wanting?' he said with all the distinctness he could summon up. 'Inspector Ghote from Crime Branch?'

'Yes, it must be you,' Frog-face said, yet more loudly. 'Very well. I have just one message for you. *Shri* Moolchand will not see you.'

He turned round and walked back into the lift

144

behind him, the liftwallah holding its doors sternly open.

And, Ghote thought, Chavan has heard every word of each and every one of these refusals. But how much of them, now we are on friendly terms, will he feel he must tell Mr Divekar something about? Will the ACP get to know I am not an officer who can secure a meeting with someone as influential as Nathumal Moolchand, that I am unfit to be an officer of the very Branch that is existing for the purpose of conducting cases involving, precisely, people of influence? Will he, or not?

What to do? Only one thing, wait and see if Chavan has somehow been fully turned from hired spy into something of a friend.

He stood there in silence, pondering, until he realised that the smooth face above the yellow nine-yard sari had raised one expressive eyebrow.

'Come, Chavan,' he snapped out. 'We are doing no good waiting here.'

He had seen himself simply stamping out, feeling somehow the sharp banging of his shoes might penetrate to wherever above Nathumal Moolchand was sitting issuing his blank refusals. But, even as he turned to make his way across the wide marble floor to the ten-foot-high solid glass doors, an alternative path ahead came into his mind.

If *Shri* Moolchand will not see me, then there is someone who must. *Shrimati* Moolchand. She will know why it was her husband, and not herself, who made the telephone call that sent their daughter on her long walk in the dark to find nothing was wrong with her aunt. When in fact, as I discovered soon enough, Smita Auntie had been wide awake playing Patience at the time Nathumal Moolchand had claimed she had not answered the customary 8.30 p.m. call.

Yes, *Shrimati* Moolchand may have a lot to tell me. And, she may very likely also know whether or not they have in their Malabar Hill house one spare set of keys to the pretty little lovers' abode on Cumballa Hill.

*   *   *

The house up in cool Malabar Hill, yet higher above the crammed and crowded city even than Cumballa Hill, looked, Ghote found, very different from the modern copy of the painting in the Prince of Wales Museum occupied by the Moolchands' daughter. Pure white in its every inch, it was, simply, enormous. On two floors, with at ground level a long-long veranda, its roof supported by a row of square-cut pillars, it extended over almost the whole of a block.

'Yes,' said Chavan at his elbow, 'once was belonging to some maharajah. But having to sell damn quick when his state was taken into India itself.'

And I am going to have to enter it, Ghote thought. It will be some kind of invasion, a one-man invasion. But an invasion by an officer—must not for one moment forget—with all the authority of Crime Branch behind him.

A one-man invasion? Yes, I think it must be.

'Listen,' he said to Chavan, 'take the vehicle back to Headquarters. I am not at all knowing how long I may be here. You can get your tiffin in comfort,

146

and I will let you know later what we may have to do this afternoon.'

With barely a *Jee, Inspector*, Chavan eagerly shot away. Tiffin before spying, if he was spying for Mr Divekar.

Very well, Ghote said to himself, now I am going to pursue, to its very end, the idea I am having of what in cold fact happened at the Cumballa Hill house the night Krishna Tabholkar was stabbed to death. How many wounds it was? Yes, twelve. At least Rahe had been conscientious enough to put that into his slim-slim report.

Taking a deep breath, Ghote marched across the wide gravelled area in front of the huge house and up the three snow-white steps to the imposing door studded with fat black iron nails, its surround so thickly carved in its every inch that it was a sculpture in itself.

*   *   *

Shrimati Moolchand proved to be a lot easier to see than her husband in his Moolchand Chambers fortress. Name given to the turbaned *chaprassi* who, at his single ring on the golden bell-button, had swung the big door wide open. Then, no more than three minutes later, there came the simple words *Shrimati Moolchand will see you, Inspector*.

He was led up to a pretty sitting room at one corner of the huge house, its windows overlooking a stretch of green lawn dotted with flower beds bright with colour.

Nathumal Moolchand's wife was dressed to perfection in a heavily embroidered Benares sari that would have made Protima even more envious

147

than the Moolchand Chambers receptionist's one. Her hair was a pyramid woven round a dazzling piece of jewellery that looked as if it must have taken her maid half the morning to construct. Her face was a picture of artfully applied make-up. Each finger of her hands bore a sparkling ring. And none of them disguised the fact that Moolchand *Memsahib* was fat. Immensely fat. Those fingers, podgy as they were, almost ate up all but the rich jewels the rings held.

'So, Inspector,' she said the moment he had been ushered in, 'what is it you are wanting here?'

'Madam, I am charged with the duty of making a most thorough investigation into the death of your son-in-law, Krishna Tabholkar.'

At once the look of acute suspicion on her full, well-powdered cheeks, and even on the wide area of her second chin, disappeared.

'Yes, poor, poor Krishna,' she said. 'The more I got to know him after the wedding, the better I was liking. So devoted he was to my Juliette.'

Ghote seized now on the opportunity of finding at a much less hostile level than he had expected the answers he wanted.

'Madam,' he said, by way of easing himself in. 'I am altogether interested in that name you and your husband were giving to your baby daughter. Juliette. Not at all an Indian name, if I may say it.'

'No. No, Inspector, I was choosing my daughter's name before my Nathumal could object. I was wanting, you see, something altogether different from the Radhas, Ranis and Lakshmis people are always giving. Inspector, are you at all knowing Shakespeare?'

'Yes, yes.'

148

'Then, Inspector, you will have heard of *Romeo and Juliet*, the famous story of two lovers.'

Ghote thought that another quick *Yes, yes* would be the only necessary response.

'So I was insisting my little daughter should be called Juliette, though I was adding some extra letters to make it more stand out. My husband was not at all objecting. He was waiting still for the boy.'

A tear or two had suddenly appeared at each richly rounded cheek. 'The boy,' she murmured, 'who was never coming.'

Ghote left a moment of silence by way of acknowledging the tragic circumstance. Yes, he thought, the sorrow of never providing an heir may very likely account for the gradual arrival of those compensating rolls of heavy flesh I see almost weighing down the arms of her chair. Sorrow often demands food, rich food and sweet.

Now, he thought, I can without difficulty bring my questioning round to where I would like it to be.

'Madam,' he said, bluntly enough, 'the sad death of Mr Krishna Tabholkar is what I must ask you about. How do you believe it was occurring?'

'Oh, Inspector, everybody is knowing that. Inspector Rahe, who was first making investigation, was accounting for whole thing.'

'Yes. Yes, madam. But . . . but, you know, questions are there about Rahe's report on the matter. That is why case has been put into hands of Crime Branch.'

'You are an officer of Crime Branch, is it?'

'Yes, madam. I am.'

A new moment of pride. Quickly suppressed.

'And you are saying that Inspector Rahe was wrong about whole affair? That my poor Krishna was not at all killed by the *goonda* who was breaking in?'

Can she know so little about the business that she really believes Rahe got it all correct in every detail, Ghote asked himself? Can she have been told scarcely anything about it?

Or . . . or is this all a clever way to avoid whatever pointed questions I may have for her? An even better way of blocking my path than her husband's *I will not see*?

Is Juliette's mother altogether as devious as her father?

One way perhaps to find an answer. Yes, try this.

'Madam, I was telling: Inspector Rahe's investigation has been found not altogether satisfactory. No trace of the individual he was thinking of as the perpetrator has come to light. All possible bad characters in Cumballa Hill area have been questioned and nothing has emerged. So we—'

Shrimati Moolchand heaved forward her beautifully dressed bulk.

'But then . . . ? Then, Inspector, who is it Crime Branch is seeking? Oh, my poor, poor Krishna.'

Now, this is seeming to be my answer. *My poor Krishna* she is saying and repeating. So, unless she is a hundred per cent clever, and it is sounding that she is very-very sincere, can it be that she knows nothing at all of anything her husband has arranged to be done? Yes, it could be. It well could be. What money-hoarding Marwari, like Moolchand, tells his wife all his secrets?

So, take one more step onwards.

'Madam, it has been suggested that if no *goonda* broke in that night, then whoever was stabbing Krishna Tabholkar may have entered the house with the aid of a somehow obtained key.'

He watched her closely, careful not to appear by half an inch to be doing so.

'A key, Inspector? But how was this . . . this *man* obtaining a key? I have heard, I think, of wicked individuals succeeding in taking a key from someone's pocket or a whole key-bunch even, and having a copy made with wax. Do criminals really do that? Or is it something I was reading in some detective-story book only?'

Another small advance. But she still may be more of cunning than she is seeming.

'Yes, madam, it is not in novels only that such things are done. But doing it is a complicated matter for any thief, often too much complicated. What more usually happens in such cases is that there is more than one key for the door in question. People sometimes lend a key and it fails to get returned, or there proves to be a second set of keys kept somewhere else.'

'Yes, Inspector, we ourselves have a second set for the house we were giving Juliette as wedding gift.'

There. There at last. My guess shown to be right.

And *Shrimati* Moolchand has shown herself also to be a truly innocent lady. Surely she is, surely.

'Madam, is it possible someone could have obtained possession of this second set of keys, or taken just only one from it? Madam, where is that set kept? Are you knowing?'

'Of course I am, Inspector. When it is something so much to do with our Juliette and my poor

Krishna, then of course I am knowing where those keys are kept.'

'And where is that, madam?'

'In a drawer of my husband's desk in the small office he has here. That, he was saying, would be the safest place. The drawer has a good lock.'

'And *Shri* Moolchand keeps the key for that drawer on his person always?'

'No, no. That would not be the best plan. Not at all. What if Nathumal he is going to Delhi one day and I am needing for some reason to visit the house?'

'So there is another key for that desk drawer?'

With an air of triumph *Shrimati* Moolchand put her two podgy, rings-sparkling hands on the arms of her chair and pushed herself up to a standing position, the large bunch of keys dangling at her side—somewhat old-fashioned nowadays—giving a brisk clatter. But it was not these she was eager to present. She dug about in the recesses of her silk-shining Benares sari and after a minute held up, high in her hand between a plump finger and a yet plumper thumb, a single shining brass key, smaller by far than any in her housewife's bunch.

For an instant Ghote wanted to thrust out a hand and grab the shiny little object. But it was for an instant only. Then he simply asked his next question.

'Madam, may we, in the absence of your husband at Moolchand Chambers, go to check that the spare set of keys is still in place?'

Bur now an obstacle.

'Oh, I am not thinking Nathumalji would want that. Private things are private things. But, if you are liking, I will telephone and ask if he can return home. If he is able to come here, I am sure he would show you those keys.'

But I am not so sure, Ghote thought. The man who refused and refused under any circumstances to see myself is not very likely to come back from his office just to show me those keys. One of which, the front-door key to the murder house, may not be there. May still, despite the passing of time, be in the possession of the *supari* who got rid of a husband no longer pleasing to Moolchand's much-spoilt daughter.

'Madam, that would be very good. But perhaps it is not necessary for Moolchand *Sahib* to quit his seat just now. There is another matter that might be dealt with first. You see, madam, questions have arisen about your sister, Miss Chunnilal, and the need there was for someone to go that night to see if she was lying ill in her Sunnyside flat.'

'If you are saying it, Inspector.'

'Thank you, madam. You see, it is seeming there is more than one account of what was happening that night. First, Inspector Rahe was told the customary call made to your sister each evening— at about 8.30 p.m., isn't it?—was not at all answered that night. But when I was talking with Miss Chunnilal, a most lively lady I found her, she was stating and declaring that she was wide awake all the time, playing a most difficult game of Patience and would, of course, have answered any call that was coming. So, madam, did you make the 8.30 p.m. call that evening?'

'Inspector, I did not. Sometimes I am forgetting, Sister Smita is not as ill as people are thinking. But I cannot say whether or not my husband made the call.'

'Cannot—'

'No, Inspector, you see, I was not in this house at eight-thirty that night. Nathumal and I were going to see late showing of that film with the new hero everyone is talking. But then, just as I was waiting in the car for Nathumal to come, he was hurrying out and saying he had received urgent telephone call—about, I think, some cricket match—and must stay in. He said I should go on to cinema, and, if he could, he would join me later. But he was not able.'

Hugging this to himself, Ghote made a strong effort to look as if he had been told about nothing more than a chance detail of the Moolchands' domestic life.

But, he said—almost sung—to himself, it is far, far from a chance domestic detail. It is confirmation, strong-strong confirmation, of the astonishing idea that began to creep into my mind when Gopal, in the kitchen of the house in Cumballa Hill, said the call about Miss Chunnilal had been made in the loud-loud voice of Juliette's father. And that was the call that made sure Krishna Tabholkar was alone at home when some well-paid *supari* quietly opened the house door and stabbed to death the man he found all alone inside.

The extraordinary conclusion blossomed now in Ghote's mind like a giant flower.

Yes, he thought, now I have solved the case of the murder of Krishna Tabholkar. My first Crime Branch investigation, and I have dealt with same in hours only.

Then a thud of dismay.

All right, I have found out how it came about

154

that Krishna Tabholkar was stabbed to death. Good. Excellent. But . . . but I am sure also the man who had that *supari* sent to carry out the killing was Nathumal Moolchand himself. Nathumal Moolchand who totally refused to see me, never mind how many times I was asking. Nathumal Moolchand whose wife, when I came to see her, as no one had done before, unconsciously has betrayed him.

Yes, I have traced down the man ultimately responsible for the murder of Krishna Tabholkar. None other than Nathumal Moolchand of Moolchand Investments. But Moolchand is one enormously wealthy man, and enormously wealthy men are people of enormous influence. However wrong that may be.

So what should I do?

At once he realised. One answer only. It is the duty of a police officer when he believes he has discovered who is responsible for a murder to report same to his superior.

CHAPTER SIXTEEN

Ghote, standing there in Nathumal Moolchand's splendid Malabar Hill house, made some excuse to *Shrimati* Moolchand for an abrupt departure. If anyone five minutes later had asked him what he had said to her, he would have been altogether incapable of telling them. Unseeingly, he went out of the big house—did the *chaprassi* let me out? Don't at all know—hailed a taxi he saw idling at the end of the road and told the driver to go to

155

Police Headquarters 'fast as you can'.

The next thing he knew he was standing outside ACP Divekar's door, hastily typed report on the Krishna Tabholkar murder inquiry tight-clasped in his hand, peering through the thick glass pane to make sure no visitor was inside. There was not. He could see Mr Divekar seated at his wide sweep of a desk, sternly upright. He was not even telephoning, not even scribbling down some passing thought.

He is waiting to hear my account of what, just only ten-twelve minutes ago, I was telling him per internal telephone. That I have found out who is responsible for the murder of Krishna Tabholkar. Found out in hardly two days what was defeating Inspector Rahe for weeks.

So, now is the moment.

He gave the door in front of him the sort of brisk tap he had learnt the ACP liked. And there came the sharp *Come* he vividly recalled.

Then he was standing to attention in front of the wide sweep of the desk, clicking heels.

The ACP looked at him, grey eyes fiercely sharp.

'Ghote. You have something to tell me?'

'Yes, sir, yes.'

And out tumbled the whole story of his investigation, the long trail of all the tiny things he had observed, and Rahe had not. The chair with its cushion deeply impressed by the weight of a pair of solid male buttocks. The curiously long time it had taken between the moment the door of the pale-purple house had first been opened to him, 'Sgt Chavan also', and the moment Gopal had returned to say Krishna Tabholkar's newly made widow would receive them. The faint smell of cigarette smoke he had been hardly aware of as he had been led through the house. The fact, too, that Tabholkar was no mere junior lecturer but a researcher marked out for perhaps world fame with a discovery in quantum mechanics.

It was then that the ACP interrupted.

'Quantum mechanics, Inspector, what the hell are those?'

Ghote scratched for an answer.

'Sir . . . They are . . . Sir, it was Professor Venugopal at Bombay University who was telling me. He was stating Krishna Tabholkar was one very promising researcher into . . . into quantum mechanics, sir.'

'And, Inspector, I was asking you what are these quantum mechanics. A question you seem unable to answer.'

'Yes, sir. No, sir. Sir, Professor Venugopal was omitting to inform me. Sir, he must have been thinking that every intelligent person would—'

An abrupt descent of wild dismay. Oh God, what have I said?

Mr Divekar's steely rigid face tautened yet more. A dull flush of coming anger seemed to be mounting up on it.

'Venugopal,' he barked out. 'Damn South Indian, name like that. And you know what South Indians are like, Ghote. Talk-talk-talk and say not a damn thing. So, if you have nothing more to your case than the idea that the victim was some sort of genius, I think you had better go away and do a lot more down-to-earth investigating.'

'But-but, sir, I have done more.'

'More? More what, Ghote?'

'Sir, more of down-to-earth. Sir, at my second

visit to the house I was questioning the maidservant, one Ritu, sir, and she was telling me how, when she was making marital bed each morning, sir, the . . . the signs, sir, after less than one year of married life had begun . . . begun to become altogether less, sir. She was indicating, with very much of wink and nudge, sir, that the Krishna-Radha love there had been in place, sir, was fast departing. And, something else, sir. I was observing that, underneath the bubbles of Surf in the sink where Ritu was washing up after a late breakfast, sir, were altogether too many vessels for one lady on her own to have used. Sir, that confirmed for me that Mrs Juliette Tabholkar, the former Miss Juliette Moolchand, sir, was having a lover.'

'Moolchand . . . '

A thoughtful look had, it seemed, crossed that iron-rigid face.

'Yes, Inspector, you do well to remind me. That lady, whatever she is called now, is the daughter of *Shri* Nathumal Moolchand, perhaps Bombay's most respected businessman. So what else have you to tell me about the former Juliette Moolchand?'

Ghote felt thrown. What is happening to my well-ordered account, he asked himself. What must I be telling next? Something more about Juliette Tabholkar? But what more? I have told all I was observing and deducing. Wait. Yes, there is this. If it will not be too much more angering the ACP . . . But why is he becoming angry?

Do not know, cannot say.

'Sir, I was also discovering that Rahe's account of Mrs Juliette Tabholkar going out to see if anything

158

was wrong with her invalid aunt, Miss Smita Chunnilal, sir, living in a flat at a block called Sunnyside, sir, and—'

'What the devil is all this, Inspector? Invalid aunts, flats called Sunlight—'

'Sir, no. Sir, it is Sunnyside.'

'Never mind the name of the damn flats, Inspector. What have they got to do with the fact that someone stabbed Krishna Tabholkar to death?'

Ghote thought like a piece of whirring machinery. Cleared his battered-about head.

'Sir, it is this. On the night of the murder a telephone call was made to thc Tabholkar house to say that Mrs Julictte Tabholkar's invalid aunt, Miss Smita Chunnilal, who is living alonc nearby, had not answered the usual call made to her at 8.30 p.m. to ask if she was all right. The caller to the Tabholkar house was stating that Juliette must go round at once to find out if her aunt had fallen, or some such thing. But, sir, I was discovering that call was not made, as you might expect, by Juliettc's mother, Miss Chunnilal's sister, sir. Sir, the call came in the vcry loud, unmistakable voice of Mr Moolchand himself.'

The ACP sat up in his chair one quarter-inch more.

'Now, listen to me, Inspector,' he barked out. 'I find it altogether irritating when any officer of mine goes rattling on and on about anything he has to report. Like . . . Damn it, like a woman, Inspector. All right, I dare say at some time in the future you may find women inspectors in the Bombay Police. But that time has not come yet. And until it does, if it ever does, I prefer my

159

officers not to gabble at me like a pack of wretched females.'

A renewed glare from the cold grey eyes.

'So, Inspector, I'll thank you to go back to your cabin, and when—when and if—I have come to my conclusion about what you have been telling me, I will let you know.'

'But, sir, I have not finished—'

'Enough, Inspector. And let me warn you. Not a word of all this is to pass your lips. Not one word. To anyone. Anyone whatsoever. Dismiss.'

*   *   *

Ghote sat, a bewildered heap, in his chair crammed between desk and cabin wall. Why, he asked and asked himself, did Mr Divekar send me out like that? All right, he was not listening to my every word with ever-increasing interest. But that seems to be his way. He was even breaking in almost at the start to ask me what are quantum mechanics. That was something I had been happy to take Professor Venugopal's word for as being of world importance. And so should Mr Divekar. If I may, inside my mind, venture to criticise him.

One thing more. I have not had a morsel to eat since Protima was serving me my breakfast *puris*, crisp as always.

Before he could rouse himself to thump his bell for Paresh and send him for a stomach-filling *vada pav* he fell back into his puzzled train of thought.

But why did Mr Divekar dismiss me like that when I had by no means completed my report? He heard nothing of what I had to tell about the final stage of my inquiry and the altogether surprising

160

answer that was eventually coming into my mind. He heard nothing about the puzzling fact that the walk from the Tabholkar house across to Sunnyside and back took Juliette much more time than anyone said it needed. But that must have meant Juliette would have been out in the darkness of the night for almost as long as one hour, there and back. And all the time her husband, who ought to have been out himself in the dark road, well capable as he was of sending packing all but the most determined *goonda*, was there at home sitting idle. Any offer he had made to go to Sunnyside in his wife's place must have been refused by her. It was almost certain she had received instructions to go herself, leaving her husband in the house on his own.

Nothing about that got to Mr Divekar's ears. All right, I did at least manage to slide my typed report, short though it was, on to that large sweep of a desk. So he may see it. Unless it is getting covered up by something else.

But if that happens, and I put those few sheets quite far away from Mr Divekar's big-big blotting-pad, I have not been able to put to him the fact that lively Miss Smita Chunnilal told me she had not had, that Tuesday night, her regular eight-thirty pip emma call from her sister, Moolchand *Memsahib*. This also: the call made to the Tabholkar house, in that loud voice that Gopal recognised as Nathumal Moolchand's, had said Smita Miss must be in trouble or at least fast asleep. But she was assuring me she had not once closed her eyes as she followed out her complicated and exciting Patience game.

Then I was never able to tell Mr Divekar about

161

my visit to the big Moolchand house on Malabar Hill, and all that Moolchand *Memsahib* had said there. The way she was so warmly calling her son-in-law as 'my poor Krishna' and her telling me also there was in her husband's desk the spare set of keys to the Cumballa Hill house, as I had thought there might be. And also how, all innocently, she had produced the little key to the drawer in the desk in which, she said, were the key or keys needed to enter the pale-purple house, though she had not allowed me to inspect the bunch in its locked drawer.

More even. There was what she told me about the regular Tuesday evening visits she and her husband made to see a film, and how at the last moment that Tuesday night Moolchand *Sahib* had come out to the waiting car and told her he had just learnt something urgent to do with a cricket match. So she had gone on her own to see some new star without telephoning, as usual, to her sister.

If I had been allowed to tell Mr Divekar all that, I might have managed also to say Nathumal Moolchand is now making money, apart from his huge regular income, from fixing cricket matches. One blot on an influential name.

Then Mr Divekar would have been doubly convinced I had solved the Tabholkar murder.

Oh, why was I not insisting on putting my report into his hand itself? But I did not. I could not have done it.

And at the outset I was thinking that the mystery would be a small case only, fit for a newcomer to the Branch. But, no. Now I believe the person who arranged that complicated plot to get rid of a

162

husband no longer cared for by his precious daughter (to be replaced, in due course, with a more suitable match) was none other than Nathumal Moolchand himself, the man Mr Divekar called *Bombay's most respected businessman*. If so, this will be not at all a small case. It will be the biggest case Bombay has seen for years.

Then something else slid into Ghote's troubled head, something between himself and his conscience. What if, in a way, Mr Divekar is right to have taken the Moolchand case away from me? For however long or short a time? What if, led away by the train of discoveries I was making, I was myself becoming too ambitious? And Mr Divekar was worried that I might go on to manufacture extra evidences. Yes, it is true I was seeing in front of me, or half-seeing, the shining reputation I would acquire in bringing down the great Nathumal Moolchand, although I would never have manufactured evidence to support my case.

And—this is the truth of it—doing that would be altogether going beyond what I am knowing is right for me.

But, all the same, even if taking away the case was best for me, why did Mr Divekar send me so suddenly back here to my cabin? And how long will it be before, after he has come to his conclusion about what I told him, he is calling me back?

And what was it he was actually saying? It was not *when I have come to my conclusion*. It was *when and if*. If, if. Why should it have been that *if*?

Does it mean it will be days and days, weeks and

weeks even, before I am hearing one word more about Krishna Tabholkar's death? Will I have to sit here without any duties whatsoever, doing nothing at all even to earn my pay, just because ACP Divekar has ordered me to wait for his convenience? Can he really be such a high and mighty layer-down of laws?

But then a new idea, coming as it were from a great distance, entered his head. Simply this: if I am relieved of any responsibility for the investigation into Krishna Tabholkar's death and given no other duties, then I am free to pursue— yes, hundred per cent free—to pursue the case of the death of my peon, Bikram.

CHAPTER SEVENTEEN

A torrent of thoughts, thoughts Ghote had been full of until the moment he had so unexpectedly been given his first proper Crime Branch case, thoughts pushed till now far to the back of his mind, rushed in on him again. At their most vivid. First had come that electrifying moment, truly impossible to forget, when he had raised half-inch by half-inch the mysterious shopping bag in his waste bin and had found inside it Bikram's severed head. Closely there followed the utterly unexpected moment when ACP Divekar, informed about the head, had simply said *Just dispose of the damn thing*. And, worse perhaps than anything else, there had been the hiding of that unthinkable object deep inside his own home. Then, with the thing he had done confessed to his wife, there had

164

come Protima's heart-lifting decision to back his barely formed notion of investigating, on his own, Bikram's murder.

Which led me, his thoughts ran on, to believe that Bikram had been nothing less than a blackmailer. Then to tracing him to the slum where he lived and encountering there Rekha Salaskar, shrilly complaining about her stolen shopping bag and accusing hulking, splay-teethed Atul of snatching it.

It was at this very point, it struck him now, that ACP Divekar had given him, out of the blue, his first Crime Branch investigation, so long hoped for, the 'small case' of stabbed-to-death Krishna Tabholkar, inefficiently investigated by Inspector Rahe. Small the case had seemed then, though in the end it has become, yes, by no means small. But once Mr Divekar gave me that first proper Crime Branch task I consigned all thoughts of Bikram to indefinite storage.

Now, however, as if a comet had reappeared after an absence of hundreds of years, Rekha Salaskar came fully into his head again, trailing a long tail of bright unearthly light. Fiercely demanding Rekha, and everything she had gone on to tell him about the man called Atul.

Must get her a brand-new shopping bag, and soon. Must-must.

But now . . . now it is the matter of finding Atul, surely Bikram's killer. But Rekha was able to give me no clue at all to where he can be found. So is it my task somehow to trace him out among all the many hundreds of possible places he may frequent in teeming Bombay? The man who, I am truly thinking, hacked off poor stupid, drunken

Bikram's head.

Think. Think.

And . . . and, wait, I believe I do have a line to follow. It is this. Neat little Paresh was telling me about Bikram's regular visits to beer bars, and, in particular, to his favourite disreputable place, the Beauty Bar. Paresh had gone on to explain that one of his fellow peons had once in a malicious way followed Bikram from Headquarters to the place tucked inside a big building in Waudby Road, not too far away.

A lead. Yes, a definite lead.

Ghote could barely keep himself in his chair. But, just as he put his hands on either arm to push himself up, a moon-face loomed over the cabin's batwing doors. Sergeant Moos.

'Ghote *bhai*, are you having one-two minutes to spare? There is something . . . '

One-two minutes to spare? How dare he think I may . . . But . . . but, no. No, the truth is I do have, or I ought to have, many minutes to spare. What time it is now?

A quick look at his watch.

Yes, not even four o'clock. So not at all likely that a person like Atul will be hanging about in the Beauty Bar now. I must really wait till evening. For once, then, welcome Sergeant Moos, with all your whorls, your islands, your bifurcations and whatever else you are bursting to tell me about.

*   *   *

It seemed to Ghote as if hours and hours of blank time had gone by, not just while Moos had been emptying his mind of his current fingerprint

166

complications, but even later, after he had declined Moos's offer of a cold drink at the pricey Edward VIII Juice Nook, that misfired celebration of an abdicated king. He sat on behind his desk until, outside, he saw the sky had begun to darken and evening must be only a few minutes away.

Then he let himself get to his feet and hurry off to Waudby Road.

There he found, without trouble, the big building Paresh had told him about. Yes, that is the sari shop here at street level, its windows still ablaze with light, though its door is firmly closed.

A few yards along the narrow street beside the tall building he made out the unobtrusive entrance to the floors above. Its door was not locked. Hesitantly he entered. No, no noticeboard, as I hoped to find, showing where each of the big building's many small businesses is located. And no sign at all for anything called Beauty Bar.

Nothing for it, then, but to explore in turn each of the six floors above, to go along whatever corridors and side passages I may find until . . . until at last I come across some sign or other telling me I have found what I am looking for.

Before too long virtue was rewarded.

But not until Ghote had trudged and trudged round each of the big building's floors until he had got to the sixth. There at last he spotted, at the very far end of its long main corridor, a flickering bluish light. Peering hard, he made out it must come from a small illuminated sign. He broke into a trotting run.

Oh, thank the gods, it is a shining blue sign. And, yes, it reads *Beauty Bar*.

Not without caution he took a peep through the

167

half-open door.

He saw, chiefly by the harsh light from the distant neon tube, a single biggish room with a few small tables dotted about, drinkers slumped at just two of them, the walls no more than bare plaster defaced here and there by coarse pencil-scrawled slogans. Though far from being deserving of its triumphant name, he saw eventually the place did possess, hung above its makeshift bar—no more than two trestle tables set at right angles to each other—a framed colour print, dulled almost past recognition. It showed, just, an English beauty of the last century. Yes, it must be because of that time-hazed picture that the bar had, at some time in the far past, gained its name.

All right, that much established.

He took a careful step inside.

But, as he looked round, he realised that, peer about as he might, nowhere among the scattering of tables was there any sign of the man he had confronted, in total silence, out in the slum in Matunga: Atul, of those unforgettable crocodile teeth.

All right, too early perhaps for him to come.

So what now?

Behind the bar, perched on a stool beside what looked like a tall store cupboard, there was the man who must be the in-charge, a bushy black from ear-to-ear moustache stretching across his face. Try him, half-asleep though he seems to be. But, no, half-asleep he may be now, but when a minute or two ago he must have seen me peeping in at the door I noticed him making one quick assessment before he decided I was neither a *badmash* hoping to steal nor a uniformed *jawan*

168

hoping for a free drink. Such an alert fellow will not tell me anything about any of his customers. I can be sure of that.

Still, this is very much the sort of place I can imagine Bikram drinking at, and perhaps being accosted by someone who was nothing other than a *supari*, a killer for hire. I will wait here as long as I can.

Shall I, before I get a smokescreen drink over at the bar, take a closer look at those two slumped bodies at their different tables? Yes, the one with that half-inch of rum still in his glass, judging by the grimy green towel and pot of fluffy soap, brush still in it, he must be a kerb-squatting street barber. Perhaps once or twice he has given Atul a shave? No, I don't see someone like Atul much bothering with clean cheeks.

Ah, now, extra confirmation. Under that table there is the two-inch-high wooden platform, the sort of thing a street barber sits his clients on. Yes.

But what to make of the other solitary drunk in the far corner? Nothing there to see as those obvious signs of the barber's occupation. All right, in front of the slumped figure there is a scatter of greasy playing cards. So, most likely, a gambler, just left to lie where he was after being cheated out of his every last *paisa*. Anything else about him? Might be, I somehow think. Better buy a beer, and take it across to sit beside him. Then wake him and find out what I can.

Setting down the glass of too frothy beer the bartender had served him—not a greeting of any sort from behind that cheek-to-cheek black moustache—Ghote took a better look at the slumped figure.

Right. Grey shirt, clean and, far as I can see, buttoned right up to the neck. You don't often see the man in the street dressing himself with such precision. And, look, his trouser matches exactly the grey of the shirt. So, a buttoned-up man himself? But, those playing cards, almost obliterated by the black grease on them, indicate surely the gambler.

He gave the fellow—his body was slight as a fourteen-year-old boy's—a gentle push to one side and revealed, all across the left-hand top pocket of the dark grey shirt, a clipped-on row of ballpoints. Blue, red, green, black.

Aha, a clerk, almost for certain. Things begin to get clearer.

And there is more, now that I know this much. I have all along been puzzled by how wretched shabby-looking Bikram could have found someone respectable-looking enough to make a blackmail demand to whatever high-above *crorepati* he had in his sights. Now I glimpse an answer. What if Bikram met, here in the Beauty Bar, this very clerk. A gambling addict. What a wonderful piece of luck for him. Perhaps even he may have hit on someone in the office of the very man whose secret he himself had by chance learnt? If the fellow is a clerk, he would be quite capable of putting in writing the demand for money Bikram could never have managed himself.

Probable? Well, possible at least. Supposition turning into something like fact. Hundred per cent definite? Not exactly. Likely? Could be.

Yes, it certainly could be. Because, if the *crorepati* victim has turned out to be altogether too shrewd to be caught out by a drunken peon and a gambling clerk, a death-dealing message will very likely have gone trickling down to ruthless streetfighter Atul.

All right, let me wake this wreck of a fellow and start up a conversation. Find out whether I have guessed right. Or, even, just get a glimpse of what might have happened.

Before, I gave my drunken gambler no more than a gentle push, just enough to heave his schoolboy body up by an inch or two. Now, make it one damn good prod.

'Uh? Wha . . . ? Who . . . ? Who are you?' Two bloodshot, blearily blinking eyes gradually focusing.

'I was thinking you would like someone for talking.'

'Talking? What talking?'

'Come, in a nice bar like this no one is wanting to sit on their own when they can have a friend for chat. You met friends here tonight, isn't it? Even if none of them is here now.'

A bleary look of offence.

'Friends I am having and having. Why not? Friends I was meeting when I was first coming here this evening. Cards we were playing.'

'And you were losing, yes?' Ghote said with a touch of sharpness.

Another look of offence.

'What if I was? At cards no one can always win.'

'But you yourself can often and often lose, yes? So, if you are asking me, you are better just only to have someone like myself beside you who will talk, yes, but not be robbing you.'

'No one was robbing Singh Anand. That I am stating.'

'Perhaps, perhaps not. But you must also be meeting here people who are liking to drink a little rum but are not at all card-players.'

'Certainly, I am. Do you think I am not able to talk and discuss? I tell you, I can sit and talk everything until it is day once again. And the next evening, and the next.'

'Yes, yes. I am sure. So, who is it you most like to discuss with?'

Some heavy dulled thought on the still-sleep-smeared face in front of him.

'Bikram.'

*　　　*　　　*

Ghote could hardly believe what he had heard. *Bikram.* This office clerk and ever-losing card-player had, in answer to one long-shot question, pronounced perfectly distinctly the name of my peon whose severed head I was finding, that terrible day, in my waste bin. The two of them knew each other, the clerk in some big firm's office with access of some sort to its boss and the peon in Crime Branch who had spotted one day something secret about the same prominent figure.

But, then Ghote reflected, perhaps when I was asking this fellow, Singh Anand as he is calling himself, who he was most liking to chat with, I had already pegged him in my mind as the sort of drunk Bikram might find it easy to make friends with. And just to find out who that might be was the whole and sole reason I came to this place.

So not altogether a miracle. More proper police work.

Very well, step by step a little more probing.

172

And, yes . . . yes, I think, a small lie now.

'So, you are knowing Bikram, yes? I also know something about him, though I am not at all knowing the fellow myself. But he is working at Police Headquarters, isn't it?'

'Working? Working? I tell you he is no more working. My friend Bikram is dead. Dead. He was murdered. You are not knowing that? I was thinking everyone in entire Bombay must know, even if the papers have hardly printed one word. But I tell you, the *gup* was everywhere, Bikram had his head chopped from his shoulders.'

Abruptly Singh Anand leant much closer. A familiar smell of stale rum assaulted once again Ghote's nostrils.

And now he saw in the man's eyes what could only be fear. Shut-out fear, frenziedly shut-out fear. But plain to see nevertheless.

At once he guessed what Singh Anand was about to tell him.

'I, too, may find tomorrow, or next week, or next month my head is no longer safe on my shoulders. I tell you that.'

'You are in fear for your life? Truly in fear? But why? How can that have happened to you? You are—what?—a simple, decent clerk in some ordinary office somewhere and, you say, your friend Bikram has had his head cut from his shoulders and you are in danger of meeting selfsame fate?'

'Yes, I fear it. And, though it is seeming hard to believe, I am thinking I know who has ordered Bikram's death and mine also. So I have had to leave my job in his company and come here where I hope no one can find me.'

173

Ghote put on an expression of disbelief at such a wild tale.

'But where is it you were working?' he asked, making himself sound incredulous enough to provoke a true answer.

Singh Anand leant yet closer. Then that answer came in a whisper, faint as if borne on the lightest puff of cool air coming from the sea on the hottest of days.

'Moolchand Investments.'

*   *   *

Somehow half-expecting, as Ghote had been, to hear what he had, when those two words were whispered to him he felt as if some great iron gates had clanged together with total finality. Yes, he said to himself, I have all along believed I knew who sent a *supari* to stab to death Krishna Tabholkar. But now, hearing who it was who paid a killer like the man who stabbed Krishna Tabholkar to death, I am doubly and trebly sure toweringly rich and influential Nathumal Moolchand ordered both Bikram's death and, as well, the fatal stabbing at the pale-purple house on Cumballa Hill.

And something else I am knowing. That the *supari* Moolchand used for both killings may very well be none other than the silent man with long crocodile teeth Rekha Salaskar pointed out to me in the middle of that slum. Atul.

It will very likely not be long, also, before Atul receives a new order. To eliminate feeble Singh Anand, now cowering in fear in front of me. It will not take Nathumal Moolchand, Anand's former

174

boss, long to work out that a clerk who suddenly, without warning, quit his job must be the person involved in the blackmail attempt.

So, I must, still on my own, since ACP Divekar refuses to believe what I tell him, somehow find Atul and put him in the dock at least for Bikram's murder. If—and I have no real proof of it yet— Atul was the double killer.

He sat back and looked at the man who had just told him he was in fear of having the head struck from his shoulders in the way that his co-blackmailer's had been. The fellow seemed slowly to be regaining a state of some normality.

'Tell me,' he said to him, 'do you know who it was who was killing poor Bikram, your good friend?'

'No. No, no, no, no. No.'

So that is the way of it.

'I think you may,' Ghote said pointedly. 'Tell me.'

'No. No. Who are you? Why are you asking me such things?'

Yes, Ghote thought. This will have to be the time.

He reached into his inside pocket, felt about with extended fingers until he was sure he had them firmly gripping his metal Crime Branch identity disc, then he whipped it out and planked it down on the table within an inch of neatly buttoned-up Singh Anand's all-but-empty rum glass.

Watching the clerk's terrified face, he saw on it, first, plain puzzlement, and then, as he blinked and blinked with still-sleepy rum-affected eyes, he at last contrived to make out the letters incised on the disc, and comprehension dawned.

'You . . . you are police? Crime Branch itself? But-but that is where Bikram was working. It was there one day, when he had been sent to some office with a message, he saw on a desk a paper—it must have been one confidential report—that had on it . . . ' His voice dropped down to the merest of whispers ' . . . the name of Nathumal Moolchand.'

So, Ghote thought, Anand has not told me Atul killed Bikram. But, just as I half-imagined it, I have learnt how drunken Bikram got hold of a vital secret about Moolchand. It must mean that Moolchand is being secretly investigated. Someone must have produced some evidence against him. Perhaps a business rival has gone to the Commissioner himself with what he knows, or claims to know, and Commissioner *Sahib*, with very much of caution, has passed on the allegation, whatever it is, to . . . to someone high up in Crime Branch who can be absolutely trusted. Probably to ACP Divekar himself. Or, possibly, to someone senior enough actively to investigate on his own. Possibly, say, Superintendent Ghorpade.

But even Mr Ghorpade may not be able to discover whether this allegation is the truth or not. Nathumal Moolchand may be safe from that. The allegation itself, even, may turn out to have been made out of no more than simple shot-in-the-air spite.

So, more urgently than ever, I must find Atul and save Singh Anand's life, as well as arresting the man who killed Bikram. My small private case.

CHAPTER EIGHTEEN

Early next morning Inspector Ghote kissed, first, his wriggling baby son, and then his wife before setting out on an errand that had been niggling at him for longer than he liked. He was off to buy a shopping bag. The night before, sitting at the white bakelite table in the kitchen over the wonderfully aromatic murgh sadah Protima had cooked, he had listened to her opinions about shopping bags, in more detail than he had thought possible.

I am, he had reflected then, sitting once again where I was putting down that blood-heavy shopping bag with Bikram's head inside, and here I am still far from being able to bring to justice the man who killed him.

'You see,' he had explained to Protima, 'this old woman, Rekha Salaskar, was very, very helpful to me when by chance I was finding her in her slum out in Matunga, and I am thinking she may still help me. So I would like to replace the shopping bag snatched from her hands by that thorough *badmash* Atul with, not just whatever bag I happen to see somewhere, but with something she will feel is altogether better.'

'Of course,' Protima said. 'If she, no more than a slum-dweller, has been helpful to a police officer, then she is deserving of reward. That is altogether right.'

She had gone on then to consider the really desirable qualities of shopping bags. Apparently, Ghote learnt, they should be double strength at the bottom seam—'if they are just only made from

177

a single piece of folded-over gunny they can wear out much too soon with all the heavy things being dropped into them.'

She had gone on to explain that handles should be bound, if possible, with leather so fingers do not become painfully sore by the end of each trip to the market. There should, too, be small interior pockets, one on each side, high enough up for the money put into them to be reached, but far enough down to be safe from *paar-maars*.

Ghote had listened with something like amazement.

'I had not at all thought,' he interrupted, 'there were so many differences it is possible to have in something I am every day seeing women, and men also, carrying to the markets.'

'So now,' Protima retorted, 'you are beginning to learn, Mr Police Officer, that a housewife's work is almost as complicated as . . . as an inspector's in Crime Branch.'

Ghote left it at that. He had, he hoped, got into his head the bulk of what his wife had told him. He should be able to find now without too many difficulties an ideal bag. And—he made a mental note—when he had secured one such for Rekha Salaskar, that fiercely determined woman, he would, after waiting a little, buy another just like it as a replacement for the one Protima currently possessed, which he saw did not altogether come up to the high standard she had laid down.

*   *   *

However, in the morning he made the mistake of setting out in too much of a hurry to complete his

178

errand before going to his cabin where, there might be, just possibly, some *bandobast* papers already on his desk. It was an understandable mistake, he told himself eventually, for a mere inspector of police, to go at once into huge Crawford Market, within easy reach almost opposite Police Headquarters. Though he had never before been inside, his father had told him, when they had first come to Bombay, that 'the iron-roofed building has been standing here many, many years. Carvings on the front are work of the father of my favourite author, old Rudyard Kipling.' So he had felt he did somehow know all about it.

Amid its many far-stretching alleys he thought he would be bound to find in just a few minutes some vendor of shopping bags. It was, however, only as he hurried past high-piled stalls by the hundred, offering every sort of fruit—bananas, yellow, pinkish, red, long and thick, short and stubby; papayas and pineapples; oranges, big and small; grapes and grapefruit—that he came to realise he had seen no bags at all anywhere.

Turn back? Give up? But I have set out to get Rehka a first-class bag, and that I will get if I have to pay through nose to do it.

On past yet more ranks and rows of vegetables of every description, their vendors crouching either above or at the foot of the huge cunningly arranged mounds, shouting out to would-be customers, but still not a shopping bag in sight. He began, at last, to come to the conclusion that somehow he was on a wholly mistaken expedition.

Eventually, he found himself back to where he had entered the huge building and, almost pleadingly, he asked a vendor of the earliest deliciously smelling strawberries, one of the joys of the month of Baisakh, where it was possible to buy a simple shopping bag. The man gave him a pitying smile.

'Not here at all, *sahib*,' he said. 'No, you are in Bombay's best and biggest fruit and vegetables market. Best in whole world also. Here you will not find anything that has not been grown, anything you cannot eat.'

Then, in face of a rueful expression, put on in fact for the strawberry vendor's particular benefit, he learnt he would not actually have far to go.

'Leave the market, *sahib*, and just round corner near where they are selling, cheap, all sorts of meat hardly fit to eat, there you are bound to find a stall piled with shopping bags, big, small, strong or ready to fall apart, bright-coloured, or altogether plain. Whatsoever you may be wanting.'

Ghote hastily purchased a newspaper-cone of strawberries, high-priced though it was, well knowing that, now it was already past his time for being at his desk, he might never manage to eat them. He thanked the man and hurried out of the market's clamour and overwhelming odours, both pleasant and nose-prickingly rotten.

Ten minutes later, in possession of just such a shopping bag as Protima had described, he hurried across wide, traffic-jostling Carnac Road, and into the busy expanse of the Headquarters compound and at last reached his cabin.

Bandobast duties once more be awaiting me? Or, will it be that the ACP's smarter-than-smart Thomas has brought a message to say I must report to the cabin above as soon as I arrive?

180

But, scrambling round to sit at his desk, he saw there was nothing at all there for him. No pile of orders for the day's duties to be fitted somehow together, no messages of any sort.

All right, if I am expected to sit idle here for yet another day, then first perhaps I will eat these strawberries but then I will feel free to go about my own business. To go, with this bright new shopping bag, to that Lady Hardinge Road slum and, if I can find her, to Rekha Salaskar.

Then his phone rang.

Oh, no.

'Ghote?'

It was Mr Divekar, the incisive voice unmistakable.

'Yes, sir? Yes, ACP *Sahib*?'

'Come up. I have something to say to you.'

Something to say to me? What will that be?

Strawberries tipped, in all their bright freshness, into the waste bin in its dark corner. One hasty look into the little wooden-framed, blurry mirror hanging where Inspector Patil had once put it— yes, smart enough, I think—and then, shoulders straightened, off up the winding stone stair to the balcony above.

Quick glance through the glass panel in the door. Yes, the ACP sitting there, bolt upright, at his desk.

What else did I expect?

Sharp tap on the door. The answering barked *Come*.

He entered.

Heels clicked crackingly together.

'You wanted me, sir?'

'Yes, Ghote. Sit.'

181

Sit? Told to sit in one of these six chairs lined up in front of the desk. I have never been asked to sit before. What does this mean?

'Sit, man, when you're told.'

He managed to slide himself on the nearest chair to hand.

'Yes, sir?'

'I have been looking again at your report on the Krishna Tabholkar murder, Inspector, and I have to say you have done some good work there. Yes, good work.'

Praise, Ghote thought. Praise. I am being praised by ACP Divekar for solving the murder at the house on Cumballa Hill, that pale-purple copy—But, no. Don't think now about the ancient painting the house there echoes in that extraordinary way. No, just only savour those words of praise.

'Good work. But not good enough.'

The snapped-out words came to him like the downward thrust of a spear. Or like perhaps—the thought flickered—the downward sweep of the cleaver or sword that had made the first deep cut into wretched Bikram's neck.

'No, Ghote,' the ACP went on, 'I have to tell you it has been decided . . . I have decided that the case you presented accusing *Shri* Nathumal Moolchand is simply not strong enough. What, after all, is there? A single rebuff at Moolchand Investments office, a few dents in the seat of an armchair, a servant washing some dishes, stains said to be on bedsheets . . . What do you think a first-class defence pleader will make of all that? I tell you, I wouldn't myself like to be in the box, as you would be, in those circumstances. Not by any

182

means.'

Unfair, Ghote thought. Yes, unfair of Mr Divekar to quote against me those small, if to my mind significant, clues. Yes, if there was nothing else at all in that report I see after all now lying there under one of the ACP's silvery weights, then I would agree *No case to answer*. But there is more, more, a great deal more.

He was about to pour out the details of all he had done and seen both at Cumballa Hill and at the sprawling white mansion on Malabar Hill, where finely dressed but housewifely *Shrimati* Moolchand had actually let him glimpse the key to her husband's desk in which the set for his daughter's new house was locked away. But at that moment he was struck by a terrible thought, as overwhelming as if an enormous rain-sodden sheet had suddenly been dropped down over him. Yes. Once the ACP has made his decision—with, who knows, the backing of the Commissioner himself—it is not going to be altered. Ever.

For a moment he hesitated. Was there nothing, something, anything . . . ? Then he pushed himself up from the chair he had been instructed to sit on, gulped once and said, 'Very good, sir.'

Again he clicked heels sharply, and then wheeled round and left the big cabin, its seven-bladed fans above briskly whirring.

*   *   *

Back in his own cabin, Ghote put into its place again Inspector Patil's typewriter on which he had written the brief report the ACP had asked for when he had telephoned him; the report, he had

183

said, that showed only what chutney a defence pleader would make of the case. Then, almost too depressed to sink into his chair, he found himself asking: can I be wrong in all I have discovered? Was I wrong in saying Krishna Tabholkar was not stabbed to death by a chance intruder—how little likely that was—but by a *supari* hired to get rid of him? Can I be yet more wrong and is Nathumal Moolchand, in fact, a deeply honest businessman who has never had one evil thought in his head?

For a little he sat and wrestled with his thoughts.

Piece by piece then awkward facts that made nonsense of such a glossy picture of innocence rose up in his mind. No, Nathumal Moolchand is, I am certain, at the least a fixer of cricket matches. His very wife confirmed that for me, if in an indirect way. And to cheat the common man, that unthinking cricket fan in his thousands, by bribing a way to a result that would never otherwise have happened is, to say nothing else, an act of money-grabbing cruelty.

Yes, and now I look at it there is more than cricket-fixing to be charged against Moolchand Investments, that mighty company. I begin to believe now the firm must have been seriously harmed by all the rioting and political upheaval there has been since Independence came and a whole huge part of the subcontinent was transformed into Pakistan, suspicious foreign power. Everybody who is reading *Times of India* will know that many, many businesses here have suffered badly from that. Bankruptcies there have been even by the hundred.

So, yes, now the very boss of Moolchand Investments may have felt himself forced to go in for that altogether more illegal way of making money than his customary dealings, the fixing of cricket matches. The paying-out of moderate sums to cricketers who can be tempted, and then making hefty-hefty bets on unlikely results. That sort of thing may have kept Nathumal Moolchand still afloat, at least for this while.

But yet more. Besides Moolchand being responsible—as I know he was—for having had knifed to death Krishna Tabholkar, scientist who would have brought to new India worldwide renown, I know now he was almost certainly also responsible for having paid Atul to cut off Bikram's head. And, yes, to get his head left inside Crime Branch as a warning to whoever might have learnt of whatever secret manoeuvres Moolchand Investments were contemplating. A warning that its boss is not a man to be blackmailed.

So, yes, damn it, what I reported to the ACP is a true account. All right, if you dig and dig, twist and twist, you may be able to find some of my conclusions could have doubt cast upon them. But, no, in the main what I typed out in my report to the ACP is the truth. Just that. The truth of the matter.

For a moment he saw, as if in front of himself where he now sat, the keys-jamming typewriter he had hammered out the report on. It had been just four days ago, when reaching for the very machine, that he had seen at the top of the waste bin the blood-spotted pages of the *Matunga News* wrapping Bikram's head.

Yes, what I have written about Bikram's death is the truth. What I put in my report is there in black and white. What Mr Divekar was saying about the work being *not good enough* is altogether seizing on small errors to make out all is wrong. No, what has happened is that my report has been suppressed. It has been suppressed because Nathumal Moolchand is still a man of such influence that he can have the truth just blotted out.

But what can I do about it?

Nothing.

Of course, I might resign from Crime Branch today and go to the newspapers with what I am knowing. But will any of them believe me, when they are learning that no steps whatsoever have been taken against Moolchand? The weight of Crime Branch, the weight of the whole of the Bombay Police, the weight of Nathumal Moolchand of Moolchand Investments will be in one pan of the scales, and Inspector Ghote, ex-Inspector Ghote by then, will be in the other pan. Weighing as much as a fly speck only.

So it seems I must just sit here and obey orders. Perhaps one day I may be given some petty affair to investigate, otherwise for weeks and weeks, months and months even, I will have to stay here at this desk and compile each day's *bandobast* requirements. And then type them out. On Inspector Patil's rotten machine.

Gloom, deep clouds of unremitting gloom.

But . . .

But then, from nowhere, from somewhere down at the core of his being, a thought emerged, poking its head from dank soil like a cautious mongoose.

There is one inquiry that no one in Crime Branch but myself is knowing about. That is an investigation that no one can prevent me taking to its very conclusion because no one is knowing anything at all about it. And it is an inquiry crying out to be pursued to its uttermost end. The murder of one simple peon by the name of Bikram.

CHAPTER NINETEEN

'Yes,' Ghote said, finding he had spoken that word aloud. Yes, yes, with Rekha Salaskar's help, if I can get it, I will track down Atul. I will question him then about who gave him his *supari* task, who handed over in the customary way the first half of the sum and promised the second half when Bikram had been killed. Can that, as I have come to believe, be Nathumal Moolchand? If Atul tells me something that indicates the *supari* money he was given came, by whatever route, from Moolchand Investments, I will be able then finally to kill a second bird with my same stone.

But, no. Moolchand would never let come to light the long chain of links between himself and a *goonda* like Atul. The very rich protect themselves better. But how do they? How exactly, link by link? Who was it who in the end came to Atul, with *supari* money tucked into some safe pocket?

No sooner was the question asked than an answer he had not in the least foreseen was there, shimmering in his mind.

No, Nathumal Moolchand would seek hard to protect himself from all the hazards offered by such a long chain of links. He would send to Atul someone he could trust to one hundred per cent.

He saw then, once again, the cold white marble reception area at Moolchand Chambers with, emerging from the smoothly opening doors of the private lift, the individual who delighted to pretend that I was Gujarati *Inspector Girish* before delivering to me that final message: *Shri Moolchand will not see you.* Little froggy Mr Kanjilal, the great Nathumal Moolchand's personal assistant.

A very personal assistant? One knowing half his employer's secrets and more? Yes, I believe it is very-very likely that the instructions to Atul to get rid of Bikram and to put his severed head somewhere inside Crime Branch were delivered by frog-face Mr Kanjilal.

Only one way to find whether my more-than-guess is right. To go *ek dum* to the Lady Hardinge Road slum, get hold of Rekha Salaskar again, present her with this shopping bag, tucked at this moment under the desk at my feet, and set her to work finding Atul for me. And . . . ? And then perhaps just ask him point-blank if I am right.

* * *

Just over two hours later Ghote was standing outside the makeshift gate of the Lady Hardinge Road slum, fine new shopping bag dangling from his left hand, looking as if he might be a simple man in shirt-pant on his way to a market. His journey had been a long one since there was no question of using a police car and a taxi was not an affordable expense for an inspector of police who might well, before long, find himself thrown out of the force.

If I am making one unholy mess of this business, he had said to himself, that is the least bad fate that will come to me. And the worst? If, by carrying on with my own investigation, I somehow let Nathumal Moolchand realise what I am doing, he may very well send out a new *supari* instruction. To deal with one persistent nuisance.

But, no. Ignore that. Ignore it altogether. The only thing to do.

Right, now, into the slum not by pushing open the few rusted sheets of corrugated iron of the sideways-tilting gate itself but by the entrance that sccms always to be used, the gap beside the gatepost.

Inside, it took him no more than ten minutes to find Rekha. She was standing gossiping with the Muslim woman, Faiza, whom he had summoned to soothe Bikram's mother after he had broken the news of her son's death. The news of his murder.

I wonder, he thought, if Rekha has been constantly lingering round this part of the slum, because she has something new to tell the police inspector who bought her *vada pavs* in the *dhaba* outside? Even something worth telling about the man who snatched her precious shopping bag?

It seemed that she might have. No sooner had she seen what was dangling from his hand than she turned sharply away from Faiza and strode, knife-jabbing nose thrusting forward, towards him.

'My bag? The new-new bag you have been buying for me? I knew you would get me one. I have waited and waited for you to come.'

Reaching forward, she almost snatched the neat leather-wrapped handles of the bag out of his grip.

'Yes, yes,' he said. 'I was not at all forgetting my

promise to you. But were you forgetting what you were promising to me?'

'When a *badmash* like that one has stolen my shopping bag,' she said, 'how could I be forgetting?'

'So you have something to tell?'

Would this be a better lead than my distant hope of finding whether Nathumal Moolchand's Mr Kanjilal has been seen with Atul?

Rekha gave him a quick look. A touch of slyness in it.

'Perhaps we should go again to that *dhaba* where the Pepsi is so cool?'

Trust this sharp creature—forty, is she? Thirty? Fifty?—to make a sort of side-claim like this.

But he gave her a different answer than she had hoped for.

'No. You tell me whatever you have to say. Here and now.'

With a quick dip of her head she acknowledged the defeat.

'Yes, yes. Yesterday only I was seeing in the distance here Atul himself, and at once I was getting as near to him as I was daring, and I was watch-watching. Then, as soon as he was beginning to go away, I was following. Like a shadow of a shadow.'

'And?'

'And he was going not far from here.'

'Yes?'

'You are knowing there are two slums at Lady Hard Road?'

For a moment Ghote was tempted to tell her that the proper name was Lady Hardinge Road and who the lady had been. But this was no time for

190

proudly showing off that piece of long-ago acquired information.

'Yes, two slums,' Rekha went on. 'One on this side of the road, one on the other. That one is a much, much better one. It is higher up. The ground there is almost dry even in the worst of the monsoons.'

'And it is there that Atul stays?'

'Why else would I be telling?'

A sharp reprimand. From schoolteacher to idle pupil. Ghote almost felt a tight slap resound on his ear.

'Can you take me there now? Now?' he asked, anxiety beginning to claw at him.

What if Atul has decamped, as he easily may have done?

'And afterwards some Pepsi? A *vada pav* also?'

'Yes, yes.'

*   *   *

In the enviably drier slum on the far side of Lady Hardinge Road Rekha pointed out a very different style of hut from all those Ghote had seen as he had been led by the cheekily coins-demanding boy wearing no more than red half-pants to Bikram's Hut 191. Patchy though the materials making up its two storeys were—two storeys, a really good place—it looked as if the sheets might well stand up to most monsoon downpours, wherever once they had been found, or stolen.

So will I even at this moment, Ghote asked himself, find inside there Rekha's shopping bag thief? The man with those crocodile-sharp teeth and arms looking like nothing more than two thick

191

tree branches. Atul himself. Atul who, I have every reason to believe, hacked and hacked at wretched Bikram's neck till his head had come away from his shoulders to end up at last in my own cabin.

And, if Atul is inside here, will I be able to hold him? Will I succeed in not being overwhelmed by such a practised streetfighter?

Yes, I must be able to.

Damn it, I am a well-trained police officer. I have undergone two years of hard drill in the gym at Nasik Police Training School. I can even ride a horse, with some skill. And all those hours in the gym taught me, if I can remember them, every streetfighting trick there is. Experts taught me. I was covered in bruises to prove it. We all were.

Right. The door is here in front of me. Looks fragile enough. One decent shove from my shoulder and in an instant it would be flat on the floor inside. But, no. No, just one good thundering knock will be enough. A knock that says *Police, open up*. And then we shall see what we see.

He gave a quick glance to Rekha, standing only a little behind him, and, from the way she was flexing and flexing her right hand, looking as if her nails itched to go ripping down Atul's face till the blood would come pouring down.

Right. Ready. He raised his fist.

Bang, bang, bang, bang.

The door quivered. But from inside there came not the least sound.

Bang, bang, bang.

Should I give that shoulder charge?

He had taken a couple of paces back in readiness when, not from inside the big hut but from round in the narrow *gali* beside it, there came a screeching sort of protest. 'Stop, stop, stop.'

Ghote thought rapidly. Surely if all the noise I was making thumping at the door here has produced no sound from inside Atul cannot be here after all. So . . . see who is this woman screeching like that. Why is she feeling such a need to protest?

He told Rekha he would talk to her later—a vague assurance he had little intention of keeping to—and went and looked down the length of the narrow *gali*.

Yes, the woman there, for the moment silent, looks little different in that tattered almost colourless sari from any other slum-dweller. Face, what I can see of it now she has drawn up the sari's *pallao* in that automatically modest way, lined and seamed with deep-furrowed wrinkles. Yet from her stance, sturdy on two bare, dirt-smeared feet, and full-bosomed as she is under that thin sari, she must be not at all as old as I was first thinking. Life has by no means defeated her.

He took a pace or two into the *gali*, its surface dry enough but rubbish-strewn.

'It is you who was screaming and screeching?' he asked, every bit the police officer in mufti.

'And it was you who was banging and beating at Atul's door?' she came quickly back.

Yes, not at all somebody to let herself be put down.

'And if I was?' he replied, almost as fiercely. 'I am a police officer, inspector from Crime Branch. And I am wanting a word with this man, Atul. Does he have any other name, are you knowing?'

'Atul is all. Atul. All he is needing for people to know he is not to be mocked.'

'You are one of those people, is it?'

'*Achchha*. Why should I not be? He was calling me one day to clean his hut, and then, when I had been doing that for one-two weeks and getting it also clean as clean, he was telling me I must take a shopping bag he had found, one heavy bag, and—'

She came to a sudden halt. Too much said, almost?

But Ghote knew, however quickly she had stopped herself, why the bag this woman had been ordered to carry away was heavy and where in the end she had carried it to. She it had been who had put that bag right into the waste bin in my cabin in the heart of Crime Branch. Within it Bikram's bloodied head.

He completed for her the account she had abruptly brought to a halt.

'You put that bag into a cabin at Crime Branch in Police Headquarters, yes? But how were you knowing where to go? Did Atul himself tell you?'

'No, Inspector.'

The woman was altogether more subdued now.

'No,' she went on, 'I am well knowing Crime Branch. Better-better than Atul, who would not at all like to be going into there. But I go every day. I am a sweeper there.'

'Then you are someone I very much need to talk with.'

She gave him a look of eyes-gleaming interest.

'You are truly inspector from Crime Branch, Crime Branch where I am going every day?'

'I am. It was into my own cabin there you went, the one with batwing doors looking out at the big compound.'

A look now of mingled fear and delight. And a

194

cautious question.

'Inspector, were you finding, in your cabin that ...?'

But now some hesitation showed itself.

'Yes,' Ghote said firmly. 'You were given that shopping bag, and in it there was nothing less than the head of my peon, one Bikram.'

'That swine of swines Atul,' she burst out then. 'He was making me take it. All the way to Police Headquarters, and saying I must put it, without looking, somewhere inside Crime Branch. He was making me go, with that head I was knowing nothing at all about, through all the streets from here to there when at any time a police *jawan* could have stopped me. I would have been thrown into gaol if he had seen that dead man's head.'

'Yes, that was what Atul was doing to you,' Ghote said.

'The *shaitan*. One day I will make him pay.'

A little flame of pleasure lit up in Ghote's head.

'You can make him pay very soon,' he said. 'Very soon, if you are wanting.'

'How? How? If someone is cheating Jyoti Bhatvadekar they must pay, however much of a bully they are. However much like Atul. However much of a great man, like that Pradeep Popatkar.'

Popatkar? Surely Protima's favourite wicked politician, Ghote registered, even as into his flipped-open notebook he was scribbling down Jyoti Bhatvadekar's name.

But never mind Popatkar, it is this determined woman here in front of me in this filthy *gali* that I must be paying attention to.

'Making Atul pay,' he said. 'That will come. But, first, you must tell me when I can be sure of

195

finding him. Will it be here? In this big hut he has? Or is there somewhere else?'

'Inspector, it will be here. He was telling, he will be here tomorrow itself, on the day of the big meeting at Oval Maidan when they choose who will be voted into Legislative Assembly.'

'You are sure he will be here? Atul was saying and saying it?'

'Inspector, he was. Inspector, tomorrow early you can find him while he is still sleeping here in his hut. I may not be here. I am very much wanting to be at the meeting at Oval Maidan, tomorrow. I have something I am very much wanting to do.'

'No. No, I am wanting you to be here. You must be.'

'No need, no need,' she said almost as if she was soothing a crying infant. 'No, Inspector, you can easily push down Atul's door yourself and get inside his hut. You were nearly doing that just now when you were bang, bang, banging at it. Tomorrow early, when you have got it down, you will find Atul inside, there in his bed too fast asleep to have at all heard you. He is always like that when he is coming back from his streetfighting and his drinking-drinking.'

'Good, good. Very good. So, then when I have dealt with him, you will be able ... But, tell me, where then can I find you itself?'

She looked, for a moment surprised at the question and even unwilling to give him any answer. But in a moment she spoke up with the number of her own hut, not far away.

Ghote added that scanty address to her name in his notebook. A sure way, he thought wryly, to put both right out of my mind. It so often happens.

Into notebook: out of mind. But, not to worry, if I have to search and search through every one of these hundred per cent disordered pages I will find it at last, down in black and white. Or in pencil at least.

'Good then, Jyoti, one day you can come to court and give such evidence against Atul that will put him behind the bars for more years than he is liking, if it is not sending him to hang from a rope at Thana Gaol.'

'Oh, Inspector *Sahib*, I will and will.'

She scurried away down the *gali*.

So, Ghote said to himself, *till tomorrow*. Tomorrow when, if all goes well, I will have crocodile-teeth Atul in a cell.

CHAPTER TWENTY

Ghote's hopes, however, were to meet with a reversal he could never for one moment have expected. Back in central Bombay, at Churchgate Station, he had seen it was now nearly five o'clock. So no need, he thought, to return to Crime Branch and sit waiting for an altogether unlikely summons from the ACP, in all probability at this hour no longer poised in his own cabin above me like a ton-weight perched over a flea.

In a little spurt of something like happiness, then, he headed straight for Bank Street Cross Lane and home. But it was there, sitting with Protima on the cushions-piled *takht* eagerly telling her what he had just achieved out in Matunga and of his bubbling hope for the morrow, that he met with his utterly dismaying setback.

'No,' Protima interrupted his account with all the finality of slamming closed a cell door. 'No, tomorrow you cannot go all the way out to your slum in Matunga.'

'What it is you are saying? Were you not fully taking in what I have told? Tomorrow, very early, if what that sweeper, Jyoti, said to me is correct— and why should it not be?—I will be able to surprise, asleep in his bed, Bikram's killer. You cannot have meant that *No*.'

She jumped to her feet.

'I did. And I do.'

'But . . . '

Words, not for the first time in their marriage, altogether failed him.

Protima, standing now directly in front of him, the cushions of the *takht* in a sprawled mess beside her, drew herself up to her full height.

'Listen to me, Ved's father, have you altogether forgotten what I must have told you a thousand times? Tomorrow at Oval Maidan there is the grand meeting of candidates for the South Bombay Legislative Assembly seat. Pradeep Popatkar will be there, making his final bid for it. I am needing to hear every lying word he is saying. But how can I go there and stay till the very end if I am having with me your little Ved who should be put down to sleep and has to be fed also and even be changed?'

Your little Ved. The words were the first to claim Ghote's enraged attention. Is not Ved, he asked himself, every bit as much my babe as he is hers? It is a shared life we have: if I am his father working to provide him with a home, she is his mother who must at every minute look after the helpless fellow while I am not there.

But then her yet graver offence came tumbling in on him, a fog bank of sheer incomprehension. My wife is actually saying I must give up this one good chance I have of putting handcuffs on Atul, the man who chopped and chopped at Bikram's head till it had come off from his neck. She is saying I must give up that chance as if it is no more than a single rupee coin I happen to have in my pocket. And for what? So that I can go in her place to some damn political meeting where her hated Pradeep Popatkar will be spouting off his fat mouth. Yes, she was telling me about it, I seem to remember now. But only once. Once, not a thousand times, not a hundred, but just only once.

And it is not as if a single word Popatkar says will make much of difference to whether or not he gains this Legislative Assembly seat, and with it, I suppose, all the opportunities to make big-big sums by selling his each and every vote there to whoever bids highest, to *crorepatis* needing permission for business ventures, like, it might be, Nathumal Mool—

At once a sliver of a new thought came sliding— a cobra or a krait—into his mind.

Perhaps . . . perhaps, after all, it might not be such a bad idea to go to this mighty end-of-campaign meeting. It is possible that Nathumal Moolchand will be there. Yes, yes, I see it now. If Moolchand's business is in the sort of financial difficulty many other Bombay firms are suffering because of the turmoils and troubles there have been since Independence, as I was thinking is possible, and he has had to turn to making money by betting on fixed cricket matches, then he will be very anxious to have a friend sitting in Legislative Assembly. Think how useful to him it would be to have someone in the Assembly with a chance, with more money behind him, to make himself Minister for Home, responsible for the activities of the whole of the Bombay Police, and its Crime Branch in particular.

So somewhere on the platform at the Oval Maidan among the rows of seats reserved for the contenders and their allies will Moolchand be there? Will something I see him do or say put for me in the shiny brass scales I see myself as holding up above him one more weight? Myself, unlikely though it seems, sitting in judgement on a figure of such wealth and influence.

But, yes, I am holding up those scales. I have evidence clearly pointing to him, however much for some hidden reason I have been ordered not to breathe a word about it.

So . . .

'All right,' he said, cancelling in an instant all the outpouring of bitterness he had been prepared to hurl into his wife's face, and all thoughts of getting Atul into handcuffs for one day still. 'All right, if you are insisting, I will go tomorrow to this meeting and see if I can spot any lies and weaknesses your Pradeep Popatkar may make evident. It is at Oval Maidan, did you say?'

'Yes, of course, Oval Maidan where people in their hundreds can stand and listen, or even sit in comfort on the grass. I was taking little Ved there for his airing today. Already a big stage has been put up at one end, with behind it a hundred different posters. Each of Popatkar's more boastful and lying than the next. And you are knowing how the crowds flock to such free entertainments, even getting paid to shout in support of one speaker or another. So you must be there early to make sure of a place up near the platform where you will be able to see every smirk and smile that is crossing that man's face, if at all you will be able to recognise him.'

'Oh, there will be no difficulty in spotting him out. He is fat, isn't it? You have often and often mentioned him as a fat pig, or sometimes swine.'

'And you are thinking no other politician is fat? I tell you *fat* and *politician* are almost the same word.'

Immediately into Ghote's mind there came a stream of names of political figures, from Gandhiji down, who were markedly thin. But he stopped himself from producing them.

'Do you think,' he said instead, 'that a trained police detective will not be able to pick out one particular man from a crowd of others if he is looking and looking for him?'

'Nevertheless,' Protima countered, 'I am thinking it is necessary you should have one good impression of Popatkar, and—'

She turned suddenly and headed into the bedroom.

In a few moments she was back, clasping the thick bundle of bloodied newspaper sheets, well wrapped in brown paper, that she had insisted on keeping under his second-best trousers. She put it down on the floor and began opening it up. In a moment she had thrust up towards his face the paper's front page and he saw again the photo of the man Protima had so often spoken of with unsparing disapproval.

'All right,' he said, 'it is Pradeep Popatkar. But hold the sheet more to light so I can get one better look. It is so dark always in this room, with the building opposite close enough to block out most of the sun. And there are some blood stains also.'

Silently, Protima did as he had asked. And he took a long moment finally to get a clear impression of the fat-immersed features he had seen when Protima had first pointed out the photo.

'But can this sheet only be why you were carefully keeping aside all these other bloodstained pages?' he asked, with—he could not help it—a touch of male incredulity.

'Evidence,' Protima snapped out.

A woman's idea of evidence, Ghote registered in a secret place in his mind. But he said not a word. This was no time to try to explain to his wife what exactly could constitute evidence.

*   *   *

Next morning, at an early hour, Ghote found himself standing close to the wide platform that had been put up towards the southern end of the Oval Maidan's long stretch of green grass, not browned as yet by the full summer sun. Across the wide road behind, quite eclipsing the massive, ornate, awnings-spread verandas of the Secretariat building, there for a hundred years or more, he saw that a twenty-foot-high wooden cut-out had been erected. It portrayed the Bombay politician who had happened to become a member of the Cabinet in far-away Delhi. His hands, as garishly coloured as the whole, were clasped one against the other in respectful greeting to the common man below. The common man who in the new India had his vote, along with every adult woman.

He took note then of what more concerned him, the exact arrangements on the platform. It might be necessary, he thought, should Popatkar for some reason suddenly stand up and hurry away, to follow him as he dodged through the omnipresent garlanded banners, the microphones poking up everywhere and the looming loudspeakers. If one of Popatkar's rivals on the platform said something to cause him embarrassment and he attempted to make himself temporarily scarce, Protima would want to know about it..

Satisfied eventually, he settled down—should I also sit on the grass? It may be long and long before the so-called really important figures are coming. Often enough, he remembered from the times he had been on duty at such events, a few of the dignitaries expected never actually arrived. Instead they would send some junior member of their entourage to 'represent' them. Always, he thought wryly, under the pretence of themselves having been called away to Delhi for a vital duty that could be carried out only at the Centre. The minion then would read some all-purpose message, rolling out its every lofty phrase.

*   *   *

Time passed as Ghote had thought it would, though he remained alertly standing. Nothing seemed to be happening beyond the occasional burst of chanting at one place or another in the crowd, or an outbreak of scuffling accompanied by noisy yells and heavy shushing. Every now and again some unimportant figure would appear on the platform and there would be a buzz of questioning, *Who is that? No, no, it is not him at all, he is altogether different*. But then calm of a sort would return, food would be unwrapped and eaten, a great deal of water glugged down.

Once or twice a technician going round to check the microphones would tap at one and produce an almost deafening bark of sound. Greeted, of course, with much laughter and ironic applause. But for a long stretch nothing more exciting occurred. Then, at last, the obviously important figures, to judge by their silk *kurtas* and the well-pleated *dhotis* hanging from rotund waists, began to come stepping up to the platform searching out the chairs reserved for them—and almost invariably attempting to change to one placed more prominently. There would then be some indignant opposition, plainly to be seen if conducted in moderately hushed voices, and a final decision would be arrived at, leaving a vacant seat and a sulking figure further away up the platform.

Ghote bore it all stoically. Protima had wanted a full account of what Pradeep Popatkar had said and how he had behaved. He had promised her to bring it back to Bank Street Cross Lane, and he would do so however little significant it seemed.

And I may, he said to himself, after all learn something about that other dignitary who may come, Nathumal Moolchand.

At last and at last the meeting took on a more active character. From somewhere just outside the *maidan*, rising above the deep murmur of the packed throng, had come the strident hooting of a

204

car horn being continuously sounded. Then, perhaps five minutes later, there was a stir among the section of the crowd nearest the platform, some angry shouting, some pushing and shoving and—yes—Pradeep Popatkar himself had arrived. Plainly recognisable, dressed in a *kurta* even more silky than any that had yet appeared, white-white *dhoti* descending in even more sharply ironed pleats. But, most telling of all, Popatkar had on his head a white Gandhi cap, as invariably worn by the Mahatma. Sign nowadays of the utmost political integrity, however little earned.

Ghote watched him with care, acknowledging that his face, podgy and well-contented, did certainly look very like the one on the blood-stiffened page of the *Matunga News* which Protima had held up in front of him, her precious piece of 'evidence'.

Then one by one the other important figures—in their own belief—and the other actual contenders for the vacant Legislative Assembly seat came hurrying to claim their chairs. Almost to a man waddlingly fat, each and every one of them, after the struggle to get through the crowd, plainly already sweating profusely under the comparatively mild Baisakh sunshine.

Among them, then, but making it clear he was not of them, Ghote recognised to his delight the man he had yet to see in the flesh, though from the multitude of newspaper photographs he knew him at once, the head of renowned Moolchand Investments.

So, the man has chosen to come here, and—yes, I can see now—he has taken a reserved chair just behind Popatkar. But why—no politician himself

—has he decided to appear? Why has that chair been specially kept for him? As impressive and comfortable-looking, with its two stout wooden arms, as Popatkar's own?

The answer came to him at once.

Yes, Moolchand, and Moolchand's money, must definitely be supporting Popatkar's bid for the vacant seat. No wonder there are so many Popatkar posters to be seen, Moolchand money is behind them. But why should Moolchand be backing Popatkar? Simple answer, when you think of it, though one doubtless carefully concealed. Moolchand is likely before long to need the help of someone seated in the Legislative Assembly, someone who may, with money behind him, worm his way into ministerial office. Even become Minister for Home, in charge of all the city's police affairs, and doubly able then to shield his wealthy patron should any activity of his put him in danger of appearing in court.

Yes, come to think of it, what Popatkar could become is one of those koel birds, like the ones in the Prince of Wales Museum painting. Popatkar would be like one of those birds fluttering and darting among the freshly green bushes outside that pale-purple house, soon to fly off to find a crow's nest for their eggs. What was it the English teacher at Nasik told me about koels? Yes, in England it is cuckoos, not koel-nightingales, that find other birds to do the work of hatching their eggs and nurturing their chicks.

Like, I cannot help thinking, Nathumal Moolchand will do with Popatkar. Installed in the nest of the Legislative Assembly, Popatkar, victim of an invading koel, will become an egg-nurturing

206

crow, doing for Moolchand whatever he needs done.

A flurry of reporters, shouting out questions they must know would never get answered, had followed Popatkar and fought their way to stand as near the platform as they could get.

Hastily Ghote insinuated himself among them.

*   *   *

He was still standing there an hour later, sticky with sweat under the midday sun, pressed hard from each side by equally sweaty, and pungent, happily gossiping reporters, when it came at last to Popatkar's turn to address the huge crowd.

He rose like a whale breaking through the surface of the deep sea below, retaining, thanks to his privileged chair in the comparative cool of the awnings-shaded platform, the better part of his pleated-*dhoti* elegance. Snatching the slender stalk of one of the microphones in front of him, he began to pour into it a store of rich words. Ghote, all ears on Protima's behalf, gave them his full attention.

For the first five minutes.

He had heard it all before. Not from Pradeep Popatkar's lips, but from the lips, over the years, of a hundred politicians before him. The promises that even the hungriest hearer must find difficult to believe, the appeals to whatever emotion was most likely to get a response. In Popatkar's case, he noted, scarcely listening as the lush periods rolled on, this was to the clamour for power made by the party he had thrown in his lot with: noisy, dominating Shiv Sena with its appeal to those in

207

the crowd wanting to glorify Maharashtra's past at the expense of Bombay's hundreds of thousands of non-Maharashtrians.

Look at the way, he thought, the politicians in power now are renaming streets in the city, substituting for the hundred-year-old British names that everybody knows whatever heroes of Maharashtra's past they can dig out. Lady Hardinge Road? How long will my father's little piece of history survive? And, in all probability, other places like time-honoured massive Victoria Terminus, VT to everyone in Bombay, will be given some other name. What for heaven's sake? Oh, yes, I can guess. Who could replace the world-ruling Queen-Empress but Maharashtra's own great hero of the past, Shivaji, war-winning capturer of impregnable forts. VT may become, yes, Chhatrapati Shivaji Terminus? A mouthful indeed for Indian Railways.

Then, as Popatkar, grasping his microphone as if it were a stout spar in a storm-tossed sea, added yet more air-filled promises to his much applauded references to Maharashtra's illustrious past, Ghote was suddenly shocked out of his idle reverie by a sharp elbow, thrust very painfully, into the small of his back.

CHAPTER TWENTY-ONE

Somebody was . . . no, a whole knot of people were making a furious attempt to thrust through the crowd close to the platform's barrier fence. Ghote, as he straightened himself up from the blow to his back, noticed the disturbance all round him had actually caused Popatkar to falter in the midst of his platitudes. But it will take more than this rowdy outbreak, he thought, to bring Popatkar to a final halt, even though the leaders of the tight little band of invaders have begun now to clamber over the fence in front.

Then the pressure of more invaders from behind sent him all but sprawling at the feet of the reporter next to him. A deluge of invective burst on his ears as, clawing at the reporter's shirt and trouser, he struggled to stand again. Shaking the shock out of his head, he saw then that the invading newcomers had been more successful than he had realised.

And something else, too. Something altogether unexpected. As far as he could make out, the invaders seemed to be led by a woman. At least there was a woman not all that far now from still-spouting Popatkar, and she was shouting and fighting to get yet nearer. Evidently, from the scanty time-drained sari he now made out she was wearing, she must be from the lowest section of Bombay's millions.

How on earth . . . ? And why on earth should such a person, plainly far below the standing of the personalities of the platform, want to invade it in this way? It was plain, certainly, she was not anyone who could be fitted, in any way, into the ranks of politically concerned individuals like—all right—like Protima herself. Yes.

Yes, if it had not been for little Ved needing to be looked after at home, my very own wife might, just might, have been leading such an attack on the platform where her despised Pradeep Popatkar was, for all the windiness of his words, gathering up to himself vote after vote after vote.

Then, looking yet more keenly at the tight little mob, now less than fifteen or twenty feet away from Popatkar, it came into Ghote's mind that the sari-clad virago shouting hard as she could at the fat, fleshy politician, was someone he felt he somehow knew. Not that a single word she was yelling had clearly reached his ears.

But, yes, he thought, she is . . . But, no. No, I cannot put a finger on who she can be. Over the last few years I must have come face-to-face with dozens, even hundreds, of women with no better garment to their back than a washed-to-death sari. But which of them is this woman? Or . . . ? Or is she—I just think she may be—someone I have seen somewhere quite recently? Up in the Lady Hardinge Road slum? It could be. But there are two slums there, one on each side of that road. Which of them would it have been?

Wait, one thing I realise. I do know now that she is not my key witness whose shopping bag Atul snatched from her, the bag he had put Bikram's head into. She is not Rekha Salaskar, eager consumer of *vada pavs* and chilled Pepsi. Her sari, surely her only one, was at least recognisable as being orange-patterned. It was not in any way

210

reduced almost to colourlessness like the one the woman up there is wearing.

Then he realised that the nameless creature had managed now to force her way yet nearer Popatkar. She would have been right up to where he was standing with his microphone except that a *kurta*-clad dignitary, a *neta*, sitting just below has thrust out the umbrella he was carrying against the sun and has all but tripped her.

From above there came the woman's piercing infuriated screech.

And Ghote had his answer.

Yes. Yes, it is—wait. Think—yes, Jyoti Bhat-something. Yes, Bhatvadekar. The woman who screeched in just that way when she heard me battering and battering at the door of Atul's empty hut. The woman, in fact, whose name and address are in the notebook in my pocket here, just where I told myself I was bound to forget them.

Got it. She is the very woman I told to be ready one day in the future to give evidence in court against Atul, though any case against him is unlikely to come up for weeks, if not months. India's courts are always slow and steady as a marching elephant. So what is Jyoti doing here now? Yes, she has even grabbed the microphone from in front of the *neta* who all but tripped her. So what is it she means to do holding that microphone—wonder if it still works—and fighting her way nearer Popatkar?

In less than a minute he had the answer, and the knowledge came to him, despite what he had just seen, as a complete surprise.

*   *   *

211

Jyoti Bhatvadekar was turning out to be much more than a mere potential witness in the case against Atul, murderer of hopeless Bikram. She was almost unbelievably—it soon became evident—a public speaker every bit as cunning at holding an audience as Popatkar himself. If she was not as polished as Popatkar, she was a great deal more effective, despite her use of the simplest, sometimes plainly coarse, language. A woman in a thousand, in a hundred thousand.

Taking up the claim Popatkar had been making at just that minute, boasting he had brought, for his Matunga Municipal Council constituents, all the benefits of a newly constructed clean, much needed toilets building.

'Where is it, then?' she yelled. 'Where is it, Popatkar? Just where in that bright and beautiful slum of yours is such a place?'

And, yes, her microphone has not at all suffered from when she wrenched hold of it. Her question is booming out all over the wide *maidan*.

'Never mind—' Popatkar had begun to retort into his own microphone when Jyoti came in again.

'But we do mind, Popatkar *Sahib*. We do mind because there is nothing there at all. And, more, we mind very much where has gone all the money to build that place that no one has ever seen?'

'I tell you—'

'You going to tell us the truth, Pradeepji? You going to admit all those lovely rupees went straight into your own fat pockets?'

And so it went on for twenty flame-hot minutes or more. Twenty minutes during which it became increasingly clear that the huge crowd below,

212

rocking with laughter, was now entirely on Jyoti's side, accepting—how could they not?—every damning allegation she was making as she took Popatkar through his time as the elected representative for the part of Matunga he thought he had made his own.

At the end of that twenty minutes Popatkar had turned from being the majestic, rich in promises, giver of good things (at some future date, unspecified) into a vast balloon into which somebody had plunged a solid spike, leaving its gassy contents whistling out. Ghote felt he could almost hear the shrill squeal. The outrush of hot air.

No need now, he thought, as Popatkar turned and lumbered towards the nearest exit, to keep him strictly in view in the way I had it in mind to do so as not to lose sight of him, if something some other speaker up there said had caused him a moment of embarrassment. Now the speaker who has utterly embarrassed him is not any fellow politician scoring a petty point. It is the voice of the common man rising up at last. Or— acknowledge it fully—it is a woman of the people speaking out and speaking the plainest of truths.

So, back now as fast as I can go to Bank Street Cross Lane. There to tell Protima how her pet hate has been . . . no, not even deflated like an enormous balloon—he was never really that mighty—but made to look like one of those dishes of smooth curds on the pavement outside the shiny milk churns of a *dudh-wallah*'s shop when some passer-by gives it the merest accidental tap. And in a moment it becomes simply a broken-up mess.

Ghote had hardly set foot on the last flight of the steep stairs leading to his uninviting flat when the door above was swept open and Protima—she was wearing her blue-and-yellow sari—sprang out with a single sharp demand.

'Well, did that man give himself away? Yes or no?'

Ghote took one deep breath, both his feet steady on the same creaky stair, and answered.

'Give himself away? No, hundred per cent better than that. Your Pradeep Popatkar was made, by a woman from a slum, Jyoti by name, to look the most ridiculous of fools. You should have heard that huge crowd at the *maidan* roaring with laughter as she tore him to pieces.'

Protima turned in an instant from severe examiner to dazed and dazzled disciple.

'How? How was that done?' she asked. 'Come in, come in, husbandjee, come and tell me how such a thing was happening. Tell to the last drop.'

So, sitting together on the cushion-piled *takht*, with little Ved sleeping happily away in his wooden cradle, Ghote recounted in full detail just what had happened when, as Popatkar was in full votes-gathering voice, the group of aggrieved slum-dwellers from Matunga had forced their way up to the platform—'I even was knocked almost to the ground as they passed'—and Jyoti tackled the promises-spouting windbag face-to-face.

'But more and better,' he went on, 'you will never guess who Jyoti is.'

'Well, who?'

'She is none other than a woman I was meeting

214

outside Atul's hut in the slum on the north side of Lady Hardinge Road, full name Jyoti Bhatvadekar. I have it in my notebook here in my pocket. And, listen to this. She is also the very Crime Branch sweeper who was forced to take Bikram's head in our bloodstained bag, there underneath my trousers, into my cabin itself at Crime Branch.'

'And you say she utterly showed up Popatkar?'

'She did, she did. Jyoti Bhatvadekar altogether made chutney out of your Popatkar. She—'

And then Protima came out with the simple sentence he had thought he might not ever hear her say.

'So now, Ved's father, you are free to carry out to the end the mission you were so good as to take upon yourself, free to track down to the utmost ends of the earth the man who cut off the head of that poor, poor Bikram.'

CHAPTER TWENTY-TWO

Ghote at once smoothed aside the claims that overambitious Protima had made for him. All the *to the utmost ends of the earth*, as well as *that poor, poor Bikram* as she had called the rum-sodden, excruciatingly inefficient fellow. Let alone that cherishable but not wholly correct *the mission you were so good as to take upon yourself*. He experienced then a wave of warm relief at the disappearance of any more such tasks as being sent off to the Oval Maidan or, worse, worse, taking Bikram's head to the Electric Crematorium. But, at that same instant, he was struck by a shaft of deep-plunging dismay. Oh God, the task once more ahead must be, surely, a near impossibility.

How can I, once again faced with doing what I have pledged myself to do, actually manage on my own to put that crocodile-teeth streetfighter, Atul, into a police cell? Yes, out in Matunga I learnt I should have been able at dawn yesterday to break into his hut and arrest him before he had roused himself from drunken sleep. But now . . . ? Now will I get ever such an opportunity again? Atul will not, early morning after early morning, be lying there at my mercy. And Jyoti? Will she still be willing to risk his murderous wrath if for any unexpected reason something goes wrong with her plan and Atul gets to know who it was who betrayed him?

Jyoti. But then a sudden idea came to him, a star peeping through cloudy night-time gloom above.

Does Jyoti not deserve some reward, a considerable reward, for her daring in toppling promises-waving Popatkar, even if in the end machinations on high cancel what she seems to have achieved? She does. But what has anybody, anybody at all, done for her? Nothing. And what have I done for her? Nothing, again. But . . . but now, at this moment I can see what Protima and I could do together.

We could give Jyoti a reward much, much bigger than the first-class shopping bag I bought for Rekha Salaskar. We could offer Jyoti, wretchedly poor as she must be with no more than the wage a sweeper gets, and that earned with long tramps each day from Matunga to Police Headquarters and back, we could offer her the job of our servant.

We need a servant, too. We badly need one, only scarcely knowing any of our new neighbours to ask, there has never been time to properly look about for one. And Jyoti, who boasted to me how well she cleans Atul's hut, would be well capable of doing the job. It would give her, too, surely a more solid roof over her head than whatever she has in that falling-apart Lady Hardinge Road slum. All right, she would have to sleep, as many another servant does, in the kitchen. But she could be made comfortable there. Yes.

'Listen, listen,' he all but shouted to Protima. 'Listen.'

'What? What arc you now wanting?'

'Listen, Ved's mother. I have had an idea. A wonderful idea, I am thinking. Or-or, no, I am hoping . . .'

Protima, putting her head to one side as much as to say *What has got into this man now?*, sat there on her nest of cushions—hard, soft, this-coloured and that, patterned and plain—and waited.

Ghote tried rapidly to sort his thoughts into the order most likely to convince his wife that what he was about to propose was a sensible solution to a problem that neither of them had been willing to face since they had, not without doubts, taken on the flat.

At last—and it was the work only of seconds in fact—he felt he was ready.

'There is something more about Jyoti,' he said. 'More than her hundred per cent victory over your Pradeep Popatkar. Because she was not only that tremendous speaker at Oval Maidan. She is also the woman who that hundred per cent *badmash*

217

Atul just only ordered and commanded one day to sweep out his filthy hut and when she had once done that, and made it as she was telling me herself *clean as clean*, he was forcing her do it each and every day with not a *paisa* of reward. Still she must be doing same. But . . . but . . . '

He came to a halt.

This was it. The make-or-break moment.

Yes, but what, he asked himself suddenly, what will I do if Protima rejects this suggestion I am about to put? She has found objection after objection to other suggestions of mine. What if she says now it would be impossible to hire as a servant a woman about whom she knows nothing? A woman she has not even once seen? A woman from some disgusting slum out in Matunga? A woman who would bring with her a thousand deadly diseases to pass on to helpless Ved?

A hundred other similar thoughts went whirring through his mind. What even if I have misjudged her character altogether when I was thinking she cannot but welcome this woman who has defeated her hated Pradeep Popatkar? What if she is not truly as kind-hearted as I have always believed? Or what if she will somehow resent that it is myself and not her who has had the idea of employing Jyoti?

Have I been wrong about Protima ever since I was first falling in love with her?

And then . . . then at once the answer came to him, the sun rising over the horizon. No. No, no, no, no. I am not wrong about the wife who has given birth to my first son, my heir, the little one.

'Listen,' he said, 'it is an idea I have had.'

'What? What? Sometimes when you are having

an idea, it is just only something to laugh.'

'Perhaps this is. But I am not thinking so. Listen.'

He found he had gripped hard with his teeth on his lower lip.

'You are knowing,' he managed to say, 'we have not at all succeeded to find a servant, but Jyoti has been sweeping Atul's—'

'Atul Patul,' Protima broke in, 'what do I care if she has been sweeping even that Mr Divekar's house? Jyoti is going to come here. She must. She must come to us. To sweep, to wash the vessels, to cook when I am not, and, above all, to tidy and tidy and tidy.'

'Yes, yes. It is what you have never had time to do since we were coming here. Yes, in one day only with Jyoti here things will be better and better. Your slipper, that has been for some time itself tucked somewhere under the cushions of the *takht*, will be put neatly away, and-and . . . and, yes, that terrible bundle of bloodied-over newspaper that has been underneath my trousers will, in one moment, be burnt to ashes.'

'But no.'

'No? What are you meaning *No*?'

'No, however much a good servant Jyoti may be, she must never, not in any way at all, touch that *Matunga News*. It is evidence. Evidence against the man who took off Bikram's head and wrapped it up in those newspaper sheets.'

Ghote thought for a moment. Then he knew he must speak. He must not too much let Protima believe she is always right.

'But, no,' he said, if with not a little care. 'You are not knowing too much about the evidence of blood. You have seen just only what they are saying in the papers. But they are never telling full story there. You see, to be evidence to put before a jury, with a scientific witness to explain also, you must be able to match the blood on whatever object you believe was the murder victim's with that victim's own blood. And where can we now find any of Bikram's blood? Nowhere. His body is altogether lost in the sea, and his head has been burnt to ashes. At Electric Crematorium.'

With an effort, a small effort, he managed not to underline the fact that it had been Protima herself who had insisted on the head being taken into that final destination.

But he had reckoned without a woman's determination that what she believes must, despite any male argument, be the truth.

'That is all very well, your body this and your crematorium that. But I am telling you: that packet of bloodstained newspaper is evidence, and evidence it will stay where it is, there underneath your trouser. Jyoti or no Jyoti.'

'Have it your own way,' Ghote said. As he had said not a few times before.

But, he added in the secrecy of his heart, I am knowing what I know.

Then, from the bedroom behind them there came a wailing cry. In an instant Protima was on her feet, *takht* cushions descending beneath her.

She vanished into the bedroom. The wailing ceased.

A few moments later she came back in, Ved in her arms.

'Now, my little one, now you are wrapped safely round and all pinned up,' she said, 'you can go to your great big, brave *Pitaji*.'

220

Ghote took his son into his arms and jiggled him carefully up and down.

But, he thought once more, am I fit to carry out any less easy task than keeping this child of mine for some minutes happy?

All too soon the truth was upon him.

'Now,' Protima said, once more radiating undirected determination on his behalf, 'tell me, Ved's father, when will you set off to arrest this terrible Atul?'

Here it is, once again. The impossible task that must be completed *ek dum*.

'That is not at all as easy to do as you are making out. What use is it if I am setting out just only this minute without any solid plan for action? Or even if I am waiting till tomorrow morning, when in any case I ought to be sitting in my cabin expecting orders.'

It was the best answer he could find.

And, of course, it did not in any way satisfy the wife who had no sooner thought of the final outcome of anything than she imagined its achievement was simply a matter of jumping up and setting out.

'No, sitting and sitting idle gets you nowhere. Nowhere at all.'

'But—'

'No. No *buts* and buttering. This is no time for making your *chapattis* easy to eat. You have a hard-hard task in front of you, one also that you must keep altogether secret from such poke-and-pry people as Assistant Commissioner Divekar and-and what did you say his name was?'

'Whose name?' Ghote asked, already more than a bit bewildered by his wife's leaping mind.

'Whose name? Whose? How can you ask? The officer you were telling who-who . . . who, I don't know what, was in some way seeming to be kind to you. If what you thought about him was at all right.'

By this time Ghote had managed to guess who she had meant.

'Superintendent Ghorpade?' he asked. 'The senior officer who was welcoming me so kindly into Crime Branch itself and has spoken to me often since?'

'If that is his name. You are the one who should have it in your head.'

Oh God, he thought, we are back already to Protima always knowing best, even when she is not at all knowing anything.

But, at once, he withdrew in his mind that allegation. Yes, Protima is harrying and harrying me. But she is doing same because, like myself, she has been seized now with one iron determination to see justice done for Bikram, whatever inexplicable obstacles Mr Divekar has put in the way. Has put, at second hand, into her way also.

'Just only let me think for two-three moments,' he said. 'Then I will be able to tell you how I believe I can get one firm hold on Atul.'

'But you will be careful, husbandjee. You will not take any foolish risks?'

Yes, this is my true wife speaking now, he thought. The wife who has always and always put myself before herself. Who has thought and worried about whatsoever scarcely frightening work has by chance been awaiting me.

'But, no,' he said, as he had more than once said before, 'this work will not be too difficult to

222

manage. You could say it is not even truly dangerous.'

Oh, that lie. How often, when there was trouble up in Dadar and I was the Assistant Inspector sent to deal with it, did I soothe her with sweet talk like this?

'Truly, my husband?'

'Oh, yes, truly and truly. Yes, Atul is a somewhat violent man. After all, he was killing Bikram in that vicious manner. But Bikram, poor fellow, was not the sort to stand up against him in any way. One grab from that man and he would have been powerless. It was then, then that his head got hacked from his shoulders. But now Atul will be up against somebody who has had full training in combating such *goondas* as himself, with handcuffs at every minute in his pocket. Then you will see.'

*   *   *

The plan that had come into Ghote's head, if cloudily, was simple enough, for all the not-to-be-guessed-at hazards that might be concealed along the way. He would go each day to Matunga, as soon as he had occupied his seat at Crime Branch for long enough for it to be as unlikely as ever that the ACP would call him up to hear that something was to be done about Nathumal Moolchand.

Then, when he felt he was comparatively at liberty, he would make his way to Matunga and the slum on the northern side of Lady Hardinge Road where Atul had his double-sized hut. And there he would tuck himself away in hiding nearby until Atul appeared, however long he had to wait.

Sooner or later, he reasoned, Atul is bound to

223

come back there, even if it may be a week or more before he does. He cannot go off streetfighting and boozing day after day, however much that appeals to him. Nor could such *supari* work as he might be paid to do—was he at the orders of other *seths* than Moolchand?—keep him away from his home for ever.

Making himself sound thoroughly eager, he laid all this out to Protima, and, somewhat to his surprise, seemed to gain her agreement.

* * *

It proved to be a long wait that sent-to-limbo Ghote had to endure day after day out in Matunga. Each morning he went, promptly to time, into Crime Branch and sat unmoving at his desk, more and more in a fever of apprehension that the telephone beside him would ring, would have immediately to be picked up, would carry to his ear a ferocious summons from the ACP. Then, when no call came, he would set out on the wearisome journey to Matunga where, crouching in a new place of concealment each day, he fixed his eyes on the door of Atul's double-storey hut, its roof gleaming with hammered-out *vanaspati* cooking-oil tins stolen from heaven knows where.

Returning home from Matunga late each day, he had to face the increasingly determined questioning of his wife.

'Well, were you seeing him? Yes or no?'

Or a few days later it might be, 'So once again you were lurking and loitering in that place to no purpose. Are you thinking no one will notice you there? That no one will notice and warn that

224

goonda who cut poor innocent Bikram's head from his shoulders?'

And yet later again, 'So *No luck* you are all ready to say. But why do you think luck is not coming your way? Let me tell you. There is nothing lucky to come. Nothing.'

But, the very next day, as it turned out, luck, of a sort, was waiting for him. God Ganesha, to whom he had consistently blotted out every impulse to offer a prayer, seemed to have rewarded the unspoken, even unthought, urgency of his pleas.

Scarcely had he arrived at the day's chosen place of observation than the door of the hut opposite him opened and, with crocodile teeth crunching at the remains of a late morning meal, Atul stepped out. For a minute or two he stood, sniffing greedily at the cool morning air. Then, with a backward jerk of his shoulders, all in one moment he set out in a plainly determined manner, heading for the slum gate.

Ghote, as he set off in pursuit, let a thankful thought appear in his head. Yes, I would have altogether missed my opportunity if, first thing, I had stayed in my cabin for only ten minutes more. I easily might have done that. Say, Sgt Moos, head full of whorls and bifurcations, had appeared at the doors, unshakable. But now Atul's broad back and heavy shoulders, moving slowly away, are well within my sights.

All right, as Atul steps into Lady Hardinge Road itself, crowded now with people going to the markets, I can go full pelt after him and be bound to be able to follow, screened by the crowd, almost as closely as his own shadow.

Ganesha's blessing, it soon seemed, was staying

225

firmly with him. A few seconds after Atul had tugged open the slum gate, a much sturdier affair than the one on the opposite side of Lady Hardinge Road, Ghote, already sweating from the sudden exertion that had brought him close behind, was able to poke his head up and spot the tall figure of his quarry heading in the direction of the Matunga Road station.

There could be little doubt that this must be his destination. But, once there, he could catch trains going either north or south. Which of the two he wanted was anybody's guess.

But it will be not at all any guess of mine, Ghote thought with a spurt of total determination. I am not going to lose the fellow now when at last and at last I have him under my eyes.

He set off at a loping run, knowing any more vigorous a pace would risk the sound of heavy shoes pounding the pavement alerting Atul, however far off he was. Soon he had got himself near enough to feel certain of getting to the station almost at the same moment as his target, yet far enough back to be sure, if for some chance reason Atul should look round, he would not be able to make out anyone following clearly enough to realise he was being trailed. Near enough too, he reckoned, to make sure no intervening bodies would lose him sight of his quarry even for a few seconds.

The chance of that, he thought, is certainly here. Look how many morning shoppers there are, women and men, almost every one of them dangling from one hand or the other a shopping bag almost indistinguishable from the one Atul happened to snatch from Rekha Salaskar.

The next moment precisely the situation he had feared came about. While Atul was still some distance from the station two stout Muslim women, each black-*burkha*-clad, walking close together, abruptly changed course and put themselves just behind Atul, hoping perhaps that a man as broad-shouldered and forceful would carve out an easy passage for them.

Ghote cursed. All very well to be pleased in general there were parts of Bombay where Hindu and Muslim lived comfortably together. But I could do without those two fat creatures blocking my view.

What if Atul gets to the station just as a train has come in? Suppose he jumps aboard it, whether it is heading north or south. He will give a clean slip to me. Worse, it may be he has all along wanted to go south. To the city's hub. Where, it is possible, even more than possible, he has agreed to meet someone, someone of importance, someone perhaps with *supari* money in his hand. As it may be, that froggy little mouthpiece of Nathumal Moolchand's, Mr Kanjilal.

He burst then into an unashamed run, leaping out into the roadway, careless of the traffic steadily plunging its way along. But he found he had left rather too much distance between himself and Atul. Or perhaps, Atul, seeing the station in sight, had quickened his pace and, unlikely as it might seem, the two waddlingly fat Muslim housewives were now being drawn rapidly along in his wake.

He peered round to get a better view.

And a truck, attempting to pass a lumbering bullock cart, on the wrong side, gave a glancing blow to his shoulder, hard enough to send him staggering back to the safety of the pavement. For a minute or so it left him too dazed to resume his care-nothing pursuit.

Which meant it had come to an end.

CHAPTER TWENTY-THREE

Above the jabber of talk from the onward-pressing shoppers—what crowd in Bombay ever passed up the chance of talk and chatter?—Ghote distinctly heard the sound of a train, that must have pulled into the station almost at the same moment that the truck had hit him, noisily starting off again.

Ganesha's gift thrown away.

But, no, he thought. No, my life is not ruled by Ganesha's whims, useful to me or not useful. I rule my life.

He set off at a fierce walk, despite the pain that at once shot up again in his side.

If Atul, he told himself, has really gone to meet somebody somewhere in the Fort area, not at all far from the cabin at Crime Branch where I should at this moment be patiently sitting, I may really have lost him altogether. But if that train was, after all, a northbound one, then Atul could still be inside the station.

He forced himself into a lumbering run.

Hurrying at last into the station itself, he saw at once there was a packed crowd waiting for a southbound train. And, yes, Atul's head, crowned by its tangled mass of black uncombed hair, was there among the press of people.

He felt a leap of delight. Immediately, there

228

followed a thud of dismay, impossible to reject. Not thirty or forty yards away from me there is a stick-at-nothing *goonda*, powerful enough to have cut off Bikram's head, if not with a single stroke of cleaver or sword, at least with the four vicious hacks I saw when Protima and I made our examination all that long night. How can I ever manage to take him?

But I must. I must. A glance to the right to make sure no train heading for Churchgate was in the distance. No, nothing. Nothing yet.

Very well, now I must get near enough to Atul to be able to slip into the carriage next to whichever one he enters, where I will be unseen by that hulking figure. After all, it is only my guess that he will stay on the train till we are reaching Bombay Central. He may be going to meet whoever it is he has in mind at any of the—let me see—yes, ten stations between here and Churchgate.

A bare two minutes later, clearly to be heard above the ear-dinning chatter of the crowd he was thrusting his way through, came the first wail, warning of the near approach of the train.

At once Ghote began yet more urgently slipping and sliding through the crowd of would-be passengers, cunningly as any seller of balloons or bangles aiming illegally to squeeze themselves on board. At every moment he kept fixed in view Atul's head, still easily to be seen. Once or twice even glimpsing, or so he thought, the projecting crocodile teeth.

But, no, damn it, he said to himself, although I had more than one good look at the fellow, even from my watching-place just only fifteen-twenty minutes ago, he has seen me only once, when behind the dyers' hut in Rekha's slum I found him leaning against that half-dead palm tree. And he may not then even have taken in who I was, for all that he at once hurried away. Really he no more knows there is a Crime Branch inspector on his heels than he is knowing my name.

Yes, I could probably, if I wanted, place myself in the same carriage now, standing at his elbow, and he would have no idea who was there. But I will not. Somehow I feel he might sense that an enemy was breathing the very same stale-smelling rail-carriage air as himself. No, the air in the next coach, equally thick with the sweat-smell and *paan*-chewing breaths of its four or five hundred crammed passengers, will be fine for me.

The powerful engine of the incoming train, steam squirting from a dozen different places, passed slowly in front of him now, its heat sending out hotter-than-hot waves that, for a moment, even dried the sweat on his face.

In half a minute more the whole train came to a full halt. At the held-apart sliding doors all along its length the waiting passengers began their frenzied assaults, barely letting anyone alight and forcing back those staying inside, determined to make room where there might seem to be none. Even women, he saw, were attempting almost as fiercely to secure places in the *Ladies Only* coach.

Just in a second's quick glance, before adding his weight to the forward-thrusting people in front, he was able to make sure he had positioned himself so that Atul—matted-hair head clearly visible—was in the next carriage.

Then, pushing hard past the books-bag of a student lounging well clear of the carriage interior so as to catch the breeze as the train once more sped along, convenient handrail hard-clenched in his left hand, Ghote registered with a trickle of pleasure that, safely on board now, he would soon be able to lean out himself as they came to each station on the way to see if the tall *goonda* was alighting.

As, with a mournful departing hoot, the train began to pull away, he added his own hand to that of the student still clutching at the rail. He found at once it was almost too hot to hold.

*   *   *

The precautions Ghote had taken proved, in fact, unnecessary. At none of the ten stations on the route was there any sign of Atul leaping out from the next carriage. It was not until at last they were pulling into Bombay Central that, pushing his way towards the window at the end of the carriage against the tide of his fellow passengers moving forcefully towards the nearest doors to get out, he was able to catch a reassuring glimpse of Atul also beginning to barge his way forwards.

Quickly he started to push, almost as ruthlessly as Atul himself, to get to a point where, as the train slowed to a halt, he could, like half a hundred other over-urgent passengers, jump down to the platform below and run forward a few paces till he was sure of his footing. Atul, he reckoned, would almost certainly be only just behind him. In a few seconds the big *badmash* would be likely to overtake, as he heads for wherever it is he wants to go.

That was exactly what happened—if his plan was

231

somewhat spoilt when Atul, in his stop-at-nothing race away, brushed, as he passed, so roughly against him that a new jab of pain shot up his side from when the too-ambitious truck driver on the road to Matunga Station had attempted to get past the bullock cart.

He gritted his teeth and, despite the pain, increased his pace. Atul, he saw, had unashamedly sent sprawling aside a man, by the look of him a clerk, who had been making his way to whatever office waited to swallow him up.

Yes, he said to himself, risk or no risk, I will have to get yet nearer if the fellow keeps on at this care-for-nobody pace.

Breaking for a minute into a trot, he closed the gap until, like the two generously fleshed Muslim women who had blocked his view on the way to Matunga Station, he was swept completely into the tall *goonda*'s wake as they crossed the black-and-white tiles of the station entrance.

Oh, how I would like, he thought, to be wearing at this moment one head-to-foot *burkha*, Government issue for the purpose of disguise.

But, *burkha*-wearing or in simple shirt-pant, he found it not too difficult, in spite of the pace Atul continued to set, to hang no more than a few yards behind. Until he realised, with a dart of uneasiness, that they were hardly any distance from Police Headquarters.

Surely, surely, the fellow cannot be making for the buildings surrounding the compound that my cabin itself looks out on? All right, Atul would be safe from recognition there. His name and photo will hardly appear on any Headquarters Bad Character roll. If they are anywhere, it will be on the roll at Matunga PS. So can he actually be going to meet someone in Crime Branch itself? No, even if it was an officer there who spotted the document or letter that had suggested Nathumal Moolchand was worth investigating, they would never agree to meet a fellow like Atul inside the building. And even if, across so many miles of humanity-packed Bombay, he does have a link to some peon at Headquarters he would never dare meet him in such a dangerous place. Even in the days when Jyoti was working as a Headquarters sweeper in the early mornings, much earlier than I was taking my seat there, Atul would never have contacted her there, if indeed he had ever needed to.

I was taking my seat there . . . The thought interrupted his hurried reasoning. Ought I to be at this very moment keeping warm that seat in case I am given at least some work, even if I am not to have the explanation from the ACP that I was meant to be waiting for? Perhaps now he will even be wanting to put me on some simple case just come in?

But, whether I ought to be sitting there or not, there is no question at this moment of going back into my cabin. I am following Atul—yes, this is Waudby Road—to see who it may be, in this top-of-the-tree part of the city, he is, surely, hurrying to meet. To meet, and to put out his big fist for the first half of a sum of *supari* money—it really could be—with instructions to eliminate yet another awkward figure standing in some rich man's path.

Then—his attention had actually wandered for a moment—he just glimpsed Atul's crown of tangled black hair as he plunged into the side turning beside, yes, that glittering sari shop on the ground

233

floor of the rabbit warren of a building hiding in its depths the Beauty Bar.

He realised at once that this must be where Atul had been drinking when he had made himself a false friend to Bikram before luring him to wherever it was he killed him.

So, will I go into the place again, now myself? Atul will be there, little doubt about that. And if . . . if someone else is there with him, someone like—it is not impossible—Nathumal Moolchand's Mr Kanjilal, then, if I can manage to get a look inside, I will have one more good reason to believe Moolchand is the man who employed Atul, both to put Bikram out of the way and earlier to rid his cherished daughter of a husband she no longer wanted. But . . .

But inside there I must—yes, my task, my duty— arrest Atul. And he will be no pushover.

All right, I have got, bulging my trouser pocket, the handcuffs I have imagined myself snapping on his wrists. But that was in imagination only. How exactly, in a few minutes' time, will I in reality bring about a situation where Atul's wrists, thick as they are, will be just where handcuffs can click round them?

I cannot see how. Not at all. And yet I must go in there, where Atul may be leaning across one of those round wooden tables, listening to some person opposite, whether Kanjilal or a different *supari* messenger. Atul, the man who was able to catch hold of poor Bikram in this very place and lead him away, a goat to the slaughter, taking him where, like a temple executioner of sacrificial animals, he could behead him. Atul of—never mind those crocodile teeth—of those tree-branch arms, of those streetfighter's tricks and treacheries.

What to do?

Then an idea, born of desperation, came to him.

Yes, there is one person, perhaps, perhaps, I could ask for help. I could ask Sgt Chavan. No longer, as when we went to investigate the murder in the house on Cumballa Hill, a solid mass of surliness, full of resentment at ACP Divekar giving him the task of spying on this new inspector. Now, thanks to the moment I was able, by asking him straight out if he had been ordered to report on me, to win a smile from that sombre face, hopefully thereafter I have had him as something of a friend.

* * *

A moment to decide. Yes, Atul's business with whoever he is meeting inside there will not last just only five minutes. A delicate negotiation like the one he will be making may easily take half an hour, more even with drink having to be offered, drunk down, offered again. So . . . so, yes, almost certainly there will be time.

He turned round and set off, at a pelting run, for Crime Branch. In less than ten minutes he was there. Completely ignoring his own cabin—what if phone is ringing, Mr Divekar on the other end?— he hurried to the room where the Branch's sergeants wait to be allocated tasks, remembered from the day Superintendent Ghorpade had shown him round the building.

And there he found Chavan.

I am in luck, truly in luck, he told himself.

Chavan might have been out on an investigation anywhere in the city. But he is not. And, better and better, there is a smile on his face as he is seeing my head round the door.

He beckoned to him.

'Listen,' he whispered when he came out, 'there is something urgent I want your help with.'

'Inspector.' A grin. 'At your service.'

Little more than ten minutes later, standing outside the narrow side door of the Waudby Road building, Ghote, who had not risked any delay by explaining earlier the situation in the Beauty Bar, put Chavan fully into the picture.

'It is my chance to arrest a first-class *goonda*, one Atul. A killer even. You know the Beauty Bar inside here?'

'*Jee*, Inspector. Almost every Other Ranker in Crime Branch knows that place. Five-six arrests I have made there myself. It is what they are calling one *den of thieves*. And you are saying Atul is there? Atul himself? Well I am knowing him. I was coming to Crime Branch from Matunga PS, you know. Even in those days Atul had one hell of a reputation for streetfighting. And worse.'

'Right. So, unless in the past fifteen-twenty minutes he has left, he is in there now, in the Beauty Bar. And, I suspect, about to receive *supari* money.'

'Yes. Yes, that work he does also.'

'He does. He took *supari*, I am strongly believing, to do that job we investigated up in Cumballa Hill.'

'*Achchha*. If we can arrest him now, clearing up that Number One killing would be a first-class feather in your cap, Inspector. In mine also.'

Ghote let that pass.

Every bit as cautiously as once before he had
peered in at the half-opened door of the Beauty
Bar, Ghote tried now its closed handle.

It began to slide round.

At least not locked, he thought. Almost I was
expecting it would be. If Atul is conducting the
sort of business inside that I believe he is, he might
quite likely have ordered that absurd curly-curly
moustache bartender to lock the door in case of
some chance customer.

Gently easing the door just half an inch open, he
put his eye to the crack of pale light at its edge.
And, yes. Yes, yes, yes. There is Atul sitting, in my
full sight at the only occupied table. He is leaning
forward and talking—no, not to froggy Mr
Kanjilal—but to a stout suited-and-booted man.
Some other *seth*'s secret messenger? Very likely.

So now? Now I have got to, yes, go in there and
. . . and take Atul.

No. No, first make sure of my backup. I am likely
to need all the help available. Absurd to see myself
as if I am that American comic-paper hero, the
one who goes wherever he wants, up, down,
outside, inside, and thanks to superhuman powers
can do in a minute whatever is needed to bring an
evildoer to justice.

He pulled the door closed, turned and went very
quietly along to the far end of the long, echoey
corridor to where he had stationed Chavan. There
he whispered to him to move up to a doorway
within easy reach of the Beauty Bar.

'Be ready,' he hissed. 'Ready for anything. Atul

may get past me somehow. If he does, stop him.'

Chavan smiled.

'It would be one pleasure,' he said.

Creeping back to the door again, Ghote thought *Surprise must be the one advantage I will have. Will it be enough?*

*   *   *

Ek, do, teen. He flung the door wide.

Atul, he realised at once, had in an instant guessed who he was, long though it had been since that single silent encounter behind the dyers' hut. In one instant he had sent crashing to the floor the little table he had been sitting at. His suited-booted companion scurried, in a fat man's buttocks-shaking run, for the narrow door behind the bar to vanish, together with the bartender. And then Atul was crouching, ready for battle like Krishna in the Mahabharata.

Battle came all too soon.

Ghote, before he could even begin to shoot out the kick that he had in half a second planned to direct at Atul's groin, found himself lifted from his feet.

Oh, God, the thought swept through his mind, why didn't I take Chavan in with me? Absurd ambition to make the arrest myself alone.

But tree-branch arms had gripped him. They were lifting him high and then they flung him back against the half-open door behind. It crashed closed. His head, jerked backwards, struck it with a thunderous crack. For a moment he saw nothing.

Then, as Atul, between two bear-like hands, lifted him up again, sight began swimmingly to

238

return.

His eyes, it seemed, directed themselves of their own volition to Atul's waist and a broad leather sheath there with at its top the heavy handle of a long knife.

Atul standing, legs widely planted, dropped him to the floor now, thumpingly as a sack stuffed with ground turmeric. And he saw, blurred though his vision still was, a bear-wide hand fasten itself round the handle of that knife. And in a moment pull out a broad-bladed dagger almost as long as a small sword.

So this . . . that was . . . The thought came into Ghote's confused mind *So that was what he used on Bikram.*

Behind him he heard the door given a full-shouldered thump. Chavan. Chavan just in time.

But Atul must have heard Chavan's hard-running steps every bit as soon as they had come muffledly to his own ears. The long knife clattered to the floor. The legs-straddled body above him flung itself forward. And then, clearly as a single plucked note from a sitar, there came the sound of a key being snapped round in the door's lock.

Quick, the knife. Must reach it before Atul. Take hold of it. Or knock it to the far corner.

But, no. No, not possible. Too battered to do more than think. To see myself, clearly-clearly, heaving round, stretching out towards the glinting blade at the very edge of vision. But it is nothing more than seeing myself. My arms and legs lie where they have been dropped, soft lengths of floppy tubing. All connection to the brain altogether lost.

As if in a curious upside-down film, he saw now

239

Atul moving slowly into view above him, watched him reach lazily down. Saw him pick up the heavy glinting knife.

This is *The End*.

The thought, like one of the bordered captions in the village cinema tent, occupied every inch of his mind. *The End*.

Move, he instructed himself. Move. Move away somehow. Move away from that knife. Before it comes sweeping down. But the instruction was ignored. The message, not even a single one of the urgent cries within it, got to where it would be acted upon.

Inert. He lay inert.

He saw, half-saw, the knife lifted high. He saw Atul's crocodile teeth grimacing in triumph.

Then one of his five senses, all in a moment, came back to life. He heard. He was able to hear. He had heard, he knew then, the locked door somewhere behind and above him burst open to a shoulder charge far heavier than the one Chavan had managed before. A full long run up a side corridor? Must have been. And . . .

And there is Atul, caught off guard, staggering helplessly back under Chavan's burly weight, banging into another of the heavy little tables and tumbling to the floor.

Senseless? Yes.

As Ghote managed now painfully to raise his head an inch or so, he saw that Atul had indeed been knocked fully as unconscious as, till this moment, he had been himself. Chavan, once Mr Divekar's sullen spy, was on top of him, grinning like a maniac.

Filled in a moment with energy, Ghote put a

hand to his back pocket and, careless of the blasting pain all his new bruises sent through him, managed to extract the handcuffs. Then, at a painful crawl, he went over towards Chavan. Still half-kneeling, he at last got the cuffs one by one round each of Atul's thick wrists.

Click. Click.

CHAPTER TWENTY-FOUR

Standing next day once again in front of the door with the single thick glass pane in it, Ghote told himself, as earlier he had given his brain instructions, time and again, that he had not only succeeded in arresting the man who had severed Bikram's head from his shoulders but that he needed now only the backing of the ACP to be able to get enough out of Atul—never mind the methods that might have to be used—to put Nathumal Moolchand in the dock.

And yet . . . yet . . .

No, he told himself. No, no. No, nothing can go wrong now. This will not at all be a time when Mr Divekar sends me, without any explanation, back to my cabin to, at his plain order, do nothing about the murder of a stupid but innocent peon, however much it had been a murder at the heart of his much cherished Crime Branch. And, equally, I will not now be instructed, as I once was, to wait to hear the outcome of his 'consideration' of the plain facts I told him as lying behind the apparently motiveless stabbing of Krishna Tabholkar.

241

No, nothing like that can happen now.

He peered once again through the glass panel in front of him. Mr Divekar was at his desk, alone.

A sharp tap on the door.

Come. The barked reply seemed to be twice as loud as his tap, brisk though that had been.

He entered.

Standing then between the two centre chairs of the six in front of the wide sweep of the desk, ringingly he clicked heels and faced the two grey marble-eyes beneath their fierce grey eyebrows.

'Well, Inspector?'

Ghote forced his Adam's apple not to gulp. By the least twitch.

What I have to do at this minute is to remind Mr Divekar what Chavan, whom I told to report to him about what he had done, has already informed him of.

'Sir, as you have learnt through Sgt Chavan, who with hundred per cent commendable courage—'

'I know all I need to know about Chavan, Inspector. If praise is due, I am the one to give it.'

So, Chavan has done what I asked. He has told him Atul is under arrest, charged with attempting to murder a police officer, to wit myself. Good man.

'Yes, sir.'

Mr Divekar gave a stir of impatience.

'Right now,' he snapped. 'Out with whatever it is you have to say, Inspector. I have work to get on with, whatever other people may be doing.'

Now. Now it is the moment to tell him the whole of it. To tell him how, by the end of this day, we could have more, much more than the attack on myself, with which to charge Atul. We could have

242

his admission that he stabbed to death Krishna Tabholkar, Nathumal Moolchand's son-in-law, on instructions passed down from Moolchand himself.

It is the moment.

Ghote produced now, for the second time, every item of the evidence he had discovered earlier. Finally, despite the ACP's claim to be the one and only dispenser of praise, he repeated how Chavan had saved his life and enabled him to make his arrest.

Mr Divekar, at the end of it all, sat in silence.

Now am I to hear, at last, recognition of what I have discovered?

'Very well, Inspector.' Words came. 'You have made out a case against one of the most influential figures in the world of Bombay commerce. You have added to that an accusation affecting a prominent Bombay politician, one likely to become, after the forthcoming elections to the vacant Legislative Assembly, as I am given to understand, State Minister for Police Affairs.'

But, no—it was Ghote's first thought—I do not at all think Pradeep Popatkar will be that man. It seems Mr Divekar has heard nothing about the Oval Maidan meeting and the way bottom-of-the-heap Jyoti Bhatvadekar took Popatkar so much to pieces that he has lost any chance of winning that Legislative Assembly seat.

Thank goodness, he added to himself in a little jet of delight, I was never passing on to Mr Divekar Protima's demand that he should vote for anyone other than Popatkar.

But the ACP had snapped out something more.

And I was not hearing him. Must I now ask . . . ? No. No, thank God, I did somehow take it in. He has said *The man, in short, who will have absolute power over yourself, and, I may add, whose backing I shall be able totally to rely on.*

He saw those two marble-hard grey eyes were coldly glaring at him.

So, do those last few words mean—can it be?– that Mr Divekar himself is the officer inside Crime Branch who was asked to investigate whatever illegal activity some rival had said Moolchand was contemplating? Was his the paper about Moolchand that dead Bikram had chanced to see and to read?

Yes, it could be. It really could be. But no time now to think more about that. Mr Divekar is relentlessly going on.

'So, Inspector, you can see, as you have hitherto obviously failed to do, that what you have told me is a matter that requires the very gravest consideration before any action is taken. Any action whatsoever. So do not let me hear that some rigorous interrogation of the man, Atul, has taken place, not without my explicit instructions. In the meanwhile I shall put all this, strong evidence or much less strong, before the Commissioner. Then we will see.'

And Ghote knew, despite Mr Divekar's still being ignorant of what had happened to Popatkar at the Oval Maidan, it was nevertheless defeat for himself. Despite the case I made out, despite all I risked and all I have done, Nathumal Moolchand, backed no doubt by some other politician who he will manoeuvre into the Ministry for Home, will sit where he always has, in a fine, wide office in his tall white-gleaming Moolchand Chambers. He will still, and for ever, be there, protected by that

244

glossy reception-counter with its ice-cold, gorgeously sari-clad guardians. Unmolested, unmolestable.

'Yes, sir,' he said as the ACP, rigid-faced, looked implacably at him. 'I understand.'

'I should hope you do, Inspector. Dismiss.'

*   *   *

Black thoughts reeling and rolling in his head, Ghote acknowledged to himself that there was nothing to be done. Nathumal Moolchand was to be left safe in his lofty tower, despite the evidence Atul could produce that he had ordered the killing of his own son-in-law. And this, too, he realised, means that Atul is not to be charged with murdering poor Bikram. Any case on those grounds that might come into court would inevitably involve Moolchand. When Atul is asked why he went to the length of hacking Bikram's head from his shoulders it will be bound to come out that he did it on orders. On whose orders? On Nathumal Moolchand's, via his personal assistant, froggy Mr Kanjilal.

So, not only is my case, my not-so-small case against Moolchand to be buried out of all sight, but my truly small case against the man who killed poor, drunken Bikram is to be buried with it. My vow to find his killer, even if I had to work entirely on my own, will, like any piece of rubbish attacked by some municipal sweeper pushing his way along the gutters with dirt-encrusted broom, simply be swept away.

All my hopes are crushed. I had believed it was certain this time that Mr Divekar would recognise

245

that I am a detective who is at least knowing his business. I thought even he was bound to say *Shabash, Inspector, good work*. But what did he say? *Dismiss*. Dismiss, as he has said to me time and again. Dismiss, and forget about your peon whose severed head got deposited in your own cabin. *Dismiss*, and lose the Darab Dastor case with all its promise of some decent kudos. *Dismiss*, and take on instead the small, small matter of a stabbing up at Cumballa Hill (and have Sgt Chavan even then watching over you the whole time). *Dismiss*, even when I was presenting him with my altogether detailed account with the plainest suspicion pointing at all-powerful Nathumal Moolchand. *Dismiss*, and wait till you hear what is going to be done about that. Or, what is not going to be done.

So now, here I am back at my beginning in Crime Branch, if not on *bandobast* duties once more likely to be on them again tomorrow, and for months, perhaps, to come. Out of the way. No more than a buzzing fly waved, with arms flapping, out of a window.

And meanwhile what will Mr Divekar do, when he at last sees in the newspapers, if he ever does, that Pradeep Popatkar will, after Jyoti denounced him so effectively at the Oval Maidan, hardly take the vacant Legislative Assembly seat? Will he manage somehow, by some political manoeuvring or other, to get him after all made an MLA for somewhere else? Then become Minister for Home, in charge of police affairs?

Yes, poor Jyoti, all that good work of yours will come to nothing then. All that will be left to you is that you now have a good *kaam* as our servant.

So, if tomorrow I find it is *bandobast* again for me, I will, when my life is over and I find myself waiting for my next one, at least have that one small item in the credit column.

All right, what time it is? Only half past three. Well, never mind. I am doing nothing here. I will go home. *Ek dum.*

*   *   *

Back at his desk next day he sat, once again, waiting. Will Mr Divekar's Thomas appear in just only one-two minutes with the first orders for my *bandobast* work? Will I not only find I am back to that, but back to it for all the weeks and months I was once thinking that the task would be mine?

So he sat there in his chair, staring into space. Once or twice, twisting himself round to ease his numb legs, the waste bin swam into his consciousness. Into his mind then each time there trickled a stream of thoughts about what he had seen there on that fateful day, about what he had done when the sight of the bloodstained newspaper sheets had made their full impact on him, the moment when he had realised that the weight in the bag in the bin was Bikram's severed head.

Then, a moment of almost comic relief with the thought of Protima's confident assurance that the bloodstained newspaper sheets must be evidence. Her pathetic, amateurish observations about the blood being able to be identified.

'Ghote, are you busy itself?'

Did I hear some voice saying that?

He looked up.

247

And there, appearing over the batwing doors of the cabin, like an orangey moon, was an all too familiar face. Sgt Moos.

'Busy?' he answered that half-heard inquiry. 'No. No, Moos, my dear chap, I am not at all busy.'

'Then, if I may, I am wanting for a chat. You know, just only a few minutes ago there was coming into my head—it was when I was thinking about that day in the history of the world when Sir Edward Henry, in India itself, came to conclusion that fingerprints, differing so minutely as they do, could provide a method of identifying any person whatsoever whose fingers have been pressed to an ink-pad and then to a sheet of purely white paper.'

And at that moment, through the haze of Moos's ruminations, Ghote knew how it might be possible, after all, to prove that Atul was the man who had wrapped up Bikram's head in the sheets of a copy of the *Matunga News*.

CHAPTER TWENTY-FIVE

'Moos,' Ghote said, 'come in, come in. Sit, sit. You are very person I am wanting to talk.'

If this had been a less tense moment, Ghote would have had the greatest difficulty in not laughing aloud at the expression he saw on the face of the Number *Ek* fingerprints expert in all India. A look of purest incredulity. Someone, at last, had said straight out that they wanted to talk with him. To talk about—it could be nothing else—his single obsession, the very hint of it in the ordinary way inevitably bringing a splatter of excuses: ingenious, fantastic, illogical, whatever.

Moos, hardly managing to push to one side the nearer of the chairs in front of the desk, sat down.

'Listen,' Ghote began at once, leaning across the swept-clean glass upper surface of the desk that he once thought might remain bare for as long as it was his to sit at. 'Have you ever lifted a fingerprint from a sheet of . . . well, shall we say, a sheet of newspaper once soaked in human blood?'

Moos, sitting there on the chair which he had managed to place at an exact right angle to the desk, pushed out his lips and thought.

And thought, and . . .

'No, I never have,' he said. 'But I believe I could do it, yes, I believe I could. Of course, there would be difficulties. If we had in Bombay some of the equipment that is . . . '

Ghote felt he could see the next words slowly arriving in Moos's head. And arrive they did. 'Equipment that is ten-a-dollar in America—I refer, of course, to the US dollar—then what you are asking could almost certainly be done. Here, I am not so sure. But it is something I have often thought of trying to undertake, yes.'

'But if . . . if I was to bring you a bloodstained page of . . . of, say, the *Matunga News*, would you be able to find on it prints clear enough to compare with those of a man already on Bombay Police files?'

'When could you bring it?'

It was all Moos said.

*　　　*　　　*

Ghote—he had left Moos getting the new records

of Atul's fingerprints—found when he had gone, almost running, all the way over to Bank Street Cross Lane that Protima must be out at the market. He was not displeased to find the flat empty. He had had certain worries about whether he would be allowed, even when he had told Protima what Sgt Moos had promised, to take away her *evidence* that it was Bikram's blood that had stained the *Matunga News*.

So, as soon as he had closed the flat's door behind him with no answer to his *It is just only myself*, he simply hurried into the bedroom, knelt there and extracted from beneath his second-best trousers Protima's brown-paper parcel. With the packet held carefully under his arm, he hastily descended the creaking flights of the old stairs, careless now of the noise he was making.

Back at Headquarters he went, not to his own cabin, but, hardly daring to tell himself what he was hoping for, to Moos's one, tucked into its obscure corner of the compound. Now, even though it was fully day—the Baisakh sun shining above—he could see strips of almost glaring electric light at both top and foot of the door.

He gave it a sharp knock, perhaps twice as loud as the tap he had learnt to give the ACP's door.

But no *Come* sounded out in reply.

Is Moos not there? Despite the bright light from inside?

The purest panicky thoughts came crowding in on him. *Moos has died, terribly overworked—Moos has for the first and only time realised a task is too much for him—Fire broke out here while I was hurrying over to Bank Street Cross Lane.*

It was the sheer ridiculousness of this last wild

250

surmise that brought him back to simple reality.

Come or no *Come*, he pushed wide the door and entered. Moos was crouching, deeply intent, under the intense light of the specially imported lamp he had once told Ghote, at length, how he had fought to get installed. In front of him was a startlingly brilliant white card. On it ten black-ink finger marks.

'Those are Atul's itself?' he burst out before he had had time to think.

'Yes, yes,' Moos replied, abstractedly. 'Chavan had not yet properly filed this card. Bad practice, you know. Bad practice.'

'And you have taken in some of the most prominent features on it? Some whorls? A bifurcation, perhaps?'

'Inspector, I have altogether memorised each and every one of these ten prints, every feature of each one of them. It is my business to do it.'

Ghote decided now not to ask any more stupid questions. Instead he unwrapped from the packet Protima had made, carefully as if it contained a rajah's store of jewels, the sheets of the *Matunga News* and handed them to Moos to put under his microscope. Peering down beside him at the topmost sheet, he thought he could even himself distinguish roundish smears that well could be fingerprints.

And, oh God, he thought then, they may be my own. That day when I had suddenly decided I could not go to the ACP without hurrying back to my cabin from his very door so as to put in place again that vital piece of evidence, the shopping bag with Bikram's head still inside it. Did I touch any bit of those bloodied sheets and leave my prints on them? I may have done. I was ready to confess to Mr Divekar that my prints might be there. And, yet worse, now also there may be Protima's, left from the night we had wretched Bikram's head on our kitchen table.

And whose else's may there be? A hundred—no, be reasonable—half a dozen other people may have at least handled that newspaper, even before Bikram's blood was left on it.

So, will Moos be able to find even one truly damning print? One that will establish almost beyond any possibility of doubt that Atul was the person who wrapped up that head? Effective evidence.

He bent down beside Moos to look more closely.

'Shadow!'

At Moos's fiercely muttered objection he shot back out of the way.

What if, under my shadow from that powerful light above, there was the one print that might give us the answer? And Moos, distracted, has missed it?

But, no. No, I can see, even from back here, that his magnifying glass is actually hovering over that exact area.

Has he found it? The print that will say all?

Evidently not. The magnifying glass has moved on.

Is he never going to find a print that checks against one of those black-ink marks on Atul's card?

Time to beg God Ganesha for help? No. I am a totally rational man. Well, almost totally rational. I will not give way to superstition. A police officer should not. But then how many of my colleagues, certainly up in Dadar, probably here also, have under the glass sheets over their desks a colour picture of one god or another? If only *For luck*.

What seemed like hours of waiting in the dark, beyond the intense light pouring down on Moos's searching, passed before Moos lifted up his bent head and laid aside the magnifying glass.

'Yes? Yes? You have found it?'

'No, no, my dear chap. You do not at all understand. Nobody I am talking with ever does understand. This is very difficult work. Utmost concentration is needed. And that is meaning there are times when it is necessary to take one short rest.'

'Yes, yes. Of course, you should rest from time to time. I am well understanding that. But . . . '

But can I suggest not very much of rest will do the trick?

No. No, let him sit there as long as he is wanting, rubbing his tired eyes even. Just so long as in the end he is finding what must, must, be there.

Time went by. Or, Ghote told himself, some minutes have gone by. Cannot be more than twenty. No, even fifteen. Perhaps ten.

He settled himself to wait again, even closing his own eyes. To wait and wait.

Then a voice. Yes? Is it . . . ? Yes, Moos's.

'Fourteen prints on right-hand forefinger so far. Enough altogether to constitute proof here in Maharashtra. In Karnataka, you are knowing, they will accept just only twelve, very easy-going fellows there, but in France they are insisting on seventeen. Here, however, we are content always with fewer than the Europeans. So, yes, I am willing to go into court, if same is necessary, and swear that on this Page One of the *Matunga News*, howsoever bloodstained it is, there is a print, perhaps there will be more even, that is proof positive the sheet was handled by the man Atul after the blood had been spilt upon it.'

'Moos, Moos, my dear friend, my good friend—little long though I have known you—will you come out with me to . . . yes, to King Edward VIII juice bar and celebrate?'

'Well, Ghote, that is a generous offer. But I think I would like to make sure, before night is falling, that these newspaper sheets are stored under fully proper conditions. Chain of evidence, you know. Chain of evidence. But tomorrow, perhaps tomorrow, if no urgent case is before me, then, yes, a visit to that juice bar will be very welcome.'

Ghote left then, almost staggering under a flood of overwhelming fatigue.

But he was hardly halfway to his cabin—yes, a few minutes with Dr Hans Gross will calm me down—when he heard a distant voice calling out his name.

For a moment he decided to ignore it. He had too much to triumph over. But then he thought *After all, I might as well answer. Whoever it is.*

He looked round.

It was Superintendent Ghorpade.

Thank goodness, I did not pretend not to have heard him. He is the one officer in Crime Branch who has treated me with true kindness, and he is of such seniority.

He hurried over.

'Yes, sir? You were calling to me?'

'I was, Ghote. It's been some time since we had a word, and I think now there is something I might pass on to you. In the strictest confidence, mind. And, may I say, I believe from what I have observed about you that this confidence will be kept as strictly as if it had never been asked for. *Malum?*'

'Yes, sir. Understood, hundred per cent.'

'Well, let me put it this way. Don't be altogether surprised, Ghote, should you hear at some time in the not-too-distant future that ACP Divekar has, on health grounds, retired as Head of Crime Branch.'

Idiotically, Ghote found himself on the point of saying something like *I was not at all knowing Mr Divekar is in poor health.* Then he grasped fully what exactly it had been that Superintendent Ghorpade had said. Mr Divekar was to relinquish his post. On, of course, the often-used excuse of ill health, standing for the unsayable word *corruption.*

'Sir,' he answered, 'I will put same into very, very back of my mind.'

'Good man. So, I suppose you are just now on your way home. So off you go. Never any harm for an officer who has no particular work in front of him to go home. Didn't you tell me, when you first came, that you have a newly born son at your place in—what is it?—yes, Bank Street Cross Lane? So, go there now and see how the boy and your wife too, naturally, are getting on. It is never an altogether easy time for a new mother.'

With a nod of goodwill, Superintendent Ghorpade strolled away.

*   *   *

Ghote stood where he was and let the implications

of all that had just been said to him pass slowly through his mind.

Miracles, he thought. Do miracles sometimes happen? Because beyond doubt a miracle has happened to me. In the depths of despair, all progress in the career I am just starting in Crime Branch looking as blackly unhopeful as possible, a chance encounter with Mr Ghorpade has altered everything. No, wait. Was it so much by chance? Or was Mr Ghorpade actually keeping an eye out for me after what Mr Divekar may have, by chance again, mentioned to him about myself and my never-to-be-spoken-of discovery?

But whichever it was, there is no doubt that a miracle has taken place. A great black towering rock lying straight in front of my path is to be miraculously lifted away as if it was, not massive stone doubly weighted with shining ambition, but a mere illusion. ACP Divekar, who has ordered me into what I might well have called *purdah*, kept away from all important business in Crime Branch, condemned almost to perpetual *bandobast* duty, has gone. Or almost gone. He is to retire *on health grounds*, which is as much as to say he has been found out as being too closely linked with criminal activity. As occasional senior officers have been in the past.

So now, perhaps, I have hope again. Hope for a decent career, hope to be given from time to time, with intervals perhaps for humdrum *bandobast* duty, cases that I can solve, working away to the best of my abilities. That much hope. And it is enough.

256

CHAPTER TWENTY-SIX

Ghote, despite Superintendent Ghorpade's advice to go home to his wife and child, felt he had to have some moments of peace to let this new view of his world settle into place. He walked slowly across the busy compound, pushed the batwing doors of his cabin open, went, almost stumbling, over to his desk, slid round to his familiar chair and slumped.

But before he had been there five minutes the phone at his ear rang out, shrillingly.

Who . . . ? What . . . ? But . . . but can it still be the ACP?

It was.

'Ghote?' The familiar bark.

'Yes, sir? Yes, ACP?' The familiar answer.

'Come up. I want a word.'

Click. Call ended.

But, Ghote thought, somehow that is not the voice of the ACP as it was each time he was ringing before. That *I want a word*. He might have been speaking to a fellow senior officer, to Mr Ghorpade even.

Well, only one way to find out what that *word* may be.

Yet once more he ascended the spiral of stone steps to the balcony above. Once again he peered through the thick glass pane of the ACP's door. But now he thought—it still seemed almost impossible that it should be true—Mr Divekar is, to all intents and purposes, no longer Head of Crime Branch. He is a man about to retire *on*

257

health grounds.

He saw that, inside, the red-leather chair was not occupied.

What . . . ? Why . . . ? The ACP has never not been sitting there, upright as a pillar. An unmoving, unmovable pillar. So why . . . ?

Then he thought he saw, some way back into the big room, that the ACP was striding about in the wide area behind the desk, to and fro, six yards one way, abrupt turn, six yards the other way.

Will he in a moment or two come back and take his seat?

It looked as if he had little intention of doing so.

But he has summoned me. *Come up.* And, on the point of retirement through ill health or not, a summons from Mr Divekar is not to be ignored.

He knocked. If not quite as timidly as the first time he had tapped at the door, at least in a sort of considerate manner.

And—did I hear what I think I did?—a voice from the inner depths of the big room saying, muttering, something that indicated I should enter.

He turned the handle in front of him, pushed the door wide, stepped in.

'Ah, yes, Ghote.'

And then a silence. A silence that seemed to Ghote to go on and on and on as Mr Divekar continued to pace up and down.

But at last it was broken.

'Ghote? Yes, take a seat, man. Or, no. No.'

But is this marcher, far inside the room, the Mr Divekar who has more than once confronted me, iron-hard?

It seems not.

258

In a voice almost as far from iron-hard as could be, the ACP muttered, murmured even, 'Come round. I want to talk to you, and I need somehow to stay on my feet.'

Ghote—is this a dream? Did I fall asleep standing outside here?—made his way, ever cautiously, round the wide sweep of the black desk.

And then went over to where Mr Divekar, in his uneasy pacing to and fro, had come to a halt.

'Yes, sir? Is there . . . ? Sir, can I at all help?'

Internally Ghote experienced a feeling of total bewilderment.

Did I say that? Did I ask the ACP whether I could help him? Myself, Inspector Ghote, last recruit to Crime Branch, asking the head of the whole outfit whether I could help him?

'Help?' The voice was plaintive.

Not a spark now of the old instant fury? No, definitely not. This was as if another man altogether was speaking.

'You know, Ghote, that I am retiring early?'

'Yes, sir.'

No, must say more than just only *Yes, sir.*

'Yes, sir. I was talking, by chance—it was by chance only—to Mr Ghorpade, sir, and . . . and he was mentioning same.'

'Quite right. The news will be announced very shortly. It's as well everybody knows as soon as possible.'

'Yes, sir.'

What else to say?

Once more the ACP—the former ACP—began his striding-up-and-down walk. Ghote, placing himself beside him, did his best to match his pace.

259

Abruptly then, as they wheeled round at one end of their six-yard march, words came pouring out from between the firm-set lips to which Ghote had listened more than once in pure dismay.

'Health grounds?' came the familiar snapping voice. 'Isn't that what they're going to say? Health grounds. Well, let me tell you what it is I have been *suffering* from.'

For a single topsy-turvy, *ulta pulta* moment Ghote thought he was going to hear what medical condition it was that the ACP had been afflicted by. But then he knew he must simply keep silent and wait to hear whatever it was he was going to hear.

'Yes, Ghote, what I have been suffering from, suffering almost ever since I was appointed Head of Crime Branch, is nothing other than ambition. Ambition, perhaps good enough in its way, but not if it is ambition run riot.'

Ghote could only listen.

He had at various times, conducting investigations, come across Catholics—both bad and good—who had, they eventually told him, gone to confession and hoped in that way to rid themselves of the sin they had committed, the crime which in the end it had fallen to himself to extract his own confession to. So he had often wondered about this practice, about what exactly happened in the confessional, jutting out from which he had often seen pairs of calves, ankles and feet with *chappals* dangling from them when a kneeling man was confessing to some sin. To a peccadillo, to a murder.

But none of his idle speculations had prepared him for this. Had prepared him to hear the man

260

who had been until a few hours ago, or perhaps still legally was, Head of Crime Branch, confess that he had fallen victim to the sin—was it a sin?—of overweening ambition.

And a moment later he was yet more astonished.

'And, do you know, Ghote, what it was that had been gradually convincing me that it was altogether reckless ambition I had become gripped by?'

He wondered whether he should answer, try to answer.

But he did not need to trouble himself.

The little side door which they happened to be facing had opened softly and Thomas was standing there, in his right hand the ACP's familiar large flower-patterned teacup on its flower-patterned saucer.

Thomas must, at once, have seen the look of fury that had appeared on the ACP's face, because he stammered out, 'Tea, *sahib*. It is time, exact time, for—'

'Out. Out. Get out.'

It was all that needed to be said, to be shouted. Thomas vanished. The little door closed behind him firmly as if never once, however long it had been there, it had opened.

'Yes, Ghote,' the ACP went on, as if no interruption had occurred, 'it was you. You, Ghote. Each time I had occasion to rebuke you for some lack of drive, some failure to pursue the case I had given you—the Cumballa Hill stabbing, whatever—you simply put in front of me—I am sure you had no idea you were doing so, no idea at all—an attitude of plain straightforwardness entirely devoid of any desire to satisfy inner

261

ambition. And that, in the end, was what undermined me. So, when the Commissioner told me that I appeared to have exceeded my proper limits in attempting to shelter that man Moolchand from the results of his illegalities, I at once realised it was what indeed I had been doing, and out of sheer ambition. And, of course, after that it was *health reasons.*'

And then it was that Ghote realised that for himself it truly was all over. All the obstacles that had seemed to be in front of him, a mountain range, the high Western Ghats, had vanished as if they were no more than piled layers of vaporous clouds. No need any more to pursue Atul in an impossible one-man crusade. Convicted, as he is bound to be, of the attempted murder of Crime Branch Inspector Ganesh Ghote, justice will have been satisfied, without him being charged and convicted of the murder by beheading of one Bikram, a peon. Nor will there be any need now to have Atul additionally tried, with all the unwelcome adverse publicity Bombay Police might attract, as the knife-wielding intruder who came to the door of that pale-purple house on Cumballa Hill so oddly resembling a painting enshrined in the Prince of Wales Museum. By his one conviction, Atul can be seen to have paid for both murders.

No need, either, for any awkward inquiry into how Bikram's head had become *disposed of*, burnt to ashes at the Electric Crematorium.

No need now to worry about rewarding Jyoti for her vital help up at her Lady Hardinge Road slum. She has been rewarded, as she had said and said to Protima, by having our flat's roof—more or less resistant to monsoon rains—over her head and a decent bed rolled out nightly for her in our kitchen, happy to clean and tidy and tidy for us. No need either to worry any more about fierce little Rekha Salaskar in the other Lady Hardinge Road slum. She has her new shopping bag in her hands, far better than the one Atul snatched from her.

And, finally, no need for me to contemplate a whole career devoted to *bandobast* duties. No, I have shown, if only before my inner judge, that I am altogether good enough to hold my Crime Branch post. I found out who murdered Bikram and put his severed head into the waste bin in my cabin. Then, when I was at last given a proper Crime Branch investigation, in little more than a few hours I discovered that it was no chance intruder who had killed Krishna Tabholkar but Atul, a *supari* sent with just that object. And, yes, I presented the case against that seemingly invincible *crorepati*, Nathumal Moolchand, as the man who ordered Atul to commit those two murders, and though at the time I believed that case had been smothered in thick blankets of concealment, now I can rest assured that Moolchand's days of glory will be short-lived.

Yes, *bandobast* duty will fall to me here sometimes, fall to me as often as it falls to every other inspector in the Branch, and with that I will be happy. Altogether happy.